music. A compelling read, this beautifully crafted novel will make you want to expl... *Candis*

When Nicky Pellegrino's Italian father fell in love with and married a Liverpool girl, he shared what all Italians know – that you live to eat instead of eating to live. This mantra is the inspiration behind Nicky's delicious novels. Now living in New Zealand and working as a journalist, Nicky hoards her holiday so that she and her husband can return to Italy to meet up with family, eat the best mozzarella and research her books. To find out more visit www.nickypellegrino.com

By Nicky Pellegrino

Delicious
Summer at the Villa Rosa
(*originally published as* The Gypsy Tearoom)
The Italian Wedding
Recipe for Life
The Villa Girls
When in Rome
The Food of Love Cookery School

The Food of Love Cookery School

Nicky Pellegrino

An Orion paperback

First published in Great Britain in 2013
by Orion Books
This paperback edition published in 2014
by Orion Books,
an imprint of The Orion Publishing Group Ltd,
Orion House, 5 Upper Saint Martin's Lane
London WC2H 9EA

An Hachette UK company

3 5 7 9 10 8 6 4

A CIP catalogue record for this book
is available from the British Library.

ISBN 978-1-4091-3613-2

Typeset by Deltatype Ltd, Birkenhead, Merseyside

Printed and bound by CPI Group (UK) Ltd, Croydon, CR0 4YY

www.orionbooks.co.uk

Tell me what you eat, and I will tell you what you are.

Jean Anthelme Brillat-Savarin

Food of Love

Luca Amore thinks he knows how the next eight days will unfold, give or take a few minor variations. Things have a habit of going the way he plans them.

Right now he is making sure everything in his kitchen is arranged exactly how it should be. The first day's menu is chalked up on the blackboard and there are four clean aprons hanging on the hooks beside it. Plates are stacked; cutlery and saucepans are shining. He has scrubbed the wooden boards where dough is kneaded and rolled; laid out a tray of almond cakes as a welcome; thrown open the shutters to show off the view.

Generations of Luca's family have cooked in this kitchen in the house at the top of Favio's steepest flight of steps. The view from its windows has barely changed in all that time. Pink and gold buildings climb a rocky spur, the cathedral at their centre. Drying laundry flutters on terraces. Date palms reach for the sky.

Since he was a boy, this view has been Luca's to enjoy. His grandparents lived in the house and often his mother brought him here, stopping on the steps to catch her breath, complaining every time.

Now his grandparents are gone and the place is his. At first Luca thought he might live here instead of in his mother's house. He began to renovate, replacing cracked tiles, freshening walls with a new coat of paint.

It was the kitchen that brought him up short. With each small thing he changed, he felt he lost a little more of the Amore women who had been there before. The modern six-burner stove, the long granite counter, even the dining table he stripped and restored; all these things pleased him yet somehow undid his connection with the past.

His nonna, countless great-aunts and distant cousins: some of his best memories were of seeing them gathered here, working dough with cool, capable hands; noisy, wide-bodied women, always bickering over something, the best recipe for a pasta al forno, or some half-forgotten slight. They filled this kitchen completely.

To the very last, his nonna loved to cook, bent and old but still conjuring the flavours from food. Luca missed her and the others. As he modernised the room, replacing and reshaping all that was familiar, he searched for a way to brighten his memories of them.

For over ten years now, Luca has run the Food of Love Cookery School. His guests come from all over the world to make his nonna's dishes, spiced with saffron and cinnamon or flavoured with the chocolate that Favio is famous for. Luca teaches them all the most important things: how to tell good olive oil from bad; how to know fake gelato from the real thing.

In early summer he takes them to collect capers from the flower-covered bushes that grow wild from the town's rock walls. They taste the local Nero d'Avola wine and caciocavallo cheese. They shop for sardines or sweet Pachino tomatoes at the market in the morning, and sleep each night in the Amore family's beautiful old house.

Season to season the schedule may vary, but for the most part every course is the same. People come together, food is cooked and friendships are formed. On warm evenings they sit out on the terrace sharing limoncello and life stories. There are good times; there is laughter.

Then, on the final day, suitcases are packed, farewell messages written in the visitors' book and promises made to keep in touch. A week or so later, a flurry of thank-you cards arrive; often e-mails too, with photographs of the dishes they have re-created at home. But the messages soon stop coming and Luca is too busy with his next group of guests to mind.

Over the years, so many of them have faded from his memory. He can't put names to faces in his photo album. The ones that do stick tend to be the complainers, or the guests whose food intolerances make menu-planning a mission. Those who have squabbles and dramas; who lose handbags and hats; or suffer heart flutters that turn out to be severe attacks of indigestion.

Luca loves his job. Cooking is a joy and he is always interested to meet new people. But it is also a pleasure when everyone is gone and he is left alone. He enjoys mornings like this one, with the house empty and his. Once he has restored order, if there is enough time, he likes to make a few cavatelli just for himself, feeling the dough beneath his fingers; deftly pressing it into pasta seashells on the wooden board the way his grandmother taught him.

Today there is no chance for that. The new guests aren't far away – four of them, all women. Luca checks his notes and memorises their names. From England there is Moll, who says she is passionate about food, and Tricia, who works as a lawyer. From America, Valerie, who is the eldest. And all the way from Australia, Poppy, who says she has never visited Italy before and will eat anything but offal.

Luca assumes this new group will be much like all the rest. Still, he is aware there are things he cannot tell from the forms they have filled in. He doesn't know exactly how much experience each has had in a kitchen; if they will understand how to knead dough with the heels of their hands until it is firm enough; if they will have healthy appetites or worry about their waistlines; if they will drink just one glass of wine or a whole bottle at dinnertime.

There are other, more important things about this group, but Luca doesn't realise it yet. Right at this moment, all four are standing by a baggage carousel at Catania airport. Moll, Tricia, Valerie and Poppy. This is what Luca doesn't know about them.

One is hiding a secret. Another is hoping to find love again. One is desperate to escape her life; one has already managed it.

As he sets out mineral water, a bottle of Prosecco and five glasses, Luca has no idea how different this cookery course will be to any that has gone before ... or how it will change his life entirely.

Welcome to the Food of Love Cookery School in the lovely baroque town of Favio in southern Sicily. Here is your apron, your cavatelli board, your maps and itinerary. Don't worry, there is no need to take notes; the recipes will be given to you at the end. Just relax and have a good time. Your holiday is beginning ...

Poppy

This is going to be an adventure – the first of many, I hope. My life has been short on adventures so far. I've been busy doing the things I ought to and not what I really wanted. But that's changed now. This is my time.

Why did I choose to come here? Well, my family on Dad's side comes from Sicily. My grandfather left when he was a child but has never lost his accent or his love for the spicy sausage he could never persuade us kids to eat. He was born in Ortygia – we'll be going there on day four, I think. Oh yes, I've been desperate to come to Sicily for ages, but it's such a long, expensive flight from Australia and, well, Brendan didn't want to.

Brendan's my ex-husband. Our divorce was finalised three months ago. It was all very amicable. I pretended to be sad because he seemed to expect it, but the truth is it wasn't so hard. We don't have kids, not even a cat. The house sold quickly, we divided up our stuff, split savings and shares – our divorce was as unexciting as our marriage really. We were together for ten years, and in all that time I never travelled anywhere on my own. I've been feeling a little nervous, to be honest. Being in a strange country – it even smells different, doesn't it? – well, it's wonderful but a little daunting, too.

Oh yes, go on then, I'll have another glass of wine. I know it's getting late, but I'm too excited to go to bed yet. And it's lovely out here on this terrace. What a view! I love how everything is crumbling and hundreds of years old; completely unlike Sydney, which seems so organised and new in comparison. You don't get that same sense that there may be a lovely secret waiting to be discovered around every corner.

Do you know anyone who's been on this Food of Love holiday? No, me neither. I booked it on the spur of the moment because I liked the look of the website. It was a risk, I guess, but it seemed like the only cooking holiday in this part of Sicily. I read Luca's blog, watched the clips of his cooking classes, and one night, after a few Chardonnays, I decided to go for it.

Dishy? Yes, I guess he is. It's a pity he wouldn't stay and have a few drinks with us, but I suppose he must do so many of these courses. And it's great that he leaves at night so we've got the house to ourselves, much more relaxing somehow.

I'm pleased there's only the four of us, too. A bigger group would have been impersonal, don't you think? This way we'll all get a go at making the dishes he shows us. Not that I'm such a great cook. I love eating, and that's why this holiday appealed to me so much – it's a chance to taste real Italian cooking rather than the samey stuff they serve up in restaurants; tomato sauce slopped over everything, all the flavours so totally expected.

I'm planning to do a lot more travelling now I'm single again. I'd like to backpack round India, visit Vietnam and China, South America; so many places. But this holiday seemed a wiser choice for my first trip, a safe way to make a fresh start.

Day One

(i) The joy of shopping

Poppy woke early and completely. Jet lag, she supposed. Twenty hours on a plane, then dealing with the time difference between here and Sydney, was bound to take its toll. As she sat up in bed, her head throbbed a little and she remembered all the wine she had drunk last night and wasn't surprised.

There was no point trying to get back to sleep. Yawning and stretching, she climbed out of bed. She went first to the window to take another look at the view. It was still fairly dark, but the cathedral opposite was lit, and around it street lamps gleamed brightly enough for her to make out crooked rows of buildings crowded shoulder to shoulder on the rocky outcrop. This town must be built on two steep hills, she realised, with the main street running along a gully between them.

As soon as it was light enough, she would go out and explore; get some exercise. Last night's welcome dinner had been lavish. Luca had escorted them to a nearby restaurant, where he took charge of the ordering. To begin with there were *arancini*, moist balls of rice filled with meat and cheese, fried until they were golden, and so delicious Poppy hadn't been able to resist reaching for more. Next came a ceramic pot filled with a steaming soup of broken spaghetti and leafy greens, and assuming it was the main course she had taken a second ladleful.

It had turned out there was more to come, much more. A sweet-sour caponata of aubergines, courgettes and celery; meatballs cooked with lemon leaves, dense pork sausage bright with flecks of chilli. The only thing to do had been to keep on eating. This morning a long walk up a steep hill was definitely in order.

Poppy dressed quietly so she wouldn't wake the others, although the walls of the old house were probably thick enough to muffle the sound of her moving around. It was 6 a.m. and the sky had lightened. She laced up her sneakers, tied back her long dark hair and was ready.

At first her pace was brisk. She ran down the flight of steps, continued past last night's restaurant, now all closed up, and turned into a narrow lane. There she was faced by yet more steps, these leading all the way to the cathedral. The climb forced her to slow, and by the time she reached the top, she was breathing hard. Resting for a moment, she turned and scanned the houses on the hill opposite until she found the one she had just left, glowing rosy pink in the first rays of the early morning sun.

Favio was a town of stairways, she discovered. They snaked between the houses and linked the winding alleyways. If she took a walk like this one every morning, she would be much fitter by the time she left Sicily in nine days' time.

Her route took her past two more churches, three elderly men gathered on a bench for their morning conversation, a couple of skinny dogs and an old woman harvesting something from a large bush growing from a rock wall.

'*Buongiorno, signora,*' Poppy said (she had been having weekly conversation classes). 'What are you picking?'

Straightening and smiling, the woman held out her basket and Poppy saw that it was filled with hundreds of small green buds.

'What are they?' she managed to ask.

The woman spoke a great jumble of words that Poppy's

ear wasn't practised enough to separate and understand.

'Sorry, my Italian isn't very good,' she apologised.

Smiling again, the old lady offered her a handful of the fresh green buds. Looking at them properly, Poppy knew exactly what they were – capers, just like she bought in jars at home, except these were fresh and firm.

After that, she noticed caper bushes growing wild everywhere, cascading over walls and pushing their way from crevices. She picked more of the buds as she went, filling the pockets of her hoodie. Later she might ask Luca how best to preserve them.

Poppy thought about Luca as she walked on up the steep incline. Last night she had found him intriguing. Over dinner, while everyone else was talking about who they were and where they came from, Luca had given away very little. He was born in Favio and studied for a while in England – that was all she knew. But how old was he? Did he have a partner? Were there children? He was careful not to touch on it.

Once he had left and they were sitting out on the terrace, Tricia had said she thought he was dishy. But it wasn't his looks that were striking, not really. Didn't most Sicilian men have dark hair, brown eyes and tanned skin? It was something in Luca's manner, the way he looked you in the eye when he was talking, yet seemed reserved at the same time.

Poppy glanced at her watch. There was still an hour before he would arrive to prepare their breakfast. She was heading downwards now, back towards the cookery school, and wondered if she might find somewhere open for a coffee along the way.

On the main street, there were signs the town was waking. A white van with leafy bunches of sprouting broccoli strapped to its roof was making a delivery. There were groups of schoolgirls in burgundy uniforms; a nun wearing sunglasses; men smoking cigarettes. People hurried past dressed for their offices, and Poppy felt that delicious freedom of being on holiday whilst others had to work as usual.

At the end of the street was a piazza, where she found a bar with tables set out beneath three tall date palms. She smelt coffee and the sweetness of pastries. Inside, a man in a business suit was taking a few moments to drink an espresso and scan the day's newspaper headlines. Poppy found a table in the sun and practised pronouncing her order: '*Un cappuccino e un cornetto con crema, per favore.*'

Of course, the waiter spoke English. Everyone under the age of about forty seemed to. Still, she didn't regret all those conversation classes she had taken. They were part of the build-up to her trip, like reading the guidebooks and planning a holiday wardrobe; a way to stay excited.

Poppy finished her milky coffee and her pastry, but no one came out to ask if she might like anything else. She suspected she could people-watch from this table for half the day without ordering another thing and no one would try to move her on. It was so different to her favourite café at home, where there was always another customer hovering for a table and the staff were friendly but brisk.

Back in Sydney it would be evening by now, and people would be eating dinner or gathering in bars. Brendan might still be working, though. This was when he liked to call potential vendors or drop fliers in their mailboxes. Poppy wondered how he was getting on without her. There had been a couple of offers under negotiation, a new listing that looked likely; still, generally things quietened down in the real-estate business this time of year.

Most people she knew had been amazed when they'd continued to work together even after their marriage ended. But there didn't seem to be too many issues so far. The things that irritated her about Brendan were the same as always. He could be too pushy; he had a tendency to gloss over the negatives of a property and a habit of never taking no for an answer.

When they had parted, she'd suggested breaking up their business partnership too, but he had been persuasive. 'We're a great team; you know that. We might not want to live together but there's no reason why we shouldn't work together, is there? Two are better than one. Just give it a go.'

He had even dropped her off at the airport on Friday, kissed her on the cheek and told her to have a good trip. And now there were to be days away from work, no clients calling at crazy hours, no Brendan at her side running her schedule; days free of all her usual responsibilities. She felt almost giddy with relief at the thought of it.

Poppy considered ordering another coffee, then changed her mind. She was hot and sweaty from her walk. Better to take a shower before Luca came with breakfast.

Already the climb up the steps back to the house felt a little easier. She called out a greeting as she opened the front door. 'Hello. Anyone up yet?'

'Oh, thank goodness.' It was Tricia, one of the English women. 'There's been a disaster. I've forgotten my hair straighteners. No, don't laugh, I'm serious.'

Last night, Poppy had noticed how poised Tricia seemed, with her sleek chestnut hair and lovely clothes. Now she made a different picture, her bathrobe sloppily fastened, skin all shiny, hair a frizz.

'It's the humidity,' Tricia complained, running her fingers through it. 'It's gone completely feral. Please tell me you've brought some hair irons.'

Poppy shook her head. 'Sorry, no, I haven't. Can't you pull it back into a ponytail?'

'That's what I was going to do, but it needs to be straightened first.' Tricia's voice rose. 'Oh bugger. You seemed like my best bet. I'll wake the others and see if either of them has a pair. Pray for me.'

Iron her hair? Poppy was on holiday and wasn't planning to bother ironing anything, even clothes. Marvelling that Tricia was so concerned with her appearance, she showered quickly, dressed in light linen and was the first one down to breakfast.

Luca was there already with the moka pot on, laying out pastries and sliced fruit. He looked up and smiled. 'Good morning, did you sleep well?' he asked, his English gently accented.

Sliding on to a stool beside the counter, she reached for a glass of orange juice. 'Yes thanks. I expected to be awake half the night after that huge meal, but it was fine. In fact, I felt hungry again when I woke up!'

The moka pot bubbled and hissed. 'That's good,' Luca told her, lifting it from the stove. 'It helps to have an appetite on this holiday. But don't worry; we eat a lot, but we walk too. You won't have a problem.'

As he was pouring the coffee, Valerie and Moll appeared. 'Good morning,' they chorused. 'Yes, coffee would be lovely. Oh, and look at these pastries. How delicious.'

Valerie took the stool next to Poppy, spreading a napkin carefully over her lap. Poppy thought her one of those women who must have been a real stunner once. There was still a fragile beauty left in her face: she had high cheekbones, soft blue eyes and silvered hair caught up in a tortoiseshell clip. And there was a gracefulness about her too. She made a stark contrast to Moll, with her clumpy shoes and sensible haircut. Still, the pair of them had been getting on well enough to seem like old friends

They were exclaiming over their breakfast now, and full of curiosity. What was in those little half-moon-shaped biscuits? Oh, almonds and candied orange. What about the ones that looked like mini Cornish pasties? Chocolate and beef ... no ... really?

Poppy tasted one. The flavour was unusual: there was the bitter dark crumble of chocolate, a hint of spice and also an earthiness that might have been the meat but she wasn't certain.

'They're called *'mpanatigghi*,' Luca told them. 'And they're part of our Spanish heritage, it's believed. But we'll talk more about that when Tricia is here.'

'Oh, she's upstairs having some sort of hair crisis,' said Moll, who had one of those voices that tended to carry. 'Valerie lent her some straighteners, but apparently they're not the ones she likes, so she thought she might be a while. She said to start breakfast without her.'

Luca shrugged. 'No problem, there's plenty of time.'

When she did appear, Tricia was transformed. She wore a silk top and matching bracelet in a shade of green that set off the chestnut of her now-smooth hair.

'Good morning, everyone.' She ducked her head, as if embarrassed. 'Aren't I awful? I'm so sorry to have held you up. I'll just have a quick espresso and then be ready to go.'

'No hurry.' Luca poured another coffee and offered her a plate. 'Take a few moments to have something to eat.'

'Yes, see if you can guess the mystery ingredient in these,' said Moll, pointing to the *'mpanatigghi*. 'I bet you never will.'

Tricia shook her head. 'I'm not a cake-in-the-morning person. Just some fruit for me, thanks.'

Moll frowned. 'You really should try one, you know,' she urged. 'They're quite different to anything you'll have eaten in England.'

Tricia shrugged off her words. 'Just coffee and fruit,' she insisted, an edge to her voice.

Apparently unfazed, Luca passed her the plate of sliced fruit and returned the moka pot to the hob.

'Before we go to the market, I want to talk to you about the flavours of Sicily,' he told them. 'Don't make the mistake of thinking Sicilian food is the same as Italian. We've been invaded so many times, by the Greeks, the Arabs, the Spanish – all have left something behind to enrich our cooking. Nevertheless, it is a simple cuisine. We eat what comes from the land and the sea; and we care about the ingredients as much as the finished dish.'

'It was the Arabs that introduced the spices, wasn't it?' Moll guessed.

Luca nodded. 'You'll find we use cinnamon and cloves, almonds and pistachios; we mix fish with cheese, which horrifies the rest of Italy. We cook with fairly limited ingredients but still dishes vary from village to village, from family to family. What I will show you is the way the Amore family have eaten for as long back as anyone knows.'

Poppy was beginning to feel uneasy. For the first time she wondered if a food holiday had been the smartest idea. These other women seemed to know a lot more than her. What if she couldn't keep up?

'So Sicilian food is essentially *cucina povera*, right?' Moll remarked now, confirming Poppy's suspicion (she'd never even heard the term before).

'Yes,' Luca agreed, approvingly. 'It comes from the poor people making do with whatever they had. There is also the richer, more sophisticated cooking of the aristocrats. The divide between the two remains even today – many of the old people in Sicily still won't cook with cream because of it.'

'Were the Amore family rich or poor?' Tricia wondered.

'They certainly weren't wealthy,' Luca told her. 'But my nonna was a curious woman and far more open-minded than most. She loved to cook and liked nothing better than discovering new recipes. Many of the dishes I will show you come from her.'

'What's the most unusual thing you're going to teach us?' asked Moll.

'I think perhaps the chicken with chocolate and Prosecco,' Luca told her. 'But we're getting ahead of ourselves. Today we're going to make a simple pasta dish with a sauce flavoured with the local sausage and a little cinnamon. For the main course, the recipe will depend on what looks good at the market – baked anchovies, stuffed cuttlefish or swordfish, with vegetables and lots of good olive oil. So are we nearly ready to go shopping?'

There was a rush to find cameras and handbags, to apply sunscreen (Poppy) and lipstick (Tricia). Valerie turned back at the last minute to change her shoes and Moll wavered over whether she should take a wrap.

Luca waited patiently at the door until everyone was ready.

'Here we are at last,' Tricia said.

'Yes, so sorry to keep you,' Valerie added, her accent clipped Manhattan.

'There's no hurry,' Luca reassured them. 'In Favio we don't move all that quickly. We take our time to enjoy life.'

Outside, the heat was building. Together they strolled up the shady side of the main street, past the shabby baroque palazzos Poppy had noticed earlier that morning, and through a maze of narrow lanes filled with curious little shops and hidden-away restaurants until they reached a small piazza with a market at its centre.

This market was a makeshift affair, and lively. Between canvas-covered stalls were flat-bed trucks piled high with wooden crates of vegetables, and caravans serving snacks of piping hot *arancini*. Shoppers haggled with traders, or clogged the narrow spaces between the stalls as they gossiped with friends and neighbours.

Everyone seemed to know Luca. Stallholders called greetings; women kissed his cheeks; men slapped him on the back. 'So you've got yourself another group of foreigners? All women again, eh?' they joked. 'How do you do it, Luca?'

Poppy was dazzled by the noise and colour. This seemed such an exhilarating way to shop for food. She had always hated pushing a trolley up and down the soulless rows of fizzy drinks and instant noodles in her local supermarket. Here, everyone seemed happy and the place vibrated with life.

To her right, an old man was standing behind hessian sacks of dried beans and lustily singing his favourite arias. To her left were fishermen wielding cleavers and dealing with the morning's catch. There was the metallic smell of meat, the brininess of seafood, and many of the vendors called out to them, offering morsels to taste.

'Try my artichoke wine, it is good for the digestion.'

'No, no, *bella, bella*, come here, taste my salami made from my own black pigs.'

'Try my olive oil, my Ragusano cheese, my sweet Pachino tomatoes; the best you'll ever have, I promise.'

Valerie had wandered over to examine a stall piled high with tomatoes of every size and shape. Moll was busy photographing jars of fat green olives.

Poppy heard a slight lull in the shouting and noticed the heads of several of the male stallholders turn. She wondered why; then saw for herself what they were staring at. A woman, very slender, very beautiful, wearing a short dress with perilous stiletto heels, steering herself directly towards Luca, a wide smile on her face.

'*Ciao, caro*.' There was a whisper of scent and a tinkle of gold charms on a bracelet as she took his arm and kissed him on both cheeks.

'*Buongiorno*, Orsolina, how are you today?' he replied, brightly.

'I am well, as always.'

Turning to face the group, she kept her hand on Luca's arm. 'Good morning, everyone,' she said in sing-song English. 'Welcome to Favio.' She spoke as if the town belonged to her, gesturing with her free hand towards the disintegrating palazzos and the cathedral high above them.

Once the proper introductions had been made, Orsolina turned away and began talking to Luca in quiet, rapid Italian.

Tricia raised her eyebrows and whispered to Poppy, 'Hey, so what do you think? The girlfriend?'

'Maybe.'

'Well, if she's not his girlfriend, then she wants to be. I can always tell.'

'She's very striking.'

'Yes, but overdone. Those shoes are Manolos. Bit much for Monday morning at the market, don't you think?'

'How does she manage to walk in heels over these uneven flagstones?' Poppy wondered. 'I guess women like her are born able to do it.'

Luca was trying to finish the conversation. He pointed towards the fish stalls, saying something that provoked a frown, and then Orsolina shrugged, throwing her hands in the air. 'OK, OK, I will see you this evening, then,' she said in English, more loudly. 'Come early if you can.'

'Definitely the girlfriend,' Tricia decided, but Poppy wasn't convinced.

Once they began to shop, Luca moved quickly and seemed certain about what he wanted. The swordfish were in season, very fresh, and he would like some steaks sliced thinly so he could prepare them the way his nonna preferred. He would take some sausage flavoured with fennel for the pasta dish; vegetables for a sweet-sour *fritteda*, and that would be lunch.

As they left the market, laden with bags, they passed a stall heaped with nothing but odd-looking leafy greens with curling pale green tendrils.

'Luca, what are those?' asked Poppy.

'Ah, they are the vegetable you had last night in your soup. They're called *tenerumi* and they come from the tops of our Sicilian squash. Very refreshing to eat, and good for you too. You won't find them anywhere but here, I think.'

'Do they use the whole plant in the soup? The stalks, leaves and tendrils too?'

'That's right. Perhaps I'll buy some another day and show you. But right now we have enough food. It's time to go and begin cooking.'

'Never mind the vegetables,' Tricia hissed as Luca turned for home. 'Ask him about shoe girl.'

Poppy laughed. 'You ask him.'

'I just might do that.'

(ii) Pasta, capers & warm hands

The kitchen was the largest room of the old stone house. If Poppy had been writing a real-estate advert, she might have described it as 'an entertainer's kitchen'. Any cook would covet the generous work space, the restaurant-sized oven and hob, the open shelves of matching plates and pans.

The room was high-ceilinged and cool. At one end was a blue-tiled table, at the other a wooden dresser and slatted doors that led to a pantry.

'A sympathetic renovation of a traditional Sicilian home,' Poppy thought, composing the advert. 'Lots of steps. Would suit young couple with good knees.'

She had peeped into the other bedrooms and decided that hers, with its view of the cathedral, was the pick of the bunch. Tricia had a small balcony, Valerie a bathtub, and Moll's was the most spacious; but Poppy preferred the outlook from her room. She was tempted to stay there, lying on the bed to enjoy it, but the others were all downstairs and ready to begin the first lesson: pasta-making. Poppy had tried it once using a friend's machine, rolling it thinner and thinner, then stuffing it with ricotta and spinach. It had taken hours and, in Brendan's opinion, hadn't been worth the fiddle.

By the time she joined them, the lesson had begun (Moll gave her a bit of a look). They had made a start on the sauce and everything needed for the pasta was laid out. Wide wooden boards had been fitted over the worktop and floured. There were rolling pins and ridged tools set at each place. Poppy hurried to the free space at the counter so Luca could begin his demonstration.

'First we'll mix a very simple dough,' he said, pouring a steady stream of flour into a large wooden trug. 'You'll find we Sicilians take a relaxed attitude to pasta. There are no firm rules about what shape belongs with which sauce; and usually we don't waste time filling it with cheese and meat. Our summers are hot so we have to keep things simple, otherwise the dough dries out while we're still working with it. We don't even put in any egg, just semolina flour and tepid salted water. You won't believe how easy it is.'

Once he had combined the dough, Luca divided it into four even portions, giving one to each of them to do the work of kneading and shaping.

Moll set to confidently, Poppy watching as she pressed and rolled her dough. She did her best to imitate, trying not to feel self-conscious.

'Poppy, that's very good. You can sprinkle a little more flour on the board if it's sticking,' Luca encouraged. 'Tricia, don't knead with your fingers; use your hands. Valerie, you've nearly got it.'

He stood and watched them work for a few moments, then, moving to Poppy's side of the counter, he touched the ball of dough then put his fingers to her hands. She stiffened a little, surprised by the contact.

'This is ready,' he told her. 'Feel how it is quite firm. You have warm hands, Poppy.'

'Is that good?' she asked.

'The best pastry chefs have cool hands,' Moll told her cheerfully.

Disheartened, Poppy glanced at Luca. 'Really?'

'Yes, but don't worry. The others can keep kneading while I demonstrate the next step with your dough.'

Deftly he rolled the dough until it was shaped like a long, thick piece of spaghetti that he cut into smaller pieces with a sharp knife.

'Now comes the magic part,' he promised.

Poppy watched as, holding the ridged wooden board in one hand, Luca pressed a portion of dough into it, rolling down easily with his thumb and forming a small curled shape like a seashell. He repeated the process several times, making sure everyone had seen and understood.

'Now you try,' he said to Poppy.

It had appeared simple enough but she must have applied too much pressure, as the first piece of pasta got stuck to her thumb. Poppy floured her hands and tried again. The second attempt was misshapen, as was the third.

'I'm useless. I can't do it at all,' she said.

'Yes you can. It's a knack. Look, let me show you again.'

Luca stood beside her, so very close that Poppy felt unnerved. Covering her thumb with his, he guided her as she rolled the dough into a seashell shape with one smooth action.

'It's a gentle, constant pressure,' he explained. 'Now, once more without me.'

Poppy tried and the result was OK, the next one better still. 'Oh, thanks for being so patient. I think I might be getting the hang of it at last.'

'It's easy really. When you get into a rhythm, making cavatelli is a truly relaxing thing to do.'

'I can see how it would be,' agreed Moll, who was holding her board like an expert and turning out perfect little dough shells. Valerie was doing a pretty good job too. Only Tricia was frowning with the effort of making a success of it.

Once the dough had been used up, Luca covered the cavatelli with a clean cloth so they wouldn't dry out and moved on to the rest of the meal. The vegetables were prepared; the swordfish seasoned, and the kitchen filled with the smell of cooking.

Valerie declared she had to sit down. Earlier she had complained of swollen ankles from her long flight and now she seemed tired. Despite her own jet lag, Poppy felt energised from the morning in the kitchen. While Moll busied herself setting the table, and Tricia returned to her room to freshen up, she stayed in the kitchen, watching as Luca put the finishing touches to their lunch.

'Have you always cooked?' she asked, glad for a moment to chat to him alone.

'No, quite the opposite actually. My nonna and the other women of the family did all the cooking. I never touched a pan when I was a boy.'

'When did that change?'

'I went to England to study and hated the food I ate there: stodgy pies bought from bakeries, endless fish and chips, meals from cans.' He screwed up his face at the memory. 'It made me sick in the end, literally. So I wrote to my family, begging them to send recipes. My nonna replied straight away. She told me how to make a simple *minestre* of fresh vegetables and a pasta al forno. Every week she sent a new recipe. The food I cooked wasn't as good as hers. For one thing, I couldn't get all the ingredients I needed. But it was better than the stuff I'd eaten before.'

Poppy imagined him as a young man trying to cope in a foreign country. 'And so cooking became your passion?'

'Eating was my passion at first.' Luca laughed. 'But I came home one summer and Nonna showed me other things – the cavatelli that we made today, for instance. The two of us spent hours in this kitchen, making different shapes of pasta, baking cakes. Gradually she passed her passion for cooking on to me.'

'And now you're doing the same,' said Poppy, touched by his story. 'Passing on your passion.'

'That's the idea.' Luca glanced at the pasta pot full of water coming to the boil. 'I like the thought that all over the world people who have taken this course are keeping my nonna's memory alive by cooking her recipes.'

'Did she know this was what you were going to do? Had you told her about your plan for a cookery school?'

'No, because the plan wasn't made then. She would have been very surprised if she'd known. I suspect she envisaged quite a different future for me.'

Luca tipped the cavatelli into the boiling water. 'These will only take a few moments,' he told her. 'It's time to eat. Would you mind rounding everyone up?'

Out on the terrace, Moll had set a pretty table. There was a white tablecloth held down against the breeze by two large seashells, a silver dish of sea salt, a jug of olive oil, a basket of golden bread and a carafe of chilled *rosato* wine.

'Hungry?' Luca asked as he brought out bowls of pasta lightly coated in sauce and grated cheese.

They hurried to their seats, clinking glasses and chorusing '*Buon appetito*.' Moll photographed her food carefully before tasting it; Tricia watched her, eyebrows raised.

'Do you plan to do that with everything you eat?' she wondered.

'Yes, most likely,' Moll replied bluntly.

Keen to try the dish, Poppy dug her fork into one of the cavatelli. It was firmer than any pasta she'd had before. Trying the sauce, she found a hint of cinnamon and the flavour of fennel from the sausage. Delicious, she agreed, very good indeed.

'So, Luca.' Tricia put down her fork and smiled. 'Tell us about the girl we met at the market. Is she a good friend?'

'Orsolina?' Luca wiped a crust of bread over his plate to soak up the sauce. 'I've known her for many years. She comes from Favio's original chocolate-making family. Tomorrow we'll visit their *dolceria* for a tasting and to watch them at work. They've been using the same technique for more than a century and their chocolate is quite different – some people don't like it at all.'

'Do you?' Tricia asked

'Yes, of course, it's the chocolate I was raised on.'

'And Orsolina?'

'I like her too.' Luca laughed. 'My nonna used to help out in the *dolceria* if they were short-staffed, and I worked there for a while myself, so I know her family very well indeed. They are my closest friends.'

Before Tricia could press for more, he changed the subject. 'What we're planning for this afternoon is a walking tour,' he told them, 'but if anyone prefers to take a rest, that's fine. We'll visit the cathedral, then climb up through the town until we reach the Pizzo, where we'll find the very best view of Favio.'

'I'm keen on a walking tour,' said Poppy.

'Me too,' Moll agreed.

Only Valerie hesitated. 'I'd like to, but I'm worried I won't make it up all those steps. You're all so much younger and fitter than me.'

'We can take it at your pace,' Luca told her. 'Why don't you come to the cathedral and then turn back after that if you're tired?'

Poppy remembered the capers she had picked that morning. 'Oh, wait, I meant to show you something,' she said. 'Hold on a minute.'

The green buds were still nestled in the pocket of her hoodie. She was worried they might have shrivelled, but they looked plump and firm. Scooping up a handful, she went back downstairs to show the others.

'These came from some bushes growing wild up on the hill,' she told them.

'Ah, you went foraging,' Luca said approvingly. 'There is often something worth harvesting – wild fennel and herbs; later the prickly pears which I love; and of course, the capers. This time of year I never walk up the hill without a basket just in case.'

'I tasted one and it was bitter,' Poppy told him. 'Do they need to be cooked or put in vinegar or something?'

'You preserve them in salt,' Moll told her.

'That's right.' Luca nodded in agreement. 'We can forage for more while we're up there and later I'll show you how it's done.'

Lunch ended with more coffee and a plate of almond biscuits while Luca dealt with the dirty dishes (he insisted). Poppy felt pleasantly relaxed. Leaning back in her seat, she let the conversation round the table run on without her.

'I'm never going to fit into my skinny jeans if I eat like this every day,' Tricia was complaining. 'I'll have to be more careful.'

Moll shrugged and reached for a second biscuit. 'Well I'm not going to waste time worrying about putting on a few pounds,' she declared. 'It would be crazy to miss out on all these amazing flavours. I've decided to eat whatever I want.'

'I agree with you,' said Valerie. 'Mind you, at my age, a few pounds are neither here nor there. The big problem is that everything is drooping. I can't wear sleeveless tops any more, never mind skinny jeans.'

'How old are you anyway?' Tricia asked.

Valerie looked taken aback. 'Old enough not to reveal my age.'

Tricia assessed her. 'I'd say mid fifties.'

'That's very kind of you; now add several years.'

'Truly? Well, you look great, so I wouldn't worry about it.'

'Yes, you do,' agreed Moll. 'I'm forty, if anyone was wondering.'

'Poppy?' Tricia prompted.

Reluctantly, she opened her eyes. 'Thirty-one, but only just,' she told them.

'Ah, well I'm thirty-eight and possibly too old for skinny jeans anyway, so I may as well eat the biscuits.'

'I don't feel old,' Valerie told them. 'My body may be starting to fall apart, but in my head I'm the same girl I always was. Sometimes I'll catch a glimpse of my reflection – in a rear-view mirror or a subway window, say – and it gives me a fright. It's not how I think of myself. Other people my age say the same thing.'

Holding her fingers at the sides of her face, Tricia pulled her skin taut. 'See this? I use lotions and potions every single day. Spend a fortune; layer them on. But it's all starting to go south anyway. When I turn forty, I'm having a face lift.'

'So long as you don't get a trout pout,' said Valerie. 'Like that actress ... what's her name ...?'

Luca emerged from the kitchen to clear the last of the cups and glasses. 'Are you all finished?' he asked, before taking away the biscuits.

Tricia glanced up. 'We're talking about getting older,' she told him.

'Ah, yes.'

'We've all revealed our ages ... now what about you?'

Luca laughed. His teeth were white, he was blessed with olive skin and there was only the barest hint of grey in his hair. 'I'm told it's difficult for people to guess,' he said, evasively.

'If we guess right, will you tell us?' Tricia asked.

'No.'

'Why not?'

Luca only laughed again. 'If everyone has finished, we should get ourselves ready to go for our walking tour.'

There was a fair bit of flapping as everyone got ready. Valerie needed to nip to the loo. Tricia wanted to change into shorts. When it seemed like they were set to go, Moll said, 'Oh wait, I'll just be a minute.'

By the time they assembled it was mid afternoon and the heat was at its most intense.

'The trouble is, if we go down those steps we'll only have to climb back up,' Valerie sighed.

'You do have a good point,' said Tricia. 'They're bloody steep.'

Luca urged them on. 'My nonna walked up and down these steps several times a day for the whole of her life. They're why she lived as long as she did.'

Throwing her leather tote over her shoulder, Poppy felt the muscles of her legs complaining at the descent. Already she was feeling the effects of her morning run, but she vowed to get some exercise every day if she could.

Down on the main street, they had to stop and wait while Moll and Valerie went to buy gelato, Luca following them into the shop in case they needed help ordering.

'Interesting guy, isn't he?' Tricia said quietly as he disappeared. 'If you get him talking about food then it's difficult to shut him up. Ask him about himself, however ... nothing.'

'I've noticed that,' agreed Poppy.

'I wonder what his story is. Have you had a chance to talk to him much?'

'Yes, a little bit earlier. The only thing I've learnt is that he loved his nonna.'

'Really?' Tricia sounded intrigued. 'Is he gay, do you think? Often the mysterious ones are.'

Poppy considered the idea. 'He's not like any of the gay men I know in Sydney. They're much more flamboyant. Anyway, this morning didn't you have him paired up with that woman at the market?'

Tricia laughed. 'What's her name? Orsolina? That's right, I did.'

Moll and Valerie reappeared, spooning gelato out of paper cups. Behind them Luca was still caught in conversation with the shopkeeper.

'Yes, this evening then. The usual time,' he was saying, 'at the Mazzara place, of course. *Ci vediamo.*'

The walk continued at a leisurely pace up the steps to the butter-coloured stone cathedral, through its great arched entrance to view the ornate interior, then onwards up the steep incline, stopping to pick capers wherever they found bushes. Luca pointed out places of interest along the way: in that house a famous philosopher once lived, this was where a well-known TV series was filmed, here was another church but the priest was famously cranky and disapproved of sight-seers, and now there were a few more steps and they would be at the Pizzo enjoying the view.

Valerie seemed to be struggling, so Poppy hung back too. 'I've been up there already today,' she said. 'I'll stay behind with you.'

'Thanks … I don't think I can make it.' She was very pale. 'I used to be pretty fit but I seem to have lost it completely. Really I don't know what's wrong with me.'

'I'm sure it's only the heat,' Poppy reassured her. 'There's no breeze like there was out on the terrace during lunch.'

'Well I hope I can keep up with you girls on this course. I don't want to be the one holding everyone up.'

'That's funny, I've been thinking the same thing,' Poppy admitted.

'You have?'

'Yes, but with the cooking, not the walking.'

'Oh, I see. Well, Luca seems to be a wonderful teacher, so I wouldn't be too concerned.' Valerie sat down on a bench, leaning back against the wall. 'Ah, that's better.'

'There's a bar over there. Why don't I see if I can get you some cold water?'

'That would be lovely.'

It was a small neighbourhood bar and unexpectedly crowded. As she hurried in, Poppy felt as if everyone was staring at her.

'A bottle of mineral water, please,' she asked the bartender in careful Italian.

'Ice?' he grunted back in English.

'No, just the bottle, please. Still water, not fizzy.'

Then she heard a woman's voice; sing-song, familiar. 'Aren't you one of Luca's new guests?'

Orsolina was sitting alone at the far end of the bar, smoking a cigarette, an orange-coloured drink in front of her. 'Would you like something more exciting to drink than water? An Aperol Spritz?' With a tilt of her head she held up her glass.

'Thank you, but my friend is feeling ill. I'm taking the water to her.'

Orsolina frowned. 'Ill? But where is Luca?'

'He went up to the Pizzo with the others.'

Stubbing out her cigarette, Orsolina stood. 'I had better come, then.'

'I'm sure she'll be fine ... there's no need. I can look after her.'

'I've done a first-aid course,' Orsolina insisted. 'And anyway, my car is here. She may need transport.'

By the time they reached Valerie, she was hunched on the bench, her head between her knees, and when she raised her face, Poppy saw it was quite washed of colour.

'I feel rather faint,' she admitted. 'I'm not well at all.'

Orsolina was surprisingly efficient: checking Valerie's pulse; making her describe exactly how she felt (nauseous and a headache); pressing a hand to her forehead to see if there was any fever.

'I think it's too much sun,' she decided. 'And perhaps the wine at lunch and so many steps when you're not used to them.'

'Yes, the steps,' Valerie agreed. 'If I could just lie down I'd feel better. I'm not sure if I'll make it back up to the house, though.'

'Perhaps if we go really slowly ...' offered Poppy.

Orsolina dismissed the idea. 'I'll drive her to my father's home instead,' she said. 'There are no steps to reach it and she can rest until she's well enough.'

'I don't want to inconvenience you ...' began Valerie.

'You're not in the slightest,' Orsolina promised. 'And Luca would expect me to help.'

'Well if you're really sure ... thank you.'

'I'll come too,' Poppy offered.

'No, no, I think you should go up to the Pizzo and tell Luca what's happened, or else he'll be concerned. He has plans to come to my house later, so he can collect your friend then if she's feeling better.'

Poppy hung on while Orsolina helped Valerie into a shining white Fiat Bambino and whisked her off much too quickly down the narrow street. Then she hurried off to look for the others, finding them a little way up the hill, standing on the steps of a church and listening intently to something Luca was saying.

He frowned when he heard the news. 'Why didn't Orsolina text me? I'd have come straight down. Oh well, at least Valerie is in good hands. She'll be well looked after at the Mazzara house.'

Moll was the one who seemed most concerned. 'Oh, poor Val, she was feeling wobbly even this morning. And she's older than she looks, as we know.'

'I'll go directly to see how she is,' decided Luca. 'There'll be time tomorrow to show you how to prepare the capers. And tonight's a free evening anyway. I was going to suggest you eat a pizza. I'll point out the best place on the way back.'

'But shouldn't we come with you, to check on Val?' Moll wondered. 'Perhaps there's something she needs?'

'No, no, you mustn't worry. Enjoy your evening. We'll take care of everything, Orsolina and I.'

They had been a group for only a day, but still it seemed wrong to be returning to the house without Valerie. The mood was subdued, and once plans had been made to meet later for dinner, they went their separate ways: Tricia to Skype her family, Moll to window-shop her way down the food shops on the main street and Poppy to her room for a quick rest. With her she took an Italian magazine she had found in the living room, with the idea of seeing if her grasp of the language was enough to translate a few paragraphs.

First she opened her window to let in the evening breeze; then she plumped up the cushions on her bed. When everything was perfect, she lay down to read, opening the magazine at a page that had been folded over at the corner. On it she was surprised to find a photograph of Luca wearing his dark blue Food of Love apron, a cavatelli board in one hand.

She tried to struggle her way through the accompanying article. It appeared to be about Sicilians who chose to come home, giving up the chance of lucrative careers overseas. Luca was described as being internationally successful, but that was the only bit of the story Poppy understood properly. It was frustrating; she wondered what sort of business he had turned his back on, and why. If only she could find an Italian–English dictionary, she might have a chance of making out more, but she hadn't noticed one anywhere about the house.

At 6 p.m., the bells of the cathedral began to ring, and those of Favio's other churches responded. Poppy heard the front door slam and supposed it must be Moll returning. She yawned, wishing her body would adjust to the change in time zones so she could be rid of this jet-lag muzziness. Hauling herself up from the bed before she dropped off to sleep completely, she decided see if anyone was ready for an aperitif.

She took the magazine with her down to the terrace, where she found Tricia already waiting, clothes changed again and face freshly made up.

'This view is at its nicest in the evening,' Tricia remarked. 'Everything seems softer and more golden, don't you think?'

'It's pretty special,' Poppy agreed. 'Luca must think so too. According to this article I've been trying to read, he abandoned an international career so he could return here.'

'Let's see.' Tricia glanced at the magazine, then frowned. 'Oh, it's in Italian. What does it say? What sort of career?'

'I'm not sure. It doesn't really make it clear, or at least not in a way I can understand.'

'I expect he did the article as publicity for his business,' Tricia commented. 'Look at him in his apron with its great Food of Love logo. The rest of the piece is probably about cooking. That's all he's interested in. He doesn't seem to notice anything else, even poor old Val having a fainting fit.'

'Come on, that's not fair,' Poppy argued. 'It's not as if he abandoned her. I was there … and Orsolina too.'

'Yes, she has a habit of cropping up, doesn't she?' Tricia focused on the photograph of Luca again. 'Hmm, yes, he's dishy, very dishy indeed. I can see why she sticks so close. I might do the same if I were her, particularly when he has a house full of women.'

'I don't think Orsolina has much to worry about from us. You're married, I'm freshly divorced.'

Tricia shrugged. 'Oh you never know: a few glasses of wine and a fine starry Sicilian evening, and anything could happen.'

Food of Love

Luca Amore is forming fresh impressions. The first day always tends to show him what to expect from the rest. Already he can tell that Moll is the foodie of the bunch, showcasing what she knows every chance she gets. He sees how much Tricia wants to be admired and reminds himself to praise whatever she does. Valerie is a watcher and it is difficult to be sure what is going on inside her head. Poppy is worrying she might not be good enough and needs his reassurance.

When did women start believing they had to be perfect at everything? Luca wonders. His nonna was never like that. If she cut the cavatelli in a rush and the pieces were uneven, she would shrug and say, 'It all cooks the same anyway.' She often hurried down to the shops for some forgotten item with floury hands and her apron splashed with whatever sauce she had bubbling on the stove. He is certain she never experienced a hair crisis in her life.

Luca has learnt a lot about women while running these courses. Above all he has discovered how hard they can be on themselves and each other. Goals and expectations are all very well – he has had them for himself – but these women are so driven, and then are inevitably disappointed. He sees the same trait in every group he teaches – this one is no different.

Still, he likes them well enough. All four seem to be getting on, and that makes his job so much easier. He hopes they can refrain from discussing those things that always end in fights (religion and politics). He very much hopes Valerie's health does not become a problem; he was pleased to see her looking a great deal better when he said goodbye to her earlier tonight.

Luca thinks there is such beauty in a woman's face when it is allowed to age unfettered. The softening and folding over the bones, the slight translucence to the skin, the way its colour fades to ivory. Valerie is especially elegant. She walks like a dancer, loose and straight. Her hair is grey but she wears it longer than most women her age and often piled up on her head. Her clothes are casual but considered.

Tricia is beautiful too but all made of angles and hard lines. She seems too aware of the picture she makes, and Luca is wary of her. He feels much easier with Moll and Poppy, whose faces shine with the people they are: natural and open. He thinks of them as like bowls of spring *minestre* or winter soups of pasta and potatoes – reliable, trustworthy, nurturing.

Luca is hopeful that the coming days will be free of feuds and dramas: Tricia will relax, Valerie stay well, Moll and Poppy find a balance in the kitchen. He is hopeful for fine days, good food, wine ... a happy holiday. There is no reason to expect anything else.

First impressions are not always accurate, of course. Luca has been wrong before.

Tricia

Toxic, that's my life. It's been poisoning me for years. I'm sick of fighting other people's battles. In my job I see the worst of everyone – it's all hatred and point-scoring by the time I come along. I'm there for the bitter endings, the moments after love has been snuffed out. The nicest-seeming people can turn into monsters as their families are split apart. They hide assets, tell lies; they demolish each other's characters. Some seem to lose all reason and spend weeks fighting over who is to keep the bedroom curtains, then decide on the child custody arrangements in an instant.

The kids, poor things, they always come off worst. Before I had my own, it never bothered me. Now every contact order, every leave to remove has a tale behind it to break my heart. There have been days I've cried all the way home and had to get my taxi to park round the corner for ten minutes so I could pull myself together before I walked through the door.

At first, law seemed such a brilliant career. I loved the mental discipline, being in the university library surrounded by all those leather-bound volumes. Later on I liked the formality and traditions – the wig when I'm in the High Court, the Your Honour this and that. Oh, and the battles, of course. There's nothing like the thrill of winning, that moment when you know the case is yours.

There are still days when I make a difference for a client

and feel good about myself. But mostly it isn't like that, not any more.

I could tell you some stories, things I've heard and seen. Paul has always hated me talking about it; it bores him senseless. Paul's a doctor. His clients seem less difficult than mine – well, he's an anaesthetist, so I guess they're asleep a lot of the time. Anyway, he was sick of me being so unhappy; arranged a therapist, sorted out some antidepressants. I'm sure those pills work for other people, but I hated the way they flattened my mood – life felt the same but muffled. As I told my therapist, I'm miserable for a reason. I hate my bloody job. A pill isn't going to change that, is it?

Of course I could leave, have a total career change. But I worked so long and hard for this one. Now is the time to make money, invest for the future. Plus the kids are at private schools, the mortgage is huge, Paul made a few bad investments ... You earn it, you spend it, I suppose.

So I'm trapped. What can I do that brings in the sort of money I earn from divorcing people? I'm good at this job, successful. Yet still I can't stand the idea of doing it for the next ten or twenty years till I can afford to retire.

It was Paul who booked this trip for me. It was thoughtful of him, sweet. That's the kind of guy he is. He didn't want to come with me, thought it would do us good to have a break from each other. He says I've turned into a glass-half-empty person and that's not who he married.

I don't know why I'm telling you this. It's the wine, perhaps. I can't talk to any of my colleagues, and my friends have their own problems – husbands who've lost their jobs in the City, that kind of thing.

Being here on holiday, sitting on this terrace, work and London seem so far away. I'm not a person who finds it easy to relax usually. All the things that are meant to help – lying on a beach, massages, facials – don't work for me at all. But here we have a schedule, things to do and see; it's all planned out and Luca is taking charge.

By the end of it I expect I'll have wound down completely. Then I'll go home and nothing will have changed. The same life and the same old hassle. So let's have another drink and enjoy it while we can, shall we?

Day Two

(i) For the love of chocolate

The first thing Tricia thought about when she woke was her hair irons. They were good ones. Those things Valerie had lent her were next to useless. She quite understood how it might seem trivial to other people, but starting the day with nice hair made a difference to Tricia. Her mother had drilled into her how important grooming was. As a child, Tricia had assumed all grown women had bright red toenails and was shocked to glimpse another mum's bare feet and see that they did not. Tricia's mother still painted her nails. She believed in getting ready for the day, presenting herself properly. Tricia happened to know she wore waterproof mascara to bed every night, although she had slept alone ever since Dad died years and years ago.

How annoying. She remembered exactly where she'd left those hair irons. They were on the chest of drawers, cord wound neatly, waiting to be put in her suitcase. One of the kids must have asked for something and distracted her. Zara was especially needy at the moment and Charlie full of questions. They were both in the room while she was packing, even though she had turned on the Disney Channel downstairs and given Zara her iPhone to play with.

The only thing for it was a shampoo and blow-dry, and since her hair was thick and the hairdryer only travel-sized, it was going to take ages. Tricia wondered if any of the shops in Favio might sell decent hair irons, but she doubted it. This seemed a one-horse town ... although Orsolina was groomed to the hilt, so perhaps the place wasn't a lost cause after all.

She found herself envying Orsolina. Not her looks so much, but the carefree life she imagined she must have. A nice no-pressure family business, a gorgeous boyfriend, no kids. While she loved Zara and Charlie, and Paul too even after fifteen years together, sometimes Tricia woke up and dreaded every second of the day ahead.

This morning she opened her eyes to find herself in Sicily, where there was nothing to do but have a good time. Reaching over to the bedside table, she put on her glasses (short-sighted, very) and, finding the itinerary Luca had given them when they arrived, was pleased to see it was to be a busy day of visits, tours and tastings.

It had been clever of Paul to book her this holiday. Tricia suspected he was hoping it might inspire her to use the Bulthaup kitchen they'd had installed at great expense when they renovated the house.

Perhaps she might make pasta for the family when she got home. Luca had given them their cavatelli boards to take, after all. More likely the small flour-dusted tool would be stuffed in a drawer and forgotten while she continued ordering takeaway from the place down the road and reading through a stack of briefs while she ate it.

Stretching and yawning, Tricia began her morning routine. A quick shower, lotions and potions applied swiftly, contact lenses in, arms aching as she dried her hair, then a final smooth with the rubbish hair irons (they were better than nothing). By the time she was finished, she was desperate for a coffee.

The others were downstairs and at breakfast already. They were sitting outside on the terrace, a healthier-looking Valerie among them.

'Good morning. How is everyone today?' Tricia asked.

'Very well ... fine ... great,' they chorused back.

'You must have got in late last night, Val. It was past midnight when we all went to bed, and you still weren't back.'

The faintest flush showed on the older woman's cheeks. 'Actually I spent the night at Orsolina's father's house. He wouldn't hear of me leaving. He brought me dinner in bed and made such a fuss.'

'Where was Orsolina's mother?'

'Vincenzo is a widower,' Valerie explained, the flush deepening.

'Oh yes?'

'A very nice man indeed, but no, don't look at me like that, it was all perfectly innocent. I was sick, remember.'

'Sure,' smiled Tricia, helping herself to a slice of melon and checking the moka pot to see if there was any coffee left in it.

'Anyway, you'll meet him later; he'll be at the *dolceria* to take us on our tour,' Valerie told her. 'He let me taste some of his chocolate last night.'

'Elegant American tourist meets widowed Italian chocolate-maker ...' Tricia began mischievously.

Valerie blushed properly then. 'Oh stop it. You're terrible.'

Moll was laughing too. 'Someone else might be interested in him if you're not,' she chirped in her east London accent. 'A man with his own chocolate factory ... what does he look like anyway ... how old?'

'He's very nice,' Valerie repeated, refusing to be drawn. 'A kind man.'

Tricia cut up her melon into small chunks. 'Count me out. I'm not interested in being Orsolina's stepmother,' she said.

'Not even for chocolate?' asked Poppy, reaching for another pastry.

'It would have to be pretty special chocolate.'

Valerie allowed herself a smile. 'Well it is rather good in my opinion,' she admitted.

Luca emerged from the kitchen with a second moka pot full of coffee in his hand.

'So we're off to the chocolate factory this morning,' he said cheerily, filling their cups. 'Although it isn't really a factory, because they use traditional techniques rather than machines. You'll meet Vincenzo Mazzara, whose great-grandfather started up the *dolceria*. Vincenzo believes that today's chocolate is losing the memory of the original and that his family's duty is to preserve that memory. He's very passionate about it – poetic even.'

'He sounds like an amazing man,' said Tricia, with a teasing sideways glance at Valerie.

'Amazing, yes, he is,' Luca agreed. 'He's a mentor for many people here in Favio. Usually he doesn't come out to meet the tour groups that go through the *dolceria*. But we have a special relationship, he and I, and it is fascinating to hear his philosophy about chocolate. He believes it is vital for strength and vigour, and that to eat it every day is essential.'

'What's so wonderful about this chocolate of his anyway?' Tricia asked (mostly she preferred to avoid sweet things).

'You will see,' Luca promised.

The Antica Dolceria Mazzara lay down a narrow lane that Tricia must have passed several times already without noticing. The old buildings were covered in ivy and there was no signpost on the main street to point the way.

'Vincenzo believes that if people want to find his shop, they will,' Luca explained.

The door swung open with the ring of an old-fashioned bell to reveal a small room where the air smelled of warm sugar. It was lined with wooden shelves filled with antique chocolate-making tools, framed letters and photographs of cocoa bean plantations. Behind the glass counter there were more shelves, but these were stacked with bars of chocolate in pastel-coloured wrappers and boxes tied with ribbons.

Orsolina was there to welcome them, wearing a starched white apron, her dark hair tucked into a muslin hat.

'*Buongiorno.*' She came out from behind the counter to kiss their cheeks. 'Welcome to our *dolceria*. My father will be here in a few minutes to share the story of our chocolate. But first I have arranged some refreshment for you. One moment, please.'

She passed through the swing doors that lay behind the counter, returning with a tray holding four espresso cups thick with steaming melted chocolate.

'Oh no, not for me, thanks,' said Tricia.

'But you must,' Orsolina insisted.

'Yes, live a little,' Moll told her.

It seemed easier not to argue. 'Fine, pass it over, then,' she said, struggling not to sound as irritated as she felt.

The drink was so viscous and rich it coated her mouth as she tried to swallow it. There was a hint of cinnamon and vanilla beneath the deep sweetness of chocolate, and something else too, perhaps the alcoholic sting of a liqueur. Two sips were too much and she slipped the cup back on to the tray, hoping no one would notice.

'My father gave this hot chocolate to me as a bedtime drink when I was a child,' Orsolina told them. 'He said it would sweeten my dreams and I believed him. The taste is still the most comforting thing I know.'

Fishing a tissue from her handbag, Tricia wiped her lips clean. 'But there's alcohol in it, isn't there?' she said. 'It's not exactly a children's drink.'

'What you are tasting is history,' a new voice replied as an older man appeared from behind the swing doors. He was grey-haired, olive-skinned and might have been unremarkable aside for eyes that were a clear, pale gold like those of a bird of prey. Tricia assumed this must be Vincenzo Mazzara.

'What you are tasting is chocolate that is pure and powerful,' he continued, his tone commanding, 'chocolate that reaches back all the way to the ancient civilisation of the Aztecs and has never been corrupted. I fed it to my daughter as a child and now I am honoured to offer it to you.'

There was a silence in the shop after he had finished speaking; even Moll had no words to offer.

'Welcome to my *dolceria*,' he added more warmly, although still without a smile. 'Please come through and we will show you how we make our chocolate.'

Before they entered the workshop, they were each given a white overall and a muslin cap. 'We ask you to wear these for hygiene reasons,' Orsolina explained.

Normally Tricia might have found an excuse for not donning something quite so unattractive, but the startling yellow eyes of Vincenzo Mazzara were turned towards her.

'Yes, of course,' she murmured like the others.

The room beyond the swing doors was small, not unlike an ordinary domestic kitchen, with a pale grey marble work table running down its length and a large mixer in one corner.

Vincenzo waited wordlessly until he had their complete attention. Only then did he begin.

'These days, people think of chocolate as a treat, an indulgence,' he said, sounding regretful. 'But there was a time in Favio when the sight of the *ciucculattaru* driving round town with his grinder on a cart was a familiar one. He blended chocolate to order, melting and mixing it over a heated stone, and his customers bought it as a nourishing food to give them energy. Today we make our chocolate almost as he did. It is simple and pure, blending only sugar, cocoa beans and spices.'

Tricia had the sense that Vincenzo was talking to everyone but looking only at her. She shifted her gaze to the floor, and when she looked back, those yellow wolf eyes held her.

'This is how it is created,' he continued in his slow, steady English. 'First the cocoa beans are roasted, next they are ground with sugar and then we heat the mixture at a low temperature so the sugar crystals don't melt.'

Orsolina passed him a saucepan, from which he poured a

thick, rough paste of chocolate and sugar straight on to the work table.

'Now I will demonstrate what we do to make it smooth and creamy,' he told them.

Using two blades, he scooped up a portion of the paste, transferring it to a small metal tin that he had placed on a deep wooden tray.

'And finally the *battatura*,' he announced, beginning to drum the tray against the table, banging it rhythmically for at least a minute, the metal tin rattling. By the time he stopped, the chocolate looked slick and glossy.

'You see how all the air pockets are gone.' He held it out to them.

'Is this how you make every single bar?' asked Tricia, incredulous.

'Yes, of course.'

'It seems very labour intensive. Couldn't you get a machine to do the shaking for you?' she wondered.

Vincenzo gave her a stark look. 'The Mazzara family are the oldest chocolate-makers in Sicily. This is our tradition.'

'Tradition isn't everything,' Tricia argued.

'We believe it is. Perhaps when you taste it you will understand why.'

Out in the shop, Orsolina was laying out a number of shallow white dishes filled with broken chocolate pieces for them to taste.

'First you must try our most popular chocolate, the seventy per cent,' Vincenzo instructed. 'As you taste, be sure to savour its perfume and flavour, but most of all enjoy its texture.'

Moll bit into a sample. 'It's gritty instead of velvety,' she said, sounding surprised.

'I would describe that as a sandiness,' explained Vincenzo. 'You get it because the sugar crystals have not melted so there is still the crunch of them. It is a part of what makes our chocolate so special.'

'There are layers of flavour, aren't there?' said Moll, enthusiastically. 'First you get sweetness and then the bitterness of pure cocoa.'

Tricia took a piece from the dish. 'Is there a proper way to taste chocolate?' she wondered. 'Do I melt it in my mouth or bite into it?'

'A good question.' Vincenzo's eyes turned back to her. 'Bite into it first to break up the crystals. Then the natural heat of your mouth will liquefy the sugar, creating a rush of flavour: smoky, spicy, bitter and earthy as well as sweet.'

As Tricia tried it, she was aware of Vincenzo waiting for her reaction.

'I've never had anything quite like this before,' she said once the peculiar gritty stuff had softened and melted against her tongue. 'So is this what real chocolate is meant to taste like?'

'Yes, exactly. The factory-made bars people buy do not deserve to share the same name. They are nothing but a cheap confection. Now you must have some of the flavours: the cinnamon and the vanilla, the *pepperoncino*, the salt, the orange, the white pepper. Every ingredient we use is the purest. Our chocolate is like a fine wine; nothing is allowed to adulterate it – no milk or vegetable fats, no fake vanilla flavouring or orange essence. All that you taste comes from nature.'

'Why can't we buy chocolate like this in England?' Moll wondered. 'I've never seen it anywhere.'

'We do supply a few stores,' Orsolina told her. 'But we make it in such small quantities it's difficult to find.'

'Why not produce more, then?' suggested Moll. 'You could expand your factory and have more workers and equipment, export it to countries around the world. I'm sure it would be really popular.'

Tricia had been thinking the same thing. She looked to Vincenzo for his reply.

For a long moment, he was silent. Then, rubbing a hand through his short grey hair, he frowned. 'Perhaps we would be richer in some ways if we did,' he said. 'But we would also be poorer in all the ways that matter.'

'You mean you might lose control over the quality of the product if your company grew too big?' Moll asked.

'Yes, but it is something more profound than that. We are artisans,' Vincenzo told her. 'Every day we breathe the perfume of our chocolate; we touch and taste it as generations of our family have. Our life is sweet and we don't want to change that.'

Tricia couldn't help wondering how his daughter felt. Was Orsolina content with an artisan's existence? For the love of tradition would she spend her whole life shaking chocolate, even if it did pay enough to fuel her expensive tastes for designer heels? Looking at her now, her lovely features shadowed by the ugly muslin hat, Tricia doubted it.

The others were keen to buy chocolate, Moll filling a box with bars in every flavour and Poppy struggling to choose between them. Tricia bought a couple but only for politeness' sake. She didn't see the point of taking any home. Paul never touched chocolate, and she imagined the children would prefer ordinary Cadbury's.

'Shouldn't we be moving on to our next appointment?' she asked, glancing at her watch. 'Aren't we due at a vineyard?'

Luca detached himself from Orsolina. 'Actually, you're right. They'll be expecting us for lunch, so we ought to leave quite soon.'

Vincenzo took his time nevertheless. With no regard for their schedule, he insisted on wrapping the chocolate properly, carefully tying the white grosgrain ribbons round their boxes, pressing a few extra samples on them before they left.

'Oh, no need to wrap mine,' Moll told him. 'It's for me to eat, not give away as gifts. I'm going to have a couple of squares every single day from now on … for my health, of course.'

'*Brava*,' Vincenzo said approvingly. 'You can also cook with it; Luca will show you how. Another tradition is to eat it with bread or melt it over a low heat for a bedtime drink.'

As they left, he shook each of them by the hand. Tricia was the last to reach the door. For a few seconds his yellow eyes stared into hers.

'Thank you for your time,' she said, politely.

'*Prego, signora*,' he replied. 'You're welcome. Always.'

For once Luca seemed rushed. He offered to carry their chocolate boxes up to the house and meet them back at the bottom of the steps, where he had parked his big Volkswagen people carrier.

'The vineyard is twenty minutes' drive away,' he explained. 'I hadn't realised quite how long we were spending at the *dolceria*. Usually Vincenzo only joins us for a few moments. I think perhaps he was pleased to see Valerie again, and looking so much healthier.'

Only when he had run up the steps and was out of earshot did Tricia say, 'Honestly, Valerie, when you told us about him this morning, you made that chocolate-maker sound like a sweet old man. How misleading!'

'Don't tell me you think he's dishy as well,' Poppy said.

'No … if anything, I found him intense,' Tricia admitted.

'Those eyes,' agreed Poppy.

'Yes, exactly.'

'Last night he was very kind to me,' Valerie objected, 'an absolute gentleman and not intense in the slightest.'

'Well you're welcome to him,' Tricia told her. 'He's not my type at all.'

(ii) For the love of wine

Tricia took a seat beside Luca in the front of the van, listening to the chatter of the other women behind her as she stared out of the window at the passing countryside. Stone walls criss-crossed the landscape, dividing up the ploughed olive groves. There was a flush of green over some of the pasture, but if the dry weather continued, soon it would turn gold. That was how you expected fields to look in summertime this far south – Africa wasn't so far away after all. But it wasn't meant to be the colour of a man's eyes.

Vincenzo Mazzara had made an impression on her: both good and bad. Tricia guessed he was younger than Valerie, but not by much. He had been wearing a simple white T-shirt, his belly curving comfortably above the apron slung round his hips, but other than that he seemed in good shape. Intense, she had called him. It was the coolness of his stare she had disliked. It felt as if she was being sized up or judged, and really, what right did he have?

'You didn't enjoy our chocolate much, did you?' Luca broke in on her thoughts.

'Not really.' Tricia half laughed. 'All that fuss to make it. I didn't see the point at all.'

'There are plenty of people who don't see the point,' Luca admitted. 'You can buy bars in Favio that have been mass-produced in a factory. You'll see them in shops along the main street. Some cost more than Vincenzo charges, although the ingredients are inferior. Still, the tourists don't know that when they buy them.'

'It must be frustrating for him,' Tricia remarked.

'Of course it is. But the problem is the same for the gelato makers, the *arancini* shops and the vineyards. There is always someone who cuts costs and corners, producing inferior goods they pass off as the real thing.'

'I guess there's nothing anyone can do about it?'

'Vincenzo wants to try. He has a plan and we're taking slow, careful steps; perhaps too slow for him. He gets impatient because he's not a man who cares too much what other people think of him, but with this we must be cautious.'

'Why not give in and mass-produce like everyone else?' asked Tricia.

'He's not the sort of man who gives in easily either,' Luca replied, swinging the van through a set of tall iron gates and up a narrow driveway with vines stretching out on either side.

Tricia had taken a few vineyard tours in her time, and this was much the same as the rest. A walk over the dry earth to look at vines growing in the glare of the sun, then the merciful cool of the winery, where they stared at a lot of stainless-steel vats and oak barrels. There was talk of fermentation and ageing; of the sweetness of the grapes thanks to the hot, sunny climate; of battling pests.

She tried to seem interested, but the romance of winemaking had always escaped her, and she found herself cursing inwardly every time Moll asked another question or paused to take more photographs. The only point in winery visits, as far as Tricia was concerned, was to taste the stuff, but so far none had been forthcoming.

'This is one of the biggest wineries in the area,' Luca told her. 'At the end of the holiday we'll visit a smaller one that's run on biodynamic lines that I think you'll find more interesting.'

'Great,' smiled Tricia, wondering if she looked so obviously bored.

'Soon we'll go through to taste the wines and eat lunch,' Luca continued. 'The head chef here is very good, an award-winner, although known for being temperamental. He's thrown out a couple of restaurant critics and people who have complained about things. He is very serious about food. Much of the produce he uses is grown here in the kitchen gardens.'

Tricia perked up. At their country house there had been a vegetable garden: rows of raised beds built from old railway sleepers that she spent hours tending, much to Paul's frustration. He had never understood the pleasure to be found in a row of spinach growing green and healthy, in picking runner beans from a bamboo trellis or digging up new potatoes. In the country she had cooked more often too; simple meals, but it seemed to Tricia you could taste the goodness in them. She loved that house, surrounded by paddocks and woodland. She felt herself loosen and relax the moment they turned off the motorway and saw the first road signs to the nearest village.

It had been Paul who'd wanted to sell; he used the excuse of belt-tightening in the face of such tough economic times, but she knew he found their country weekends dull. In the city there were exhibitions to go to, more than one place to eat lunch, plenty of shops and shows.

Zara's pony had been sold, belongings packed and taken home and the place put on the market. Tricia did the springtime planting anyway; put in rows of lettuce and beans, thinking that whoever bought the house might like to harvest them.

'Why don't you have some pots of herbs out on the roof terrace at home?' Paul had suggested. 'You could probably grow rocket there too.'

Tricia had imagined the fresh leaves coated with the invisible poisons of the city (diesel fumes from buses and taxis, air that had been breathed by too many people) and she hadn't bothered.

The family that bought the house were Londoners like them, and Tricia heard later from friends in the village that they visited it only occasionally. They must have been busy with other things: skiing, boating. Now and then she fantasised about buying the place back without telling Paul, and going there alone to blanket the vegetable beds with fresh compost and shop for punnets of seedlings.

'I'd be interested in seeing the gardens here,' she told Luca.

'Normally we don't, but if there's time then I don't see why not. I'll check with the chef.'

Moll was still bursting with questions and expressing a keen interest in watching wine bottles being labelled, the tour guide nodding in agreement. Tricia hung back. As soon as everyone else had disappeared inside the bottling sheds, she took her chance to slip away round the side of the winery building.

The kitchen garden had been planted on a gentle slope, close enough for the smell of cooking to drift across. It was there to be admired as well as to produce. Plants rambled over willow frames or up rustic wooden stakes. Flowers grew untidily, dots of haphazard colour amid rows of green. Smooth stepping stones had been laid as a pathway and Tricia followed them through the herb beds, pulling a few needles from a rosemary plant to rub between her fingers and inhale the resinous smell.

A man's voice startled her. 'Signora, can I help you? Have you lost your group?'

He was wearing a chef's hat (although he seemed absurdly young) and carrying a wide, shallow-bottomed basket. Tricia assumed he was an apprentice sent out to harvest vegetables for lunch.

'I'm fine, thanks,' she told him.

'You enjoy gardens?' he asked.

'Yes, I'm enjoying this one. Is there a gardener who maintains it?'

'I am the gardener,' he said in heavily accented English, offering her a smile, and Tricia thought what a beautiful boy he was. 'The others help me, of course, but I'm the one who is here first every morning. I dig, plant and weed ... finally my reward is the picking.'

'What are you picking today?'

'Peas ... For the soup we need plenty.'

Tricia fell in beside him, moving down the rows, stripping the plants and filling his basket as the sun beat hard on the back of her neck. He mustn't have minded, as he made no comment, only tilting the basket her way whenever she had another handful of pods to deposit.

'I've never grown peas myself,' she said. 'Are they tricky?'

'They can be. Here the season is short because of the heat. This will be the last of them, but still, we've had a good crop. Last year wasn't so successful.'

'Bad news for the soup. Was the head chef furious? I hear he's temperamental.'

The beautiful boy smiled. 'I think he understood,' he said.

They sent Valerie to come and find her. She was shading her eyes with a hand as she came round the corner. Smiling, Tricia waved at her. 'I gatecrashed the garden,' she called out.

'Ah, Luca said you might be here.' Valerie walked the stepping-stone path until she reached the rows of peas. 'I hadn't realised you were a gardener.'

Tricia shrugged. 'Oh, I'm not really ... I just got bored and went exploring. So is Moll still studying to be a winemaker?'

Valerie looked confused. 'Sorry?'

'Have they finished looking at the bottling plant?' she asked, a little less tartly.

'Oh yes, they're in the restaurant now, tasting the first wine. Luca thought you wouldn't want to miss out.'

Tricia glanced back at the young chef. She might have preferred to stay here with him; take a spade or trowel; pull out some spent plants; smell clean earth and green stalks.

'Lunch will be served any minute,' Valerie added. 'The food is matched to the wines. Best not to be late.'

'No, I suppose not,' she agreed, and nodding at the chef, she turned to follow Valerie back towards the winery.

*

The restaurant was cool and modern, with floor-to-ceiling windows to show off the view and glass floors so they could see all the way down to the wine barrels in the dimly lit cellar below. The others were at the table already, sipping glasses of wine, and Tricia took the free seat, facing the open kitchen, where two chefs, younger even than the one she had met in the garden, hovered over hot pans and sharp knives.

'Is there a menu?' she asked, not spotting one on the table.

'No, we leave it to the kitchen to decide what to give us,' Luca told her.

'Really? I'd prefer to choose. Would that be a problem?'

Luca seemed dubious. 'The chef here is Sicilian. This is the way he likes to do it. If there's something you don't like, then I'm sure he'll offer an alternative.'

'Can I see the menu at least?'

'I'm not sure they have one. But here's the head chef now, I'll ask him.'

Tricia saw the young gardener come into the kitchen with his basket full of peas. Resting it on a long bench, he nodded at one of the others to come over and begin podding.

'Surely that's not the head chef?' She pointed, amazed. 'He looks about twenty.'

Luca laughed. 'They're very proud of him here. Santo is a local boy, a young talent, but not as young as he looks. I expect you'll meet him, as when the Locanda is quiet like today, he brings the food out himself. Shall I ask about a menu?'

She shook her head, embarrassed. 'No, that's OK, leave it.'

'At least let me find out what he has planned for us.'

Tricia looked at the beautiful boy, moving round his kitchen in an almost animal way, quick and watchful, sinewy and strong. 'Would you mind asking if we're going to get the pea soup?'

'No problem.' Rising from his chair, Luca approached the open archway that led to the kitchen.

He and the three chefs greeted each other with very Italian embraces, a rough squeeze or two, some backslapping, a lot of laughter. They talked animatedly for a moment or two.

'They're so handsome, the men here, aren't they?' Tricia murmured.

'I used to be married to handsome,' said Poppy. 'It's not everything.'

'I guess you're right.' Tricia stared at Luca and the young chef. 'You know, the first time I came to Italy, I was in my early twenties and the guys wouldn't leave me alone – following, wolf-whistling, pinching my bottom. It drove me mad. This time there hasn't been any of that. I must be too old.'

'Perhaps they've just learned better manners by now,' Poppy suggested.

Tricia laughed. 'OK, I'm going with that. I'm not ready to be old. It can wait.'

Hearing their laughter, Luca looked over. He smiled and gave her a thumbs-up. 'Pea soup,' he mouthed.

As Luca had predicted, Santo brought out the dishes himself, laying them at each place with a quiet reverence. First came the soup, served in delicate white bowls, searing green with a curl of mascarpone on top.

'*Buon appetito*,' the chef told them. 'I trust you will enjoy it.'

Tricia tasted a spoonful. It smelt of the garden and was sweet, nutty and creamy yet still ridiculously light; it filled her mouth with its flavour.

'Dear God, that's good.'

'This is the soup of spring,' Santo said. 'I have enough peas for one more batch ... maybe two. You were lucky you didn't arrive any later than this.'

'Would you mind sharing the recipe?' Moll asked. 'I'd love to try it at home.'

'By all means, but the soup you make will not taste like mine.' It was said without a trace of arrogance. 'In my kitchen the peas are cooked within moments of being picked and podded, the herbs and leeks are grown in the garden, the mascarpone comes from a local producer and is very fresh. Without the ingredients, you don't get the soup.'

Moll seemed undaunted, as always. 'Still I'd like to try it.'

Lunch went on for half the afternoon, course after course each matched with a glass of wine. There were fritters of fava beans and wild fennel, fresh pasta dressed with salty olives and crushed pistachios, fleshy white fish in a sweet-sour sauce. Tricia kept expecting to reach her limit, but to her surprise, each new dish revived her appetite.

At the very end they were served strong coffee, sweet wine and a preserve of lemon and orange peel that Luca said had been cooked in honey and was excellent for the digestion.

'If I stop eating, that might help my digestion more,' Tricia said wryly, rubbing her taut belly.

'But each portion we had was small and the textures were very light. It's healthy food,' Luca promised.

'At home, all I have for lunch is a sushi pack at my desk or a salad from Pret A Manger.'

'That sounds terrible. I would kill myself.' Luca grinned at her. 'Please try a little of the *aranciata e cedrata*. It has the sweet-sour flavour we Sicilians love. I think you will prefer it to Vincenzo Mazzara's chocolate.'

It was hardly surprising that she fell asleep on the drive back to Favio. Waking to feel a tiny damp patch in the corner of her mouth, Tricia feared she had been drooling. Fortunately Luca's eyes were focused on the road.

'Are we nearly there?' she asked.

'Yes, you were only sleeping for a few minutes, I think.'

She yawned. 'All that wine … it was delicious, but too much. You were smart not drinking any.'

'I'm driving,' Luca said lightly.

'You could still have had a glass or two, though, couldn't you?'

'Perhaps, but I prefer not to.'

Tricia tried to recall if she had ever seen him touch alcohol. 'You didn't have any wine at lunch yesterday either. Or when we went out to dinner. Do you not drink on the job?'

'You could put it that way.'

As they turned on to the main street, the others began to stir, finding handbags and picking up the gift boxes of wine they had bought.

'Everyone is free for the rest of the day,' Luca told them. 'Poppy, there is time for me to show you how to prepare the capers you picked yesterday. The rest of you are welcome to join us.'

'I'd love to, but I really ought to update my food blog,' said Moll. 'Oh, didn't I tell you? It's just a little thing I do for fun.'

'I'm going to take a rest, I think.' Valerie was looking exhausted.

Tricia felt like time alone anyhow. She decided to explore the shops, check out the local fashion and see if she couldn't find some decent hair straighteners (she didn't hold out much hope). Luca pointed her in the right direction and she set off, browsing windows as she went.

Before long, she noticed how every third shop seemed to sell chocolate. The bars were piled in the windows, some in pastel-coloured wrappers just like the ones from Dolceria Mazzara. Tricia was tempted to try one.

She found herself almost looking over her shoulder as she entered the shop. How ridiculous. So what if Vincenzo Mazzara saw her? She was free to buy whatever she wanted.

This shop was at least twice as big as the other *dolceria*, and the man behind the counter was small and solid with very ordinary eyes.

'Just a single bar, signora?' he said, regretfully. 'Are you certain? This is the very best chocolate you will find in all of Favio.'

'Really? I was told the best stuff came from that small place round the corner.'

The man scowled, muttering something in Italian.

'I'm sorry?'

'I said that is the *oldest* chocolate shop, signora; it doesn't mean it is the *best*. In the end it is a matter of opinion. You decide which one you prefer.'

Tricia paid for the bar, stuffing it to the bottom of her handbag as she left the shop. She didn't believe for a moment she would taste a difference between this and Vincenzo Mazzara's products. Chocolate was chocolate, wasn't it? A trivial thing to get so worked up over.

Walking along the shady side of the street, she passed more places selling local specialities – *torrone* as well as chocolate, gelato of course, packets of dried pasta, cheeses and jars of preserved red peppers, trays of biscuits and cannoli. Sicilians appeared to be obsessed with food. Everyone Tricia had met so far talked of little else. And yet it was just food, something tasty to eat, fuel to keep you going. It didn't save lives or change them. Preparing it was a chore for many people she knew, including herself most of the time.

Amidst the glut of food shops were a couple of places offering expensive shoes and designer clothing. There was a bookshop and a tailor, a florist and a jewellery store; more things to buy than expected but not the one thing she wanted right now. Tricia kept going until the shops finished and she reached a row of modern apartment blocks. Turning to walk back up the other side of the street, she decided to stop for a drink at the café she had passed earlier.

She was half hoping to find one of the others there, but the only occupants were the two old men playing chess she had noticed first time round. Their table was cluttered with glasses, cups and ashtrays, and they seemed to have settled in for the long haul.

Tricia claimed a table well out of reach of their cigarette smoke, waving to attract the waiter's attention. She gave her order crisply and in English. A coffee with a jug of skimmed milk on the side, a Peroni beer, very cold; no need to bring out baskets of crisps and little snacks, but she would have a wedge of lemon in the stem of the beer bottle, please.

He took ages to return, seeming as unhurried (or painfully slow) as everyone else in Favio. Tricia appreciated that this was a more relaxed pace of life, but still she was struggling to adjust. At home if she ordered something she expected it to come in minutes; once finished, she liked dirty crockery whisked away. She didn't suffer slowness gladly: judges who spoke ponderously, clients who couldn't grasp what they were told, anyone who shuffled along – all of that drove her insane. It was a character flaw, this impatience of hers, and she had tried to deal with it, talking it through with her therapist, even paying for several sessions with a hypnotist whose room was over-warm and whose voice was so calm and measured it failed to block the rush of thoughts from flooding through her brain.

Her drinks finally arrived on a tray with all the things she hadn't asked for: a bowl of sugar, a dish of salty crackers, another of sweet biscuits. She bit her lip instead of speaking. Paul hated it when she complained, saying it spoilt every occasion. She knew he had a point so was trying to train herself to resist. At least here on holiday she could accept the way things unfolded, even if it remained impossible at home with a job to do, a family to run and not enough hours in any day.

Tricia imagined that dynamic young people like Luca and Santo must find the crawl of life here frustrating. Even Vincenzo Mazzara had crackled with energy as he shook his chocolate smooth. These were men with high standards; how did they deal with the slowness and incompetence of others?

She watched the two old guys at their chessboard, taking minute upon minute to consider each move, reaching for a piece then changing their minds, stopping to think a little longer. They had nothing else to do with their time; for them the problem was more likely finding ways to use it up.

She tried to slow her own pace to match; sipping her beer so gradually it was lukewarm by the time she finished; even breathing more slowly. She supposed a day might come when the busyness of her life would stop. After the children left home, if she and Paul retired they might be like these old men, wasting time on a pointless game as an afternoon cooled to early evening. But that was years away, and until then, every day was made up of so many things to be done.

Even when their weekends were spent at the country house, Tricia hadn't liked to squander free hours. That time was useful for activities with the children or catching up on the books everyone else was reading. She couldn't afford to lose it to nothing.

That was why she got so impatient when clients were late for appointments or waiters failed to clear her table and ask if she would like anything more. She thought of those people as time thieves, stealing perhaps only seconds or minutes but all of them incremental and important in the end.

Tricia was trying not to drum her fingers on the table when she noticed a familiar figure threading between the trunks of the date palms towards her.

'*Buona sera*,' Orsolina called out. She looked very chic again. Her hair fell glossy down her back and she had changed into a short cherry-red shift dress and a pair of matching heels. 'Do you mind if I join you?' she asked.

'Please do. Although good luck trying to get a drink in this place.'

As she took a seat, Orsolina whistled at the waiter and held up two fingers. 'They know me here.' She lit a cigarette without asking if Tricia minded. 'Every evening after work I take a drink at this bar or the other one up the steps beyond the cathedral.'

'On your own?'

'Sometimes with my father, other evenings Luca joins me; but yes, very often on my own. It's a small pause between the *dolceria* and home, a moment to be social. My neighbours pass and I say good evening, share some news or perhaps a little gossip.'

'That sounds nice,' said Tricia.

'Yes, it is.'

The waiter brought out two tall glasses filled with a clear orange drink over ice, along with more small bowls of nuts and crisps.

'This is my cocktail of the moment, Aperol Spritz,' Orsolina explained. 'I ordered one for you as well. It's good for the digestion.'

Tricia laughed. 'If everything was as good for the digestion as people keep claiming, then I'm sure I wouldn't feel so bloated all the time.'

'It's easy to eat too well in Sicily,' agreed Orsolina. 'You must have had a good lunch at the vineyard today. It is worth suffering a little for Santo's cooking, I think.'

Tricia sipped her drink. It was cool and almost medicinal, with an acid bite of citrus and a pleasing sparkle of Prosecco.

'I love your dress,' she told Orsolina. 'Where do you shop? Not in this town?'

'I try to go to Rome every season – we have family there anyway. Otherwise there is good shopping on Ortygia. Luca will take you there in a day or so, I think. Is there something in particular you are looking for?'

'Oh, just hair straighteners. I left mine at home and it's a real pain doing without them.'

'Ah, I see. Not the sort of thing Luca would think to supply in your rooms. Why don't you borrow mine while you're here? They're the decent ones – very high temperature, don't snag on the hair.'

Orsolina was talking language that Tricia understood. 'Are you sure?'

'Absolutely. I prefer to wear my hair curly in the summer anyway. Come and pick them up from the house on your way back to Luca's place.'

'That would be fantastic. You'd be saving me at least half an hour a day spent blow-drying it.'

'And then it rains and it goes all frizzy ... I know, I know ...' Orsolina smiled. 'But tell me, how do you like your Spritz?'

Tricia took another sip. 'It might be an acquired taste,' she admitted.

'Like our chocolate?'

'Yes, to be honest ... sorry.'

'There's no need to apologise. You like what you like.'

'I can appreciate the effort that's put into making it ... it's only my palate that doesn't.' Reaching into her bag, Tricia produced the other bar she had bought. 'Luca told me about the shops selling inferior chocolate, and I got this so we could make a comparison. Is it the fake stuff?'

Orsolina wrinkled her nose. 'That one is not the worst. It's factory-made by machines but still the ingredients are good. Maybe you will not even find a difference.'

'But you would?'

'The texture would be different ... the flavour ... the feel in my mouth. My father says none of the magic is in it.'

'He's very enthusiastic about chocolate.'

'Of course.' Orsolina shrugged. 'It is his life.'

'Is it yours too? Don't you get bored here?'

Orsolina twisted the gold bangle on her wrist. 'Why would I get bored?'

'It's a small town ... slow, dull.'

'If you think Favio is dull, then you don't know it at all.' Orsolina leaned forward, her elbows on the table, lowering her voice. 'I could tell you something fascinating about almost everyone that walks past this bar in the next half-hour. Really I could.'

'OK then.' Tricia lowered her voice too. 'The two old men playing cards, tell me something about them.'

'That's easy.' Orsolina tapped the side of her nose. 'They're old friends. For years, the grey-haired one slept with the bald one's wife.'

'Did the bald one know?'

'Eventually he found out. There was a feud until the wife died, and now the two men compete for chess pieces rather than a woman.'

'I don't believe you,' Tricia said.

'Why would I lie?'

'OK, tell me something about Luca, then.'

'What do you want to know?'

'How old is he?'

'Older than me ... in his late thirties.'

'And what's the relationship between the two of you?' Tricia believed in being direct.

Stubbing out her cigarette, Orsolina hesitated. 'Have you asked him this question?'

'Not yet.'

'Do it and let me know me what he says.' She gave a tight smile. 'In the meantime, is there anything else I can tell you.'

'What's his story?'

'Luca has many stories.'

'OK then, what did he do before he opened the cookery school?' she persisted.

'He lived overseas ... he was a photographer.'

'Fashion?'

'No, he photographed people.'

'Portraits, then?'

Orsolina twirled the straw round in her empty glass. 'He was in London. He made a lot of money, I think.'

'I can't imagine Luca living that kind of life.'

'And yet he did, I promise you. Now of course he's changed his life. It is entirely different. I don't think I ever see him with a camera in his hand.' Orsolina glanced at her wristwatch and nodded at Tricia's glass. 'If you're not going to finish it, then we should go and fetch those hair irons for you.'

Tricia's curiosity about Luca had only been whetted by their conversation. She had other questions, more she wanted to know. But Orsolina was on her feet, clearly not planning to confide any further.

They walked in silence up the main street, turning off down the lane where the *dolceria* lay and continuing beyond it to a wooden door set into a wall of rock.

'This is your house?'

'Yes, it's one of Favio's original cave houses. The roof is low, so mind your head.' As she unlocked the door, Orsolina slipped off her heels. 'Even I have to duck down in places, and I'm tiny.'

Inside were rough-hewn walls. Light filtered through skylights, barely reaching the corners of the rooms. What furniture there was looked simple and rather worn.

'My family has lived here since the nineteenth century,' Orsolina explained. 'Papa doesn't like to change things too much.'

'It's ... amazing,' said Tricia.

'Actually it's two houses knocked into one, so it's more spacious than it seems and modern where it counts. Cool in summer, snug in winter. Perfect.'

Tricia thought it smelt musty and was probably very damp, but didn't say so.

'Is your father home?' she asked instead.

'I'm not sure.' Orsolina called out, but there was no reply. 'He may still be at the *dolceria*, or perhaps he had a meeting. Why don't I run and get those straighteners for you.'

Tricia noticed there were framed photographs crowded

on an old sideboard. While she was waiting, she picked one up: a wedding portrait taken in the early 1980s, by the look of the clothes. Vincenzo's hair was black and curling to his shoulders; his wife seemed very like Orsolina, equally as pretty but a little plumper.

The rest were mostly of Orsolina: as a child, in her school uniform or sitting at a piano, wearing a bikini on the beach, serving behind the counter in the *dolceria*. Right at the back she found a shot of Luca. He was standing beside Vincenzo on a boat, the pair both holding fishing rods. He looked younger but not boyish, and Vincenzo's hair wasn't quite so grey. Neither man was smiling. It seemed a strange picture to bother framing, and hearing Orsolina's footsteps, Tricia hurriedly put it back where it belonged.

'I'll make sure I return these before I go,' she said, taking the hair irons from her.

'Oh no, just leave them at Luca's place. I can pick them up when I need them.'

'I really appreciate it. I'll say all my thank yous now, just in case I don't see you again.'

'You'll see me,' Orsolina replied. 'Favio is a small town. You never go too long without seeing someone.'

Back at the cookery school, Tricia set up her chocolate tasting, breaking up a bar of Vincenzo Mazzzara's and the other one bought later, and putting them on separate plates, the wrapper hidden beneath, before calling the others down from their rooms.

'OK, the all-important question is can we tell the artisan chocolate from the stuff that's been factory-made,' she said, once everyone had assembled. 'I've tried a chunk of each and there didn't seem to be the slightest difference. Now it's your turn.'

Moll was keen to go first. She took her time, letting each piece of chocolate melt in her mouth, then pointed to the plate on the right. 'That's the artisan one, no doubt about it. There's more depth of flavour and the sandiness is a little more pronounced. I'm right, aren't I?'

Tricia was irritated (know-alls had that effect on her). 'I'll tell you once everyone has had a try.'

Neither of the others seemed as certain.

'There's a difference, but it's subtle and I can't say one is better than the other,' admitted Poppy.

'Valerie?'

'I'm going to agree with Moll,' she said after some deliberation. 'To me, this one tastes as if it's made with more love.'

Tricia lifted the right-hand plate, revealing the pastel-shaded Mazzara wrapper beneath it. 'Well done! I must say, I'm surprised. I'd never have picked it myself. I guess I'm not as into food as the rest of you.'

'It's about training your tastebuds,' explained Moll, with an air of superiority. 'Experiencing what you eat instead of gobbling it down like most people tend to. If you're serious about food, really serious like that young chef who cooked our lunch today … that's what you have to do.'

'I don't get it one bit; all these men who are so mad about food.' Tricia felt contrary. 'What's it about?'

Moll looked at her blankly, as if the question made no sense.

It was Valerie who responded. 'I think it's kind of nice myself,' she declared.

'But why?'

Valerie hesitated. 'Food is sensual, isn't it; therefore surely so are the men who care about it.'

Up till now, Tricia had viewed Valerie, with her neat figure and pressed linen outfits, as far too prim to be finding things sensual.

'Really?'

'I've always loved to watch men working in a kitchen,' the older woman explained. 'Handling knives, pots and pans;

bringing together raw ingredients and turning them into something you want to touch, smell, eat with your eyes, taste in your mouth, bring into your body.'

'Put like that,' said Tricia, seeing her in a new light, 'perhaps it is a little sensual.'

'If a man can cook ... or even make fine chocolate ... then I think it follows that he's more sensitive,' Valerie declared without a trace of primness, 'and far more passionate in every way.'

Food of Love

Luca Amore is opening himself up to possibilities. Of the four women who have come to learn from him, one has started to attract him, although he is barely aware of it yet. It is more of a sympathy between them, a sort of warmth, a good feeling when they are together.

Luca is not hoping for anything to happen – quite the opposite. Right now, he is busy making preparations for the day ahead and thinking only of what must be bought. He needs chicken for the chocolate dish he promised them, saffron for the pasta.

Some things he has already in his food cupboards. He ticks them off his list, wondering if the time has come to change the recipes he teaches; perhaps he is growing bored, even if every new group still comes to them fresh. The rhythms of each day in a town like Favio cannot be expected to change much. That was part of what drew him back to this slow, safe life. Yet after all these years there is a restlessness; a need for change that Luca will always carry, whatever he tells himself. A yearning for something more.

He will introduce new recipes, he decides, not for this group but for the next. Then he will make some calls, research on the Internet and find different places to put on his itinerary. Perhaps the mascarpone producer Santo mentioned earlier might welcome a small group. There may be other new people starting up he has not heard of yet. It won't hurt to ask around.

Luca begins another list, this one of things to be updated. He decides the guest rooms might be freshened up. Should he buy new bed covers in brighter colours, or paint the walls a different shade? Is it time to replace the towels or the sachets of dried flower heads and herbs that scent each room?

As he writes, he considers asking his friend Orsolina for advice. He has relied on her for help like this over the years. She understands the importance of the way things look, and he is sure her eyes will see immediately what needs to change and what is better left the same.

Luca is satisfied at having made a start. He assumes these small changes are what are needed. If he knew how wrong he was, if he even suspected, it would concern him. Luca has reminded himself a thousand times that certain things are not for him; he has told Orsolina too. His past is his past. For the new life to work, everything about it must be different. Whether Orsolina has accepted this he isn't entirely certain, but he believes he has convinced himself.

Luca likes to make lists. He keeps a Moleskine notebook in his pocket for that purpose. Once things are written down and ticked off, he has them under his control. His lists are what he trusts. They have got him through more than ten busy years of running his cookery school, and he has no reason to think they will ever let him down.

Valerie

Oh, I tasted that in Spain ... or maybe Croatia. I'm sure I had something like it in Turkey once. Yes, I guess I've travelled a lot, although at your age I'd barely left home. I never imagined I'd see so much of the world.

It was all because of Jean-Pierre. No, he wasn't my husband, although we did have nearly twenty years together. Jean-Pierre was the most unexpected thing that's ever happened to me.

We met after I divorced my second husband. I was about to turn forty-five and feared I'd be single for the rest of my life. Lots of my girlfriends were on their own and I hated the idea. I wanted to be loved again ... in every way. So I took out one of those personal ads in *New York* magazine: 'Genuine woman seeks like-minded man' ... you know the kind of thing. There were quite a few replies and I picked out the ones worth considering.

Jean-Pierre was the first. We arranged to meet at a coffee shop and almost missed each other because I was waiting at one table and he at another. It took me a while to recognise him from the photograph he'd sent. He was much older, heavier-set, with less hair and not handsome at all. I liked him straight away, though – his smile, his voice. And to be honest, the shot I'd sent him wasn't so terribly like me either.

We met a second time and a third; took in theatre shows, ate at restaurants, had a long weekend at a little place in New

Hampshire. We kept on seeing each other until eventually we were a couple.

Jean-Pierre was a successful man. He was in the import-export business, and wealthy enough to show me what I'd been missing. He took me everywhere; we stayed in the best places. There was a house in the south of France and a lovely apartment in Paris. He had friends all over the world, owned a share in a yacht that we sailed round the islands – Corsica, Sardinia then on to Capri. Such a wonderful time we had together.

Then a year ago my lovely Jean-Pierre died. He had three strokes and the final one finished him off. After he had gone ... oh, thank you, I would like a tissue. I'm so sorry; I always do this when I'm talking about it. I can't help myself. The beginning was so romantic and the end so very sad.

Where was I? Oh yes, of course. His children inherited most of what he had – the houses and the bulk of his money. They had first claim on it all, naturally. Fortunately I had held on to my little loft apartment in Greenwich Village for all those years, so at least I had a home. And there was a nest egg; enough for me to start again, Jean-Pierre made sure of that.

I miss our life together, but I stay as busy as I can. I've been getting to know New York again, going to exhibitions and shows. I'm always doing something. I've even started working a couple of days a week at the boutique where I used to buy my clothes. They've been very good to me there.

Still, it seemed as if I wouldn't travel any more – not without Jean-Pierre. Then I saw the advertisement for the cookery school and realised how much I missed it. I'm sixty-five, and who knows how many more good years I have left. I checked my savings and thought, blow it, I can afford this.

I thought I'd managed to talk my friend Maeve into coming, but then she had hip problems and changed her mind. I might have done the same but I'd paid the deposit, and anyway I knew what Jean-Pierre would have said about me staying home instead of having new experiences. He saw everything as an opportunity. You never know what will come of things, he always told me.

I'm glad I didn't cancel after all. It's beautiful here, a special place. Meeting you all has been a bonus. At my time of life you value the chance to make new friends; it happens so rarely.

You're still so young; oh, I know you don't feel it, but believe me, you are. I envy you the years you have ahead and all the possibilities. I don't mean to sound gloomy, but I feel as if the best is behind me. It's a wonderful thing to love, but it's a risk as well. I was lucky to meet a man like Jean-Pierre. I can't expect that again.

Here I am running on about myself while most likely you want to go to bed. I can't imagine what's got into me. Perhaps it's these Italian men we keep meeting; so handsome and passionate, they've reminded me of how I used to feel. I'm past all that now. Of course I am.

Day Three

(i) Cornetti, olive oil & unexpected flavours

Valerie wasn't sleeping well. The bed was firmer than she was used to; the sheets a lower thread count. With Jean-Pierre she had become accustomed to the best of everything: room service, fresh linen every day, suites with a view. This tiny chamber, with its vaulted wooden ceiling and single window overlooking layers of crumbling rooftops, was charming enough, but she could imagine him frowning and suggesting they find something better.

She always did this, thought of what Jean-Pierre would think of every place she visited, each meal she cooked or was served. Even when she put on her clothes she considered his opinion. He had preferred to see her in bright colours and shapes that fitted her body. It had pleased him when she wore the jewellery he had given her. Not that Valerie always dressed the way he wanted, but she liked to keep him happy, and the habit hadn't entirely left her.

She was glad there was at least a bathtub here to soak in when she woke at dawn and found herself alone. The touch of warm water on her body was a comfort. She wallowed in it, staring at the toenails she had polished in coral the day before leaving New York.

Valerie had been concerned about this trip. It seemed such a risk to journey to a country where she didn't speak the language and had no friends to help if anything went wrong. On the plane she was convinced she had made a mistake; she should have stayed home, saved the money.

Now she was here and everything felt different. She had forgotten so many of the things she loved about travelling. The way every day there was something interesting to see or do. The different sounds of each place – here it was the peal of church bells she noticed – the way people dressed, lived and ate; the newness of it all. And she felt surprisingly safe, perhaps because of the air there was about Luca. He was most definitely in charge of things, yet in a quiet way that she enjoyed.

Then there were the new friends she was making. They were people she might not necessarily have been drawn to at home, but here, thrown together, she had found something to like about each of them. Tricia was spiky and fun; Moll earnest and caring; Poppy reminded her of what she had been like herself at that age: trusting, open and living on hope.

Valerie's bath water was growing chilly. Reaching for a towel, she climbed out carefully. It wouldn't do to slip and twist or sprain something. Oh, but she was cautious with herself these days: took pills to keep her brain active, performed endless exercises to stay supple and firm. Who knew getting older could be so much work?

She had chosen her outfit the night before and ironed it ready. Fine white linen pants and a little top, a turquoise wrap to hide her arms (she was conscious of them turning crêpey). Flat shoes because this morning they were to visit an olive estate and Luca had indicated there would be walking. She put everything she might require into her zippered travel handbag – her wallet, lip balm, sunglasses, Advil in case of a headache.

She didn't carry a photograph of Jean-Pierre. The way he looked was never the attraction anyway. It was his spirit, a kind of light he had about him, not a thing a camera could capture, sadly. The first stroke had mostly snuffed it out. He had been different after that; he had faded.

Valerie had never met another man with that amazing shine, but occasionally there might be one who showed a tiny flare of it. With Vincenzo Mazzara she had noticed something, more of a heat than a light, but special all the same.

She put on a little make-up and fastened her hair away from her face. Grief had aged her. It had carved new lines and robbed her skin of colour. She tried not to cry, but things still set her off: a snatch of a song they had both loved, a certain scent or a small kindness from a stranger. She had been emotional at the Mazzara house the day she fell ill. That funny cavern-like place they lived in where the rooms were surprisingly beautiful and their care so very generous. Vincenzo hadn't said a word, only offered a handkerchief and fetched a glass of brandy. She supposed he'd had his own sadness and loss, so understood hers.

With a last check of her reflection, Valerie went down to the kitchen. There was no sign of Luca, but Moll was there, busy pottering round in search of what was needed to make coffee.

'Good morning,' she said cheerily. 'Our friend seems to be late today. Perhaps he overslept.'

'Lucky him, if only I could oversleep. I'm waking so early here.'

'Oh dear, is it jet lag like Poppy has?' Moll asked.

'I suppose it must be. Flying never used to bother me at all. But I'm lying awake half the night at the moment and then I'm up with the birds.'

'Poor you, there's nothing worse than not sleeping. Would you like some coffee, or will it make the problem worse?'

'Oh, coffee, please,' Valerie said gratefully. 'I can't think of starting the day without a cup. And it's so wonderful, not like the dishwater they serve at home.'

'Everything tastes better here,' Moll agreed, discovering the moka pot in a high cupboard along with the coffee beans and grinder 'I suspect it's something to do with what we were talking about yesterday. They care so much about food. It seems to come naturally to them. Wouldn't it be wonderful to live here? In England you're never too far away from the baked-beans-on-toast brigade.'

'You can always come back. It's so near for you; such a short flight.'

'I suppose so.' Moll turned away to grind the beans. For a moment the noise was too loud for their voices to be heard. When she had finished, she added awkwardly, 'Val, before the others come down, can I just say how sorry I am. What you were telling us last night, about losing Jean-Pierre and everything, it must have been so devastating and I wanted you to know how much I feel for you.'

'Oh … thank you …' Valerie was dismayed to feel the threat of tears.

'I was thinking about it later,' Moll pressed on, earnestly. 'The most important thing is you've got no regrets. You did all the things you wanted while you had your time together.'

'That's true,' Valerie managed.

'It's so easy to put things off. To worry that you don't have the money or think you can't get the time off work. I've been guilty of that myself.'

'We were fortunate, we didn't have any of those issues,' said Valerie, regaining control.

'Still, you lived for the moment and I bet you don't regret it, even though it's over.'

'No, I wouldn't change any of it. If Jean-Pierre were here now, it's what we'd be doing still.'

Watching Moll make coffee, she thought how life might be if he hadn't died. This time of year they would be in France most likely, having breakfast by the pool, wondering if the water was warm enough to take a dip, planning a dinner party with friends or an excursion on the boat.

'He was older than me,' she told Moll. 'And he'd had some health problems over the years. Possibly that's why he was so determined to cram his life full, although I suspect he'd always been that way. Jean-Pierre was a dynamic person. He believed in following his dreams.'

Moll poured out two cups of coffee. 'That's what I believe in too, even if they're only small dreams. Otherwise your days are made up of dreary stuff like folding laundry and hoovering floors, and that ends up being your whole life.'

'Still, the floors have to be hoovered, don't they?' As she took her cup, Valerie heard the slam of the front door. She looked up, expecting Luca, but instead it was Poppy, dressed in running gear, red-faced and glowing with sweat.

'Bloody hell, those steps nearly killed me this morning.' Poppy collapsed on to one of the kitchen chairs, fanning her face with her hands.

'I can't believe you ran up them.' Moll filled a glass with water from a bottle in the fridge. 'You're crazy.'

'And fit,' added Valerie admiringly.

'Not really ... Oh, thanks.' Poppy took the water. 'I have to keep stopping to catch my breath. But it's lovely out there first thing, when it's still cool and there are only a few people and cars about.'

Valerie glanced outside where the pale morning sky was already deepening to blue. 'It's going to be sunny again,' she remarked. 'We've been so fortunate with the weather, but I do hope it's not going to get too hot.'

'Yeah, I won't be going out running if it does,' Poppy agreed. 'Not unless I find a flatter part of town.'

'Running?' Tricia appeared, looking morning-fresh in a pale blue shift dress, her hair poker-straight. 'Seriously? After all the limoncello we drank out on the terrace last night?'

'I did feel a little seedy,' Poppy admitted, 'but sweating it out helped. I'm starving now. Where's Luca? Shouldn't he be here with his basket of breakfast goodies?'

'No sign of him yet,' Moll told her. 'I was thinking of

rustling up some scrambled eggs on toast, but there's not enough of anything in the fridge.'

Tricia pulled a neatly folded copy of the itinerary from her handbag. 'It definitely says breakfast at eight a.m. and it's not like Luca to be late. Perhaps we should text him?'

'Has he given you his number?' Poppy wondered.

'Ah, no, now you mention it, he hasn't yet.'

Moll checked the fridge again to see if she had missed anything that might be breakfast. 'There's the leftovers of yesterday's melon, and a few tomatoes,' she offered. 'Or we could go down to that little café in the piazza and get something to eat there?'

'Good idea, let's do that. I'll have a quick shower first,' said Poppy. 'I'll be five minutes ... no more than ten, I promise.'

'Who gets ready in ten minutes?' Tricia asked, pouring herself a coffee. 'It's not natural.'

Valerie went out on the terrace to wait. She sat with her face tilted towards the sun. It felt good to be back in Europe. The light here was different from home, softer somehow, the sun gentler, and there was more sky than often you got to see in New York (all those high-rise buildings).

Beside her, Moll sighed. 'Imagine living with a view as beautiful as this.'

'I used to ... well, beautiful in a different way. From our place in France we looked across a field of sunflowers and down towards some woodlands. I guess I took it for granted after a while.'

'You must miss it so much.'

'Yes, of course, but I was fortunate to have it as long as I did. Most people never get a chance to live like that. Before I met Jean-Pierre, I'd spent most of my life selling beautiful things to wealthy people in a store on West 57th; never imagined I'd do anything else. It was him who changed everything.'

'It sounds like the plot of a film.' Moll was wistful. 'Nothing like that has ever happened to me

Valerie glanced at her. Plain and sensible was how she would describe Moll. Her hair was steel-grey and cut very short; she wore stretchy clothes and sturdy shoes. But when she smiled, it warmed everything about her and she looked almost pretty.

'You never know, it still might.'

Moll shook her head. 'No, I don't think so.'

Valerie wondered what Moll's story was. There was no wedding ring on her finger, but that didn't mean anything these days. Was she single? Divorced? It seemed impolite to ask.

'Still, I'm here right now,' Moll added, more upbeat. 'I dreamt of being here and I made it happen in the end. I can't complain.'

There was a murmur of voices in the kitchen, a low male one among them, and Valerie rose from her chair. 'I think this may be Luca at last.'

'Thank God,' Moll said, standing too. 'My stomach is begging for food.'

He was in the middle of an apology as they came into the kitchen. 'I overslept, I'm so sorry. Last night there was a gathering at the Mazzara house that went on far too late.'

'We were just about to head to that little place beneath the palms in the piazza for coffee and cornetti,' Valerie told him.

'Good idea.' Luca smiled, seeming relieved. 'They do the best cornetti in town and the coffee they serve is roasted locally and very good.'

After that, he was his solicitous self, taking her arm as they headed down the steps; telling Moll it was the hint of vanilla bean through the pastries that made them so good, joining in the laughter when Poppy revealed that an old man had pulled over to offer her a lift while she was out for her morning run. Still, this morning there seemed something different about him, a barely pent-up energy that reminded Valerie of how Jean-Pierre could be at times.

She watched Luca stride ahead down the main street. He was wearing bone-coloured linen trousers, a shirt bright in greens and blues and a pastel-shaded cotton sweater slung round his shoulders.

He was handsome in a way that suited his surroundings. In New York that shirt might seem garish, in London the sweater wrong; even in the South of France Valerie suspected he would look out of place. He fitted best here.

Right now his head was turned attentively towards Moll, who was holding forth about food.

'Going out for breakfast always seems rather decadent at home,' she was saying. 'But here it's an everyday thing, isn't it? You stop for coffee and a pastry on the way to work without a second thought. That must be why there are so many little bars and cafés. I love it, I really do.'

Luca nodded but made no reply (not that Moll seemed to mind).

As they came into the piazza, she pointed towards the café. 'Oh look, there's Signore Mazzara. We should say hello.'

The chocolate-maker was sitting alone at a table beneath the date palms, a plate of untouched biscuits before him. As they approached, he looked up and Valerie wondered if she saw a flash of irritation cross his face at being interrupted.

'*Buongiorno.*' Moll was advancing, a smile on her face.

Vincenzo's expression warmed and, rising from his chair, he kissed her lightly on both cheeks. '*Buongiorno*, how nice to see you all,' he said in his careful English. 'You are well?'

'Yes, and looking forward to another beautiful day in Favio,' beamed Moll.

'Please, you must join me.' Vincenzo began darting this way and that, pulling chairs from the surrounding tables and arranging them at his. 'Sit down, my friends. What can I offer you?'

Luca thought they would need a second table, and there was more noise and fuss as the waiter came to help them move it. Once finished, the three men stood apart from the group, speaking quietly and quickly. Valerie could see only the waiter's face clearly. He was frowning at something Luca was saying.

Returning to the table, their talk was all of regular things: the weather forecast, plans for the day, the recipes they would be learning later. If there had been any tension, only Valerie had noticed it.

When the waiter came back, he was ferrying cups of coffee and plates filled with crescent-shaped pastries. Valerie helped herself, tearing into one with her fingers. In France she had never liked the croissants much, finding them too dense and buttery, but this Italian version was different, lighter and sweeter.

Vincenzo nodded towards her. 'You have a good appetite,' he remarked. 'You must be feeling fully recovered.'

'Yes, thank goodness. It would be terrible to be in Sicily and not want to eat the food. It's all so beautiful.'

'Most of it is,' he agreed. 'Still, there is bad food to be found here like anywhere else. You are fortunate you have Luca to guide you towards the best. The cornetto you are eating, for instance. It was baked here fresh this morning and is superior in every way to the ones sold in the café on the other side of the piazza. But the ordinary tourists, how can they know that? They come here to Favio and take their chances.'

'Surely they have guidebooks,' Valerie offered.

'True, but the information in them can be out of date. Things change even here.'

'I expect the second-best cornetto is still pretty good, though, isn't it?' Valerie said.

Frowning, Vincenzo shook his head. 'What is the point of eating if it is not the very best?'

'To sate hunger?'

'But my hunger isn't satisfied with a cornetto that is too heavy or sweet or flavoured with vanilla essence rather than the real thing. Why should I expect visitors to Favio to put up with what I won't?'

'What can you do about it, though?' Valerie wondered.

'That is what we have been trying to decide. Last night at my house we had a big meeting, one of many, to discuss my plan.'

She was intrigued.

'Perhaps it is an idea more than a plan at this stage,' Vincenzo admitted. 'What I would like is to produce a list of the best places, a food guide for people who arrive here.'

'That's a good idea.'

'Yes, but there are problems.' Reaching for a biscuit, Vincenzo snapped it in half. 'Who sets the standards? Who decides if these biscuits deserve to be on the list? Who tells the owner of the café across the piazza that he hasn't made the grade? It is more complicated than you would think, especially in a town like this where feuds and friendships go back through the generations.'

Valerie chose one of the biscuits and took a bite. It was crisp and thin, tasting of almonds and icing sugar.

'It seems perfect to me.'

'But you have nothing to compare it to. Perhaps if you tried the same kind of almond biscuit from another place in town, you might change your mind about this one.'

'Is it really so important to have only the very best?' she asked. 'Most tourists won't know if they don't.'

'Some will, and those people matter to me,' Vincenzo insisted.

'I guess tourism is crucial here,' Valerie conceded. 'Favio is not a wealthy place, is it? Many people must survive on the money the tourists bring in.'

'Yes, but I am not interested in fleecing foreigners of their money.' Vincenzo sounded exasperated. 'This is about us squandering the chance we have to enrich people's lives. There is plenty of opposition to my idea. The waiter here, for instance, he tells me I should not do it. He says it will cause trouble. But I am not faint-hearted.'

'Clearly not.' Tricia had been listening to their conversation. 'I think you're an idealist, though.'

Vincenzo shrugged. 'Perhaps ... I have been called many things.'

'Don't get me wrong, it's a noble thing to have ideals.'

'But I suspect you might not share them?'

'To me, ideals are one thing and reality quite another,' Tricia told him.

'So the two can never come together?' Vincenzo asked. 'You believe they are incompatible? Can you honestly say that?

Valerie saw it then: an unexpected energy, the brightness Jean-Pierre once had. This man was filled with it. She put down what was left of her biscuit and held the edge of the table. When she felt like this, flooded with loss, all she could do was keep breathing.

She felt the light touch of a hand. 'Signora, you look pale suddenly. Are you feeling unwell?' Vincenzo sounded concerned.

'No ... it's nothing ... no ...'

Moll jumped up to fetch more water; Poppy wondered if Valerie was suffering from low blood sugar; Luca looked worried. Vincenzo said nothing more, but his hand stayed on her arm and she felt the pressure of his fingers.

'I'm fine, really,' she insisted. 'I just had a little moment ... you know how it is.'

'Would you prefer to stay behind today and rest?' Luca asked.

'No, not at all, I don't want to miss out.'

'Maybe I should organise a doctor's appointment?'

'Honestly, there's no need.'

'Well if you're sure, then we ought to get moving pretty soon. We're due at the Ortolo olive estate in a short while.'

'Sure, I'm ready.' Valerie tried to infuse her voice with an energy she didn't feel.

You'll be on your feet a lot,' Luca warned. 'There'll be some walking. Is that OK?'

'Yes, sure,' Valerie repeated more strongly.

Vincenzo squeezed her arm. 'I think you are a brave one, signora,' he said softly before letting his hand fall.

Valerie was glad of the long drive to the olive estate. She was grateful Moll was talkative and Luca had so much knowledge about olives to share. Resting on the back seat, her face turned to the window, she hoped the feelings wouldn't rush at her like that again. All she wanted was a pleasant day, to see trees and taste oil, to retrieve the holiday mood she'd had earlier sitting out on the sunny terrace.

The others seemed in good spirits. They were talking (shouting, really) about the chocolate-maker and his high standards. Everyone had an opinion.

'He's a classic perfectionist, isn't he?' Poppy was saying. 'Brendan is a bit like that. His way is the only way, and once he gets an idea in his head ...'

'I don't agree,' Moll argued. 'Vincenzo insists on excellence, and that's quite a different thing.'

'If you ask me, he's pompous,' Tricia declared. 'Who is he to decide what's good and what isn't?'

'But that's exactly the point he was trying to make ...'

'He's arrogant ...'

'Likely a nightmare to work with ...'

'He has high standards; what is so wrong with that?'

Valerie said nothing. She knew exactly what Vincenzo was. She had seen it before; had never expected to find it again.

*

The iron gates of the Ortolo estate were ornate and the wall of flinty stone surrounding it was a high one. Olive trees grew in rows, some with trunks so broad and knotted they must have been there for centuries.

Luca told them that olive trees were as much a part of the history of Sicily as the baroque buildings – more important really because they gave food, sustained life.

'This estate has been in the same family for more than three hundred years. It's incredible when you think of it. All the things that have changed during that time, yet what you see here has stayed the same.'

Valerie couldn't help thinking about the olive trees that grew at Jean-Pierre's old place in France. Everywhere she looked she found another memory. She wondered if that would ever change.

'You can almost breathe the history here, can't you?' said Moll as the car was parked beside a set of old stone buildings.

'Later you will eat the history too,' Luca promised. 'The Ortolo oil is my favourite. It's bold and spicy yet elegant. It has character.'

A young woman was waiting to greet them. She had dark curly hair and a face straight from a Renaissance painting, a high forehead and strong nose. She offered Valerie a steadying hand as she climbed down from the car.

'Welcome, welcome. My name is Giulietta Ortolo.' She paused while everyone organised handbags and hats. 'Now please follow me. We will make a tour of the olive groves. You all have water? Good, because today it is hot. First we will stop here, as this is the original stone olive press. Gather round so you can hear me.'

Valerie wished she had brought her hat. The sun beat down on the back of her neck as she stood with the others beside the two great circles of lavic stone. The last thing she wanted was to grow faint and trigger more concern about her health. She took a few steps back into what little shade the well-pruned trees offered and tried to pay attention to Giulietta's talk.

The view from here was distracting. The grove was planted on a gentle slope that stretched down towards wide plains below. Between the trees grew prickly pears, almonds and citrus, untidy straggles of oregano and thyme, towering cypress and carob.

While she half listened to details of the harvest (every olive hand-picked), the ancient varieties of tree and the Ortolo family's biological farming methods, Valerie thought how lucky Giulietta was to have been born into the family that owned this place.

'This time of year the groves are quiet,' she was telling them. 'If you were to come in October, you could watch the harvest and the pressing.'

'I'd love to see that.' Moll sounded regretful.

'Perhaps you might come back some day.'

Moll said nothing, and Valerie noticed her broad face creasing into a frown.

'I've seen olives harvested and pressed,' she offered quietly. 'It's not so exciting really.'

Giulietta led them on a dry and dusty walk along a track that looped through the groves, Moll and Tricia lagging behind taking photographs, while Luca fell in beside Poppy, their pace much brisker and soon taking them ahead of the group. Valerie heard them laughing and wondered what their conversation was about. She missed that easy intimacy with a man. At Poppy's age she had never imagined a time when she would live without it. She certainly never expected the invisibility that came along with grey hair and wrinkles.

It was years since Valerie had seen a man's head turn as she walked past or found herself the target of an admiring glance. Call it vanity, but her life had dulled without it. How she would have liked to flirt again, to talk to a man all night long, to feel the thrill of attraction.

Several times, after the second of his three strokes, Jean-Pierre had said he hoped she would find love again. She had cast off his words, unwilling to imagine going on without him, certain that love was the last thing she would need if she did. But she had been wrong. It was what love brought that Valerie longed for; the physical side, yes, but mostly the connection and understanding. Realising that she would never have those things again turned out to be her second great loss.

The dirt track was taking them upwards now, back to the group of low stone buildings. Valerie hoped there would be a shady place to sit down. Her breath was coming quicker, her heart rate rising, even though the slope seemed hardly steep at all. Was this old age she was feeling, she wondered, a gradual decline of strength? How long before she was whittling down her life to fit what she was capable of? It was a dispiriting thought to have on such a bright and lovely day.

Giulietta continued to talk, telling of olive oil scandals, and the swindlers who mixed in cheap seed oils or passed off stale ones as freshly pressed.

'It is a disaster, this oil fraud, and seems to get worse year by year,' she lamented. 'The risk is that all Italian products will get a bad name because of it.'

'How can you tell if an oil is poor?' Moll wondered.

'Usually the first sign is the price,' Giulietta admitted. 'Olive oil is almost never the bargain it seems.'

'But the boutique oils are too expensive. Some of us can't afford to pay those high prices,' Moll pointed out.

'I would say you can't afford not to,' Giulietta argued. 'But come, it's time to taste our oil, which is certainly of superior quality. I have two blends for you today, quite different.'

She took them to a wide terrace filled with fragments of stone amphorae and vivid ceramic tiles.

'Here you see some of my family's history,' she told them. 'But it is the oil that is the most important link to our past.'

Valerie smelt wood burning sweetly, but couldn't see a fire or imagine why anyone would want to light one in such heat. To her relief, Giulietta steered them towards a trellised arbour shaded by a leafy grape vine. Beneath it was a wooden table set with a basket of crusty bread, a couple of saucers so old their glazing had crazed, a tray of shot glasses and two small, dark bottles of oil. Valerie hoped this was not the lunch they had been promised, for she found she was hungry.

They took seats around the table (Luca still beside Poppy) and Giulietta began pouring oil into the glasses almost reverently.

'First we will taste the milder of the two, which is still very fruity,' she explained.

The oil was a sunny yellow. Holding her glass up to her nose, Valerie found it smelt of just-cut grass.

'Shouldn't it be greener than this if it's a good oil?' Moll asked.

'That's an interesting question. Some people will tell you the colour of an oil is important,' Giulietta told them. 'In fact it does not signify quality and will vary with the type of olives used. But there's another reason to disregard colour. Oil should be packaged in dark glass to protect it from the light. You won't see what colour it is until you open the bottle and pour some out.'

'So are we meant to drink this?' Tricia asked, sounding dubious.

'That's right. The trick is to take a sip, then quickly suck in some air through your teeth to enhance the oil's flavours.'

Giulietta demonstrated, taking a gutsy slurp of air before swallowing her mouthful of oil. Valerie gave it a go. She was self-conscious about slurping, but judging by the expressions on their faces, the others felt the same.

'What do you think?' asked Giulietta when they had all taken a taste.

Valerie tried to come up with the right words to describe it. The oil was full of flavour, but it was impossible to know what to compare it to. A fruit? A vegetable? She had no idea.

'I think what I can taste are tomatoes and artichokes,' Poppy said, tentatively.

'Yes, maybe. It's very vegetal,' Moll agreed. 'I like a spicier oil myself. This is pleasant, but very mild.'

'Then you'll prefer our second one, I think.' Giulietta unstoppered the other bottle, filling the remainder of the glasses with liquid gold.

This time Valerie sucked in the air more enthusiastically, and the pepperiness of the oil hit the back of her throat, taking her breath away. She coughed and spluttered, her eyes watered ... and of course, they all did the last thing she wanted and made a terrible fuss, Tricia thumping her back; Luca thrusting a glass of water at her.

'Oh no, Val, you poor thing, are you OK?' Moll fished round in her pockets and produced a crumpled tissue.

Valerie made an attempt to say something reassuring, but her voice came out as a croak.

'Don't try to speak, just breathe,' Moll told her.

'Next time try tasting it with a little bread to help control the pepperiness,' suggested Giulietta when she recovered.

Valerie shook her head. 'I think I'll stick with the first oil, thank you,' she replied, a little hoarsely. 'It appears to suit my palate better.'

She tried to laugh off the moment, but the truth was she couldn't find it funny. At every turn she seemed to show herself as frail; first almost fainting, now not even being able to sip olive oil without causing a fuss. She wondered what they thought. Surely Luca must be judging her an old lady.

Valerie wished they could see the person she truly was. If only they had known her as a young woman who could swim fast and run hard, had met her before her skin puckered and her eyebrows thinned and her face grew like her mother's (the similarity was unnerving at times).

It was awful to be so melancholy when she had spent a decent portion of her savings on this trip in the hope of having a wonderful time. But Valerie had never been able to change her own mood. Only Jean-Pierre had found ways to lift and lighten it, almost always making her laugh no matter how bleak she felt. Now he was gone and there was no one left who understood her so well. She was on her own.

(ii) Bread & battles

The smell of burning wood turned out to be coming from an outdoor oven at the far end of the terrace. Announcing that he would prepare their lunch in front of them, Luca stoked it up with olive tree trimmings.

'We will eat *scacce*, the traditional worker's meal that wives once brought to their husbands out in the fields,' he told them. 'They have always been a favourite in this part of Sicily. In my nonna's house, they were made for Christmas, Easter, birthdays and baptisms, any time when large crowds gathered and grew hungry.'

'I'm hungry now,' Moll told him.

'They take a little time to make, but I'm sure Giulietta will be happy for you to enjoy more of the bread and olive oil while you're waiting. Or you can help me. That always makes the time go faster.'

Valerie stayed in the shade, a glass of wine at her elbow, watching Luca mix dough from hard wheat flour and olive oil. He seemed completely in his body when he cooked, moving with grace and economy. It was a pleasure to see him rolling the dough into thin sheets, folding them and smearing each layer with ricotta and tomato sauce, dotting them with fat black olives and young spinach leaves sprinkled with salt, and finally sweeping the heavy tray one-handed into the oven.

'It's like a stuffed focaccia,' Moll said, also observing carefully.

'Yes, but much better because the bread is very thin rather than doughy,' Luca told her. 'Our *scacce* will need thirty minutes in the oven, so I'm going to fetch my phone and make a couple of calls. When I get back, we'll mix a salad of tomatoes and herbs, then we'll be ready to eat.'

Luca headed back to the car and Giulietta disappeared too, down to the cellar to retrieve another bottle of cherry-red Cerasuolo wine for them to enjoy with their lunch.

'Imagine living in a place like this,' sighed Moll, watching her go. 'Some people get all the luck in life.'

Tricia looked dubious. 'Yes, it's pretty, but you couldn't live here full-time, could you? Think how isolated and dull it would be.'

'You'd get used to it,' Moll argued. 'Following the rhythm of the seasons, eating from the land.'

'That's probably why they're all so obsessed with food,' said Tricia. 'There's not much else to do here other than eat and drink.'

Moll seemed taken aback. 'So you're saying I'm dull because I'm interested in food?'

'No not at all ... obviously not.'

'I think what she's saying is that their lives are very limited,' explained Poppy. 'Isn't that right?'

'Yes exactly—'

Moll interrupted. 'But aren't all our lives limited? I live in London but still stick to the same places mostly and make the same choices. It may be a great big city, but my part of it is quite tiny.'

'We have lots of possibilities, though. All they have is this.' Tricia swept a hand around at the view, at trees sloping down towards a distant blue band of sea, at weathered rock walls, a blaze of bougainvillea, a cluster of citrus trees. 'Yes, it's beautiful, but what do you do, where do you go?'

'You were telling us the other night how stressed your job makes you,' Moll pointed out.

'I know, I was ... It is stressful. I'd like more balance, less pressure, to get away more often. But still I wouldn't swap the city for being marooned in a place like this.'

Listening to her, Valerie wondered if Tricia was one of those women who were never fully satisfied, no matter what. She had friends like that, always unpicking the neat seams of their existence, redesigning rooms, buying new clothes, trying new hobbies, expecting the change to make everything better. It rarely did.

'Isn't happiness mostly a matter of learning to appreciate what you have?' she suggested. 'That's what the people here seem able to do. If you asked them, I'm sure they wouldn't say their lives were unexciting.'

'They don't know any better,' Tricia said stubbornly.

Valerie couldn't be bothered arguing. 'Everyone is different,' she replied mildly. 'And I don't suppose you can ever really know what's going on in other people's lives.'

For his salad Luca chopped fat, ripe tomatoes, tossing them with flat leaves of parsley, parings of sweet red onion and lashings more olive oil. Valerie had never consumed so much oil in one sitting and wondered what her doctor would have to say about it.

Tricia must have been thinking along the same lines. 'It's still a fat, isn't it, even if it's a healthier one,' she said, grimacing at Luca's generous pour.

'Don't worry, it's good for the skin,' Moll told her.

At last the *scacce* was pulled from the oven smelling of melting cheese and wood smoke. Luca let it cool for a few minutes before cutting it into slices that he arranged on a wooden board and placed in the middle of the table.

'Looks great.' Tricia held out her camera. 'Luca, would you mind? I'd love a photo of us with the *scacce* before we start eating it.'

'Sure.' Taking the camera, he backed up a few steps. 'OK, everyone, look happy, look hungry ... that's lovely.'

Without bothering to check the result, he handed back the camera.

'Thanks.' Tricia smiled. 'I'm sure you'll have taken a much better picture than I'd ever manage. After all, you used to be a professional photographer in London, didn't you?'

Valerie saw the surprise registering on Luca's face. 'Who told you that?' he asked.

'Oh, your friend Orsolina mentioned it the other day. So what exactly did you photograph?'

Luca stared at her coolly for a moment and then replied, 'All sorts; people mostly.'

'And you gave it up to come back to Sicily? Why was that?'

'It's my home,' he said shortly. 'Why wouldn't I come back?'

'It's a familiar enough story,' put in Giulietta, topping up their glasses with wine. 'Often young people move away in search of better opportunities, then find they miss home. I studied abroad for a while myself, but this place is in my blood, I couldn't live anywhere else. I expect you're the same, eh, Luca?'

'That's right,' he agreed.

'There aren't as many options for work here, though,' Giulietta admitted. 'You have to make do with what you can find, or start your own business as Luca has.'

'So you don't take photographs any more?' Tricia asked.

He shrugged. 'Yes, of course, for people like you who want snapshots taken with the food we've cooked. I just don't charge for it these days.'

'And you don't miss it?'

'It was time for something different.'

'I'd love to see your work,' Tricia told him.

'Oh yes, me too,' Poppy agreed. 'If you don't mind.'

'Sure, I'll see if I can dig out a few shots before you leave,' Luca murmured. 'There should be some at my mother's place.'

He turned his attention to the food after that, wolfing down a small piece of the *scacce*, then muttering something about making more phone calls and disappearing back to the car.

Once he had gone, Tricia turned to them. 'I'd be amazed if he has any intention of letting us look at those pictures. Why do you think he's so evasive? Odd, isn't it?'

'Why ask him if it's quite obvious he doesn't want to talk about it?' Moll said sharply.

'I'm curious, that's all.'

'Some people might call it nosy,' said Moll.

'Oh get over yourself,' Tricia bit back. 'Don't be so pompous. I'll ask him whatever I want to.'

Valerie hated friction. She never understood why people thought a good argument might clear the air. Arguments were never good. They were unsettling things, unpleasant every time.

'Come on now,' she said, although it was obvious Tricia and Moll were going to chafe against each other.

'Everyone has a right to privacy.' Moll was steadfast. 'Prying is just plain bad manners.'

'Fine, I'll drop it. Happy? Or is there something else bothering you? If so, we should have it out right now.' There was a dangerous note to Tricia's voice, and Valerie recognised the lawyer in her.

'I suppose I may as well say it.' Moll spoke steadily. 'This is a cooking holiday, and I'm not sure why you bothered coming just to criticise people who care about food. I mean, really, what did you expect?'

'I'm not criticising … I'm questioning,' Tricia bit back. 'I'm interested in people – that's who I am. I'm sorry if you're offended. None of it's aimed at you, Moll, so don't take it so personally.'

'Well I think it is personal.' Moll scraped her chair away from the table. 'And I've had quite enough of it, thank you. I'm going for a walk.'

Tricia stared after her as she marched away. 'What's her problem, do you think? PMT? That all came out of nowhere, didn't it? Well it wasn't my fault anyway.'

Valerie squinted at the idyllic view. It seemed life was never allowed to be perfect, at least not for long. People had the ability to turn everything ugly. Even this.

'She's a sensitive person,' she told Tricia. 'More so than she seems. I'll go and talk to her.'

Another walk in the heat of the day was the last thing she needed, and Valerie was relieved to come across Moll not too far away, sitting in full sun, eyes closed, with her back propped against the old stone olive press.

'Be careful, you'll get burnt,' she warned.

Moll's eyes opened. 'Did they send you to find me?'

'No one sent me anywhere,' said Valerie.

'I expect you think I overreacted.'

Valerie looked at the ground. If she sat down beside Moll she might never get back up. (Besides, she was wearing clean white linen pants.)

'Actually I think you had a point. If Luca prefers not to talk about himself then that's his business. But I have to admit I'm curious about him too. That's not so wrong, is it?'

'I suppose not,' Moll admitted grudgingly.

'And Tricia's job as a lawyer is to probe and ask questions. It's second nature to her. That's her personality, I guess.'

Moll sighed. 'The thing is, I don't like her. I haven't from the start. She's vain and trivial, always going on about her hair. She came here because she's got lots of money to throw around, not because she loves food or Italy.'

Valerie gave up. She lowered herself to the ground beside Moll (she could always rinse out her pants later).

'There are lots of people I don't like,' she offered. 'Heaps of them.'

'Truly?' Moll sounded surprised.

'I'm not one of those sunny types who adores everyone they meet unless there's a reason not to. I don't even have that many friends. For a long time I thought Jean-Pierre was the only one I needed, and now, well I've had to start from scratch and find new ones. Not so easy, believe me.'

'Why are you telling me this?'

'Because that's one of the things I've been enjoying about this vacation – making new friends. You're younger than me, quite different, but I like you all.'

'You're trying to get me to apologise, aren't you?'

'Not really, although I expect one of you will have to.' Val glanced at Moll's freckled cheeks reddening in the glare. 'You really should put on some sunscreen, you know.'

'Yes to the sunscreen but not to apologising.' Moll took the tube she was offered, squeezing the white cream on to her fingers and spreading it unevenly over her face, neck and arms. 'You know, I feel sorry for Luca.'

'You do? Why?'

'Well, if he was a successful photographer, there must be a good reason why he gave it up. Those people can make a lot of money. You're not telling me he does so well running a cookery school. Something must have gone wrong.'

'Now you're the curious one,' Val pointed out.

'Yes, but I'm not going to pester him with questions. Everyone is allowed to have their secrets, aren't they? I bet Tricia has a few herself.'

'I expect so,' agreed Valerie.

'And I don't care what you say, I'm not going to apologise.'

*

The atmosphere in the car heading back was tense, but if he noticed it Luca didn't say anything. He put on a CD of Italian pop music, turned the volume up a little too loud and drove faster than he had the previous day.

They arrived in Favio towards the end of the afternoon, just as the shops were reopening. Parking at the foot of the steps, Luca switched off the music but kept the engine running.

'OK, ladies, I hope you enjoyed your lunch and your trip to the Ortolo estate.' His tone was almost formal. 'Now there's an hour or two free to shop or relax, then we'll have our second lesson in the cookery school and the dishes we prepare will be our dinner. I'll say goodbye for now and see you all in a little while.'

For once Valerie almost raced up the steps to the house. It was a relief to shut the door of her room behind her. First she rinsed the dust from her good linen pants, before stretching out on the bed and closing her eyes. What a funny old day, coloured almost from the beginning by her own grey mood and then shattered by an argument.

She and Jean-Pierre had never fought. If necessary she gave way to him, but it hardly ever happened. Valerie wished she could take her cell phone from her bag and call him. He was still the first person she wanted to tell about anything that happened. Not that he would have had much wisdom to share on this occasion, but he might have been reassuring. 'Don't worry, it'll blow over,' he would have told her. She hoped it was true.

She must have drifted off to sleep, waking more than an hour later to the sound of cathedral bells ringing, her mouth dry and her eyes scratchy. Yawning, she went to the bathroom to pat cold water on her face. She thought about this evening's cooking lesson. She so hoped Moll and Tricia would be civilised to one another, even if they were too proud to apologise.

There was a gentle knock on her door and Valerie called out, 'Just a moment!' before drying her face, popping on her robe and going to see who was there.

She opened the door and Poppy slipped inside. Her long hair was wet and in a tangle, her lightly freckled skin bare of make-up, but even so there was something luscious about her. It might have been to do with the plumpness of her lips and cheeks, or the darkness of her eyes and the arch of her brows, or the way her body was rounded and soft despite all the jogging she did. Valerie thought she looked ridiculously pretty.

'Sorry to bother you, I wanted a quick moment to talk about that business this afternoon,' Poppy said in a low and anxious voice. 'What do you think we should do?'

'Ignore it,' Valerie suggested, hoping to sidestep more friction. 'Carry on as if nothing has happened. Don't worry, it'll blow over. These things always do.'

Poppy's face gleamed with the hope that the older woman knew best. 'Do you really think so?'

Valerie was struck at how young she seemed. After all those years of marriage to the bossy-sounding Brendan, it must be hard for Poppy now with no one to rely on. 'It's up to Moll and Tricia to get along with one another,' she said, briskly. 'I'm sure they'll manage it. They're both grown-ups, after all. It'll be fine.'

Poppy surprised her by kissing her quickly on the cheek. 'You're such a lovely woman, Val,' she said, before stealing back through the door.

Valerie found she had to dab her eyes with a tissue and fix her mascara before she was ready to head downstairs. It was exhausting being so prone to emotion. She was sure she had never been this tearful before in her life.

In the kitchen, Moll was busy helping Luca set up for the cooking lesson. She looked relieved when Valerie appeared.

'Good rest?' she asked, smiling.

'Yes, I went out like a light the minute I lay down. You?'

'I didn't feel like sleeping. I don't want to waste a minute of being here if I can help it. There'll be plenty of time to rest at home.'

Valerie suppressed another yawn. 'I do agree with you, and yet it was lovely having a nap.'

Luca began chalking up the evening's menu on the blackboard: *maltagliati with saffron; chicken with Favio's chocolate.*

'More of your nonna's recipes?' asked Valerie, watching him.

'Yes, she taught me both of these dishes, but the chicken was originally a Mazzara family recipe,' Luca told her. 'It came from Vincenzo's mother, I believe. My nonna was a collector of recipes. She wrote them all down, sometimes on the backs of old pasta packets rather than waste money on paper. There used to be a wonderful old book of them; she kept it in this kitchen.'

'What happened to it?'

'That I don't know. I looked for it after she died. When we renovated, we took the place apart, but there was no sign of it. Sadly, it seems to be lost for ever.'

'Perhaps she destroyed it,' Valerie suggested. 'Don't some cooks guard their recipes jealously?'

'My nonna wasn't like that.' There was pride in his voice. 'To her a recipe was a conversation. She loved to talk about food: what were the best ingredients to use, how a dish might have been better.'

'Maybe the book was thrown away by mistake. People can do silly things when they're clearing out a deceased person's belongings,' said Valerie.

She was thinking about Jean-Pierre, of course. As always. There were things of his she would have liked to keep. A Shetland knit sweater, the wool slightly scratchy; a blue corduroy cap and a soft leather belt with a silver buckle – worn, old things his children had stuffed into plastic trash sacks and given to the goodwill before she had a chance to stop them. Those clothes must still have smelt of him, the citrus in his cologne and the oil of his skin. She would have liked to wrap herself in the sweater, even put the hat on her head.

'Your nonna's book may have been caught up amongst some old clothes or shoes,' she pointed out.

'You're right,' Luca agreed. 'That might be what happened. Towards the end, her mind began to wander, so she may have put it somewhere strange. I've never entirely given up hope of finding it. In the meantime, I have the recipes she copied out for me, and there are other dishes I've tried to recreate from memory.'

'It's great that you're keeping family tradition going,' put in Moll. 'My children aren't interested in cooking at all. I've tried to show them how to make their favourites, but they can't be bothered. Without me, they'd live on tinned soup and takeaways.'

'How many children do you have?' Valerie asked her.

'Two girls, Lola and Rae, they're fourteen and sixteen. I've filled the freezer with meals for them to eat while I'm away. All they have to do is stick them in the microwave. It wouldn't surprise me if some nights they don't even manage that ... not with a McDonald's just down the road.'

'They're still young,' said Valerie. 'Perhaps they'll change.'

'I hope so. Right now, the last thing they'd want to inherit from me is my recipe book. Still, I shouldn't complain. They're good girls really.'

When the others appeared, Moll fell silent. She moved to the far side of the kitchen bench where Valerie was standing and remained beside her as Luca prepared to demonstrate the first dish. It made for an uncomfortable atmosphere, but

Tricia ignored her, directing most of her conversation at Poppy instead.

So this was how it would be, Valerie realised with some regret. The group had split in half. Like it or not, it seemed she would be Moll's companion for the remainder of the vacation.

Luca started the lesson by mixing up more pasta dough, this time golden with the powdered saffron he swirled through the flour.

'Maltagliati are the pasta you make when you're in a hurry,' he explained. 'The name means "badly cut", so there's no need to aim for perfection. A busy mamma might make them to provide a quick lunch for her family. My nonna often fed us a few to keep us going when we were working hard. Sometimes she would pound a little basil and add the puree to the dough to make it green instead of gold. It took no time at all.'

It was very simple, Valerie agreed, rolling out the dough and cutting it roughly into small squares. None of them had any difficulty; even Poppy, who had seemed so concerned at the beginning of the lesson, looked like she was starting to enjoy it now.

Rather than making a rich sauce, Luca sautéed a few colourful peppers in olive oil, adding torn basil leaves, a pinch of salt and some ground toasted almonds at the very end.

The doorbell rang just as he was turning off the gas beneath the pan. 'Ah good, this must be my special delivery, right on time,' he said, heading to the door.

As it opened, Valerie thought she heard Vincenzo Mazzara's voice. She felt her spirits lift at the thought of seeing him again, then reproached herself for being foolish.

He came into the kitchen, a couple of bars of his chocolate in one hand and a bunch of wild poppies in the other. He was wearing a blue checked shirt, open at the neck, the sleeves rolled up. 'I heard a rumour that someone was making my mamma's special chicken,' he said, dropping the chocolate on the kitchen counter.

'Actually we're making my nonna's version,' Luca told him. 'With Prosecco instead of the white wine.'

'No? Your nonna changed the recipe? I do not believe it.'

'It's better her way,' Luca insisted.

The red poppies had been tied into an untidy bouquet with a piece of grosgrain ribbon from his shop, and Vincenzo held them out to Valerie. 'For you, signora, I hope you are feeling better.'

She felt her cheeks flush. 'How lovely, thank you.'

'I picked them just before I came. I am afraid they will not last long before wilting, so enjoy them while you can.'

It had been years since a man had given her flowers. Jean-Pierre had preferred more lasting gifts, and neither of her ex-husbands had bothered after they had married her.

'I'll find a vase and put them in some water.' She knew she sounded flustered.

Moll helped her arrange the delicate stems with their papery petals, smiling as she caught her eye. Most likely she was thinking the gesture a romantic one. Valerie knew better. She had reached the age when flowers (even wild ones) were brought in sympathy rather than love. Still, she was touched either way, and thought the poppies lovely.

'Now let's return to our lesson,' instructed Luca, pulling a deep dish of marinating chicken pieces from the fridge. 'Since we're preparing his family recipe, I thought we'd invite Signore Mazzara for dinner. I forgot how scandalised he would be to discover I had soaked the chicken in Prosecco, but my nonna swore it was the secret to tender meat and a more delicate flavour.'

'Luca, my friend, at least let me prepare the chocolate the proper way,' Vincenzo pleaded. 'Or did your nonna improve that part of the recipe too?'

'No, no, I'm sure she wouldn't have dared.' Luca was laughing. 'Although she did sometimes make the dish with rabbit instead of chicken to save a little money, but I think your mamma probably did the same when chickens were hard to come by.'

Unwrapping the dark chocolate he had brought, Vincenzo began grating it, then, using a pestle and mortar, ground it into a paste along with a few cloves and fennel seeds.

The two men cooked together; Luca softening a sliced onion in sizzling olive oil and frying the chicken until it was golden; Vincenzo tipping in the chocolate mixture; Luca adding spoonfuls of white vinegar, chopped chilli, a little sugar and another splash of Prosecco.

'The rest of the bottle is for us to enjoy while the chicken is simmering,' he said, fetching the champagne flutes from the top shelf of the dresser, 'which is possibly another reason why my nonna preferred to use it.'

It was the first time Valerie had seen him take a drink. He poured himself only a half-glass, raising it quickly in a toast and drinking it down.

Vincenzo reached into the fridge for another bottle. 'Surely your nonna would have wanted us to enjoy this one too,' he said as he uncorked it.

'She would have expected it,' Luca agreed, grinning. All the same, he refused when he was offered more.

They sat at the table out on the terrace. Luca brought out mosquito coils, a dish of fat green olives, some bread and a bottle of Ortolo olive oil. As the sun set, they sipped glasses of chilled Prosecco while the smell of chicken cooking in wine and chocolate teased their appetites.

Valerie had always loved this time of the evening, when the light softened slowly to darkness and candles were lit. Everyone looked so much better: the sharp lines of Tricia's face were blunted into prettiness, Vincenzo's skin was tanned and his eyes glowed a darker gold, Poppy was a beauty, and even solid little Moll beside her seemed lovelier.

'Our third day is almost finished,' Valerie said wistfully. 'This vacation seems to be flying by. Aren't there moments when you'd just like to stop time?'

Moll nodded. 'Of course there are.'

'Soon I'll be back at home and all this will be nothing but a memory and a few photographs, like the rest of my life.'

She saw Vincenzo glance towards her. He was held in conversation with Tricia but had overheard what she was saying perhaps.

'I'm being awfully gloomy, aren't I?' Valerie apologised to Moll. 'I've been in a peculiar sort of mood all day, to be honest.'

'I'm sure that's only natural, given what you've been through,' she replied sympathetically.

Vincenzo was watching them. He seemed to be waiting for a chance to speak. Valerie smiled at him but went on talking to Moll.

'Jean-Pierre would have told me so stop overthinking things, to live in the moment,' she admitted.

'That's good advice,' agreed Moll, 'but easier to say than do, I think.'

'Often he'd take me to a beautiful place, and if I remarked on how much I wanted to come back some day, he'd laugh and say, "But you're right here now, Valerie. Enjoy it."'

'Would he really? He sounds so great …'

'Yes, he was. If he hadn't been then perhaps I wouldn't miss him quite so much. Oh dear, I'm sorry. Let's change the subject quickly, before I ruin the mood of the whole evening.'

'Why don't we see if Luca needs some help serving up dinner,' suggested Moll. 'I'd like to watch him cook the pasta anyway. At home, mine often seems to stick together for some reason.'

*

Vincenzo used the opportunity presented by dinner being served to change his place at the table, taking the seat where Moll had been, right beside Valerie. He tackled his pasta with relish, accepting a second helping, too busy eating to talk.

'You know we have a saying in Italy,' he told Valerie, once he had dabbed at his mouth with a napkin. 'My papa was especially fond of it. "At the table one does not age," he would often say. It was the reason he gave for spending so long over his meals.'

'At the table one does not age,' Valerie repeated. 'I like that. If only it were true.'

'Why not choose to believe in it? The table is a good place to be; celebrating, commiserating, making new friends.' Vincenzo put his napkin beside his empty plate. 'What can be better than the moment you sit down to a bowl of good food and a glass of wine? It is like having the best of life ahead of you.'

'You set a lot of store by food, don't you?' she said.

'Most Sicilians do, especially my generation. None of life's milestones is considered properly marked unless accompanied by a great feast. Some of it is about putting on a show, of course; we Sicilians love that. But mostly it is about the food.'

'Do you cook a proper meal for yourself each night, even if Orsolina isn't there?' Valerie wondered.

'Of course ... what else would I do? Often it is very simple: some fresh fish with a sauce of olive oil, lemon and herbs. Perhaps a caponata or a salad of vegetables dressed with almonds and chilli. I like to spend time thinking about what I'm going to eat and to shop for the fresh ingredients every day at the market; but the moment I really relax is when I begin to cook.'

'Have you always loved to be in the kitchen?'

'Yes, when my wife was with us I would cook with her. Back then there was much more food, two or three courses, and we would invite friends to share our meal and spend half the night over it.' Vincenzo smiled. 'Because, of course, at the table one does not age.'

'At home, I eat in front of the television,' Valerie admitted. 'Perhaps that's why I'm getting so old.'

'Old? No, no, I don't think so, signora.' He began stacking the dirty pasta bowls. 'But if you are distracted by the television, how can you fully appreciate the flavours and textures of what you're eating?'

'Often it's only Chinese takeout I've picked up on the way home,' Valerie confessed. 'I used to cook more when my partner Jean-Pierre was alive. He would throw dinners for ten or twenty people and I'd be in charge of the menu. But cooking for one seems a bit soulless. So does sitting at the table to eat alone.'

'I make sure it isn't soulless,' Vincenzo told her. 'I have a napkin, my cutlery nicely polished, the dinnerware Mamma and my aunts passed on to me. I make it into a small occasion.'

Valerie stood to help carry the empty bowls back to the kitchen. 'That might make me feel even lonelier,' she admitted. 'The television is my company. Half the time I'm not really watching it; I just have it on for the noise.'

He grimaced. 'The sound of a television is one thing I hate. I am always telling Orsolina to turn ours down.'

Valerie wasn't surprised; Jean-Pierre too had been firm in his belief that hours spent in front of a screen were wasted. He had preferred to be involved in life, not sitting watching it.

She wondered what Vincenzo's wife had been like, but a keen sense of what was appropriate held her back from asking more questions. At heart, she agreed with Moll: it was rude to pry. Sooner or later people would tell you the things they wanted you to know.

As the main course was served, they changed places at the table once again. Moll ended up at the far end while Tricia moved to sit at Vincenzo's other shoulder, very quickly monopolising his conversation.

'Where on earth do you go for a night out round here?' she was asking.

'The café in the piazza stays open fairly late,' Vincenzo told her. 'And there is another smaller bar up the hill that is often busy in the evenings.'

'No, I mean a proper night out,' Tricia insisted. 'With music and dancing.'

'It has been years since I have done that,' he admitted. 'I think there is a place a few kilometres away down by the beach, a discotheque where the kids go in summer. But if I go out, it is usually to enjoy a hot chocolate and a liqueur after dinner.'

'I guess that sounds nice enough; perhaps we should do it tonight.'

Tricia had barely touched her dinner. Half the maltagliati had been left on her plate, and now she was toying with her chicken, even though it was meltingly tender, its sauce delicately sweet and spicy. Valerie thought it wasteful to push such good food aside uneaten, even if you were a little distracted by the man sitting beside you.

'So who else wants to come out for pudding and a night-cap?' Tricia asked. 'Poppy? Luca?'

Moll was staring at her plate, still steadily eating. She didn't bother to respond, even as the others agreed to the idea. Valerie glanced over at her. While she might have been tempted to prolong the evening, she could see it wasn't an option.

'I can't face tackling those steps again,' she said, smoothly. 'I think I'll stay here.'

Moll looked up. 'Yes, me too. It's so lovely sitting out here. Why move?'

Vincenzo tried to persuade them both to change their minds. 'But it is good for the digestion to take a walk after dinner,' he argued. 'And the hot chocolate at the bar in the piazza is very good, I promise. It will most certainly be included when I publish my food guide. You must try it.'

'Another night perhaps,' Valerie replied. 'If you have time.'

'Of course ... it would be a pleasure.' Vincenzo flashed a smile. 'What about tomorrow evening?'

He kissed her very lightly on both cheeks before he left. His lips were warm, and there was the faintest graze of roughness from his stubble. He smelt of musk and cocoa beans.

For the briefest moment Valerie felt that shivery sense of mutual attraction. It was entirely unexpected and left her with a hope she couldn't quite bring herself to dismiss.

Food of Love

Luca Amore remembers how it ended. The ending is the part he struggles with. The rest of it might have happened to someone else. Here in his nonna's kitchen at the end of an evening, caught in the routine of cleaning up after dinner, loading the dishwasher, refrigerating uneaten food, wiping down surfaces, it is almost impossible to believe he ever had that life.

It may have faded from most other people's memories, but apparently not from Orsolina's. He knows she has a habit of holding on to what she is told. He recalls her mother being exactly the same.

But neither of them was there, so they can only ever have known the barest details. Orsolina was still a child, Luca himself just turned eighteen and trying to survive as a student in London. Everything in that big, grey city had cost more than he expected. His life shrank down until it was a meagre thing. He gave up his accommodation and slept on other people's sofas; he skipped meals and walked instead of taking buses. He might have asked his mother for more money, but he felt guilty taking what he had already.

The job started out as a favour. Harry was the student who most often let him crash overnight in his flat. Luca liked him. He was generous with food; shared his coffee and beer; made him laugh. Then Harry started skipping college, soon dropping out altogether. He told Luca he had found a nice little earner, said he could use some help.

'You take the back entrance, I'll take the front,' were his instructions as he passed over the camera.

Luca spent an entire night sitting in some bushes with a flask of coffee and a packet of sugary biscuits. Even so, it was a struggle not to curl up on the ground and fall asleep. In the early hours, he was the one who got the picture. He didn't recognise the blonde girl who slipped out the back gate wearing yesterday's clothes as the morning brightened. Harry had told him to photograph anyone, coming or going, and he followed orders. She was famous, he discovered later, a star of some soap opera. She was cheating on her boyfriend.

The girl walked right past Luca's hiding place, so it wasn't difficult to capture her. When the shots were developed, they were good and sharp. Harry swore he was a natural and later shared what seemed a dizzying amount of money.

When he asked for help a second time, Luca didn't hesitate. Standing by bins full of decomposing food at the back of a West End restaurant wasn't much fun, but again he got the shot, it was printed in a Sunday newspaper, and they split the fee.

And that is how Luca became a photographer, in partnership with Harry, who knew all about backhanders in exchange for tip-offs and eventually signed them up with an agency.

What Luca enjoyed was the challenge and the chase; the rush of adrenalin and the thrill success gave him. He liked using his brain as well as his camera. Best of all was having what no one else had managed to get. He was young enough not to consider much beyond that.

Studying was dull in comparison, so Luca dropped out too and pursued his new career day and night. He and Harry bought a motorbike, a fast one. They were earning big money and spending big as well. It was a life where everything was done hard and fast: working, drinking, even women. They all lived the same way.

In summertime, they followed the famous to beach resorts in Spain, Italy and France. In winter, it was the royal family skiing. Harry had the contacts but somehow Luca always got the better shots. They were a tight team.

Things got rough from time to time. He was sworn at and spat on. Once he was punched. He became accustomed to lugging heavy camera gear and ladders, to sleeping in cars and standing outside nightclubs for hours in the middle of the night. Often there was a crush of them, making it impossible to get an exclusive. He and Harry grew more ruthless and determined. They used up favours and friendships. All that mattered in the end was the picture.

She was the biggest prize of all, the one he most enjoyed following. After a while she recognised him, learnt his name even. 'Not today, please, Luca,' she might say if she was feeling down or wearing no make-up. Occasionally he would lower his camera, give away the shot and deal with Harry's wrath later. It was worth it for the other times, the ones when she smiled and said '*Ciao, bello*', the rare ones when she posed up for him.

That last summer they hunted her all over the Mediterranean, to a villa in the South of France, to a funeral in Milan, to Sardinia, where they rented a motorboat to get up close. He watched her through his long lens, caught her every mood and expression, examined the hundreds of images they sent around the world. In the end he knew her face almost as well as his own.

And then it all finished one night in a dark tunnel in Paris. The finish is the part Luca can never forget. It is what he struggles with.

Moll

I saved for the longest time, you know. I'm not like the rest of you; getting here wasn't only a matter of putting my credit card details on a booking form and packing my suitcase.

A social worker's salary isn't much to survive on, not when you're raising two kids alone. There's not a lot left over for extras. I haven't had a holiday for years now; hardly ever see the inside of a restaurant. A takeaway cappuccino has been a big extravagance, I've been saving so hard.

My dream trip was always Tuscany. I imagined a landscape with cypress trees somewhere outside of Florence or Sienna, and a vast, crumbling palazzo. But everything I looked at there was so expensive. And I didn't want to wait any longer, to waste another year or two putting money away.

Then another blogger messaged me on Facebook to tell me about this place. It sounded ideal. The cooking style is very different, of course, and to be honest, I prefer the food from the northern regions. But this was affordable. I could come right away, that was the thing.

Even so, I felt guilty about spending so much on myself. Lola needs new clothes and Rae could do with help saving for university. Both girls told me not to worry, they insisted I should come … and Mum helped out with some bits of money she had tucked away. The three of them ganged up on me, bless them.

I suppose that's why I struggle with women like Tricia. For

her, coming to Sicily is just this year's holiday. I expect she's busy thinking of where she'd like to visit next.

My plan was to do some travelling once the girls left home, even if I had to backpack. I've hardly been anywhere really. When I was married, we went caravanning in Cornwall, and as a student I worked the summers in bars and cafés, so there was never time to get away.

I've still travelled sort of; I've journeyed the world through my cooking instead. Food is the main reason to go abroad anyway, in my opinion. I'm more interested in how things taste than the way they look. I prefer fish markets to art galleries, ingredients to souvenirs. All I need is a decent cookbook and I can go anywhere at all from the comfort of my own kitchen: Morocco, Mexico, China, you name it.

On weekends I'm always off on little adventures. I love finding spice shops or Italian delis and just breathing in the air. I lust after new recipes and the flavours I might find in them.

Last year I was totally into Asian, balancing sweet, sour and spicy, and my cupboards were full of bottles of shaoxing and kecap manis. Before that it was Indian, grinding up cumin and coriander seeds to splash into a pan and make fragrant curries. The girls loved my Mexican phase for the burritos and home-made tacos. They liked it when I came over all Spanish and made paella. They even managed to eat raw fish and wasabi when we did Japanese.

My favourite is Italian, though. It's what I always come back to wherever else I've travelled with my saucepans and recipe books. There are no flavours that pall, no dishes I tire of. I've always loved rolling out gnocchi or pasta dough, cooking down sweet late-summer tomatoes to make a sauce, grating a chunk of hard, gritty Parmesan.

And now I'm here – not only cooking Sicilian food but actually staying in Sicily. I'm doing what Jean-Pierre always advised you to do, Val: living in the moment, following my dream.

Yes, I'm missing my girls, but they say they're doing fine without me. My Mum pops in on them every day and I Skype in the evenings.

I may never make it back to Italy; but I'm here right now, and determined to relish every minute no matter what. It's what I saved for all that time. No one is going to spoil it for me.

Day Four

(i) Swordfish, cannoli & a mystery

Moll woke to the ringing of her alarm clock, as she had every morning. She liked to give herself at least an hour to update her blog before it was time to get ready. At home she might only post a few paragraphs, often about the things she cooked, sharing little tips and recipes. Here she was spoilt with things to write about.

Today's entry was all about olive oil, of course. She didn't think it would matter if she passed off some of Giulietta's comments as her own. Really, who would know? The details of how to tell the good oil from the bad were essential, after all.

First she checked for comments on yesterday's post. Her regular followers seemed excited she was in Sicily. They were demanding recipes and more photographs, wanted to know what Luca was like and what was happening day to day. Moll was happy to oblige.

There were some things it was better not to mention, however; the scrap with Tricia, for instance. Not that she was ashamed of her outburst. Moll had never suffered fools gladly. She thought of herself as the plain-speaking type, and if people didn't like it, then too bad.

Tricia had grated on her from the beginning. Moll could tell when she was being patronised. So what if she didn't paint her nails and iron her hair; if she was a social worker not a barrister, if she lived in Hackney rather than Belgravia.

It didn't give anyone the right to queen it over her.

Once she had updated her blog she packed her laptop into its padded bag till next time. Moll loved the Internet. It had opened up a whole new life, introduced her to so many people who thought the same way she did.

Her computer was the only thing she bothered to stow away tidily. The rest of the room was a muddle. Clothes spilled from her suitcase; the dresser was cluttered with things she had pulled from it, and on the floor there were shoes, books and crumpled chocolate wrappers. It hardly seemed worth tidying up; she would only create more mess.

Indifferently, she poked about in her suitcase for something to wear. Moll had packed lots of loose tops, drawstring trousers and skirts with elasticated waistbands. Even so, after last night's dinner she had experienced that uncomfortable feeling of clothes squeezing into flesh.

Still, there were worse things in life than putting on weight, and she had enjoyed every bite of it. The pasta dish with its bright flavours of vegetables softened in grassy olive oil; then the chicken cooked in its bath of spice and chocolate. She had expected it to be rich, like the Mexican mole she once tried, but the sauce was delicate enough not to steal the glory from the meat, a perfect harmony of sweet and sour with the sudden fire of chilli at the finish of each mouthful.

Already Moll was anticipating the coming day's eating. Just a few of those little pastries for breakfast; the ones filled with semi-sweet lemon marmalade were her favourite. And then they were booked in for lunch at a restaurant in Ortygia, where Luca had promised them a feast from the sea.

She wondered if he had arrived with breakfast yet. She hadn't noticed the slam of the front door, but her room was tucked away at the back of the house, quiet and private. She couldn't hear the sound of Tricia's hairdryer or Poppy slipping out at dawn to run up and down Favio's long flights of steps. She was grateful for that.

When she booked this holiday, Moll had thought only of the cooking and eating. She hadn't considered it would mean rubbing so close to other women. As soon as they met, she had known none of them were her kind of people. Even Val, much as she liked her, was from another world.

Preoccupied with her thoughts, she dressed in black Marks & Spencer leggings and a flowing short-sleeved tunic covered in a bright print of sunflowers. She didn't bother checking her reflection. She knew what she looked like; there was no need for constant reminders.

Moll had never been especially pretty. She had cared about that when she was Lola and Rae's age. Later on, it seemed an advantage not to have to worry about the spread of flesh and wrinkles. It was amazing all the time and money some women wasted fighting the way their faces changed. Moll didn't see the point. She liked to think she had a talent for seeing beyond appearances anyway, right to the nub of people's characters.

It had been easy enough to sum up the other women on this holiday. Tricia was self-centred and vain, the type she most disliked. Val was kind-hearted and wise. Poppy was at a crossroads in her life and rather vulnerable (at least they had divorce in common).

Luca was more difficult to read. There was his passion for food and his skills in the kitchen. Beyond that, Moll could only detect a general likeability. Surely there must be something else, a side of himself he was hiding? She encountered lots of damaged people in her work. It showed up in different ways and she was used to seeking it in everyone she met. Yet she couldn't be sure about Luca. Maybe there was a buried seam of hurt; then again, perhaps not.

One thing she was sure of – he was sweet on Poppy. From the first, she had caught him looking at her with a sort of hesitant admiration. Moll imagined no one else had noticed this, possibly not even Poppy herself.

The other flirtation, the one between Vincenzo and Valerie, was much more obvious. It must have been evident to everyone by now. How sweet of him to bring her flowers. A little attention might do Val the world of good, but perhaps it might be better if it didn't go much further. The poor woman hardly needed more heartbreak in her life.

Moll was hungry and desperate for a coffee. Through her closed shutters she heard the cathedral bells ringing the hour. Eight o'clock; surely Luca would be in the kitchen by now, laying out pastries. Grabbing her camera, she went downstairs to see.

To her dismay, she found only Tricia, busy opening cupboard doors and slamming them shut again.

'I'm looking for the moka pot,' she told Moll, sounding exasperated. 'Where does he hide the bloody thing, do you know?'

'It's in the cupboard up there next to the fridge. The rest of the coffee things are in there too.'

'Oh, thanks, here it is. Hey, you should have come out with us last night. You'd have enjoyed that hot chocolate, it was thick and really rich.'

Moll didn't bother replying.

'We went to a couple of bars in the end. I can't say Favio has much of a night life.'

Tricia had found the moka pot lying in several pieces and was making a hash of putting it together. Moll watched until she couldn't stand it any longer.

'Here, let me,' she said.

'Oh, thanks.' Tricia moved aside. 'I've never been able to get the hang of those things. We've got this huge machine at home. Paul had it specially plumbed in. It's a bit of a nightmare to use, so mostly I can't be bothered. I tend to go out for my coffees instead.'

Moll wished Tricia wasn't making such an effort. She had hoped they might skirt around each other for the rest of the holiday, engage as little as possible. It was irritating to have someone she disliked be so friendly. Now she would have to do the same.

'Did you stay out late last night?' She tried to appear interested.

'Till about midnight, I think, maybe longer. We left when they started closing the bar around us. It was a good evening, actually, a laugh. Vincenzo was very charming.'

Moll was hoping one of the others might appear (ideally, Val). In the meantime, she would have to put up with Tricia's chatter.

'Charming? I suppose he is,' she said dismissively.

'His wife died years ago in a road accident, apparently. He told me she was hit by a speeding motorbike. Odd that he hasn't married again, isn't it?'

Moll supposed she had been prying. 'He must have been busy raising Orsolina and running his business.'

'Yeah, that's what he said.' Tricia looked at her. 'The two of us talked a lot about our lives, but I promise I didn't interrogate him. So don't tell me off, OK?'

'Was Poppy not with you?' Moll asked, ignoring the mention of their quarrel.

'No, she headed away with Luca a little earlier. I think they were going to walk up to the Pizzo to take a look at the view by night.'

'So it was only you and Signore Mazzara?'

'For the last hour or so, yes.'

Moll wondered what that meant. She imagined Tricia wasn't the kind of woman who worried about having a husband at home. And yet she could have sworn it wasn't her that Vincenzo was interested in.

The slam of the front door felt like a reprieve. She heard Luca's voice calling out good morning, and he came in carrying a basket she hoped was filled to the brim with bread and pastries.

'Oh, hello, you're making coffee.' His tone was cheerful. 'Good, I could do with some myself.'

'Late night?' asked Tricia.

'For me it was,' Luca agreed. 'Usually I prefer to be asleep well before midnight.'

Tricia laughed. 'You must be lightweights here in Favio. At home we don't consider that to be late.'

Moll might have contradicted her. Even on weekends she herself was in bed by 10.30 with a book and a chamomile tea, and she didn't think that was so unusual. But keeping her thoughts to herself, she helped Luca unpack the basket, pulling out crisp cornetti oozing with custard, soft biscuits made from pastes of almonds and pistachio, crusty bread rolls still faintly warm, a ripe orange-fleshed melon and a few long-stemmed strawberries.

Loading a plate and helping herself to coffee, she went out on the terrace to enjoy it. Even when she heard Valerie and Poppy's voices she didn't bother to go back inside. It was pleasant sitting in a pool of morning sunlight looking down at the town. Already she had taken scores of photographs of this view, although none really did it justice. She would have to ask Luca for some tips on how to improve her skills. Perhaps she needed a different lens. Surely if he had been a professional photographer, he should know.

'Ah, here you are.' Valerie had come to find her. 'We're all breakfasting indoors this morning.'

'I'm happy out here, thanks.'

Valerie hesitated. 'OK then,' she said, withdrawing back inside.

Moll hoped Val didn't feel as if she had to babysit her. There was no need. She had never been one of those people who craved constant company. At home with the girls and their friends coming and going, or at work in an open-plan office, she always felt surrounded. Here it was a pleasure to be alone. She noticed things. The man on the balcony opposite watering his tomato plants before the sun reached them; the sound of the woman who lived next door sweeping her floors and the smell of something baking sweetly in her oven; an old lady dragging her shopping trolley behind her up a flight of steps; a couple having a noisy argument somewhere in the houses above. All these things added up to Sicily. And it was Sicily that Moll wanted to experience, not the constant chatter of a bunch of women, their little flirtations and petty gossip.

She yawned and rubbed her eyes, gave a thought to what her girls were doing, hoped they weren't sleeping in and missing school; wondered if they had remembered to water her pots of herbs and feed the cats. There were lots of feral ones here in Favio and Moll felt sorry for them, skinny things with dull fur and sores on their backs. Luca shooed them off the terrace, said not to feed them, but she had sneaked some scraps anyway when he wasn't looking.

Picking up her empty coffee cup, Moll moved indoors in search of a refill. The others were still at the kitchen table. Poppy's plate was messy with half-eaten pastries and pieces of melon peel. Tricia's looked clean, with only a few stems of strawberries to show for breakfast. Val was smearing pale gold honey on a crust of bread.

Pouring what was left of the coffee into her cup, Moll asked, 'So what time do we set off for Ortygia?'

'Half an hour or so,' Luca suggested.

'And what's the plan when we get there?'

'Until lunchtime you're free to do whatever you like. Ortygia is packed with history. There are the remains of temples to see and the old town to wander through. Oh, and the shopping is good ... at least that's what Orsolina tells me.'

Moll didn't care for browsing aimlessly round shops. If she needed something, she bought it; otherwise she didn't bother. She flicked through a guidebook she had found on the bookshelf earlier, checking what else there was to see, while Tricia went upstairs to fiddle with her appearance, most likely, Poppy to smooth sunscreen over her bare arms, and Valerie to fetch her sunglasses.

'There's a cathedral we could visit,' Moll said when they all returned. 'And the ruins Luca mentioned.'

'Actually I'm quite keen on visiting the stores,' Val admitted. 'I'd enjoy the chance to see the local styles.'

'Me too,' agreed Tricia. 'I've been here three days and haven't used my credit card yet. That's unheard of. Amex is likely to send out a search party.'

In the van they took their places, Moll making sure not to end up beside Tricia. It was the longest drive so far, taking them past stretches of dry-earthed olive groves, wild poppies and oleander growing by the roadside, a herd of goats solemnly chewing, and the first glimpse of a wide band of Mediterranean blue on the horizon (Moll longed for a dip in it).

Ortygia was surrounded by sea and linked by bridges to the mainland. From what she had read on other people's blogs, it was a good place to find authentic Sicilian cooking. Moll had made notes about some of the things she hoped to try.

'Will there be swordfish at lunch? And fresh anchovies?' she asked Luca.

'I hope so, but who can predict what they've pulled from the sea? Only the freshest fish is served at Il Capriccio. They buy direct from the boats. One thing I can promise you is the best cannoli you'll have in your life.'

Behind her, Tricia gave a groan. 'Please can we stop talking about food for a minute? Didn't we just have breakfast?'

'I wasn't aware we'd discussed food at all yet today,' Moll said, stiffly. 'So sorry.'

She was gratified to hear Luca add, 'I can always talk about cannoli, no matter how much I've eaten.'

'What's so special about them?' Tricia asked. 'Go on, you know you want to tell us.'

Luca laughed. 'They have a long and interesting history. Originally they were made for spring festival season – this was back in the Middle Ages, when the Arabs occupied Sicily. Some say they were a way for us to reassert our national identity. Others that they symbolised fertility and protected against evil spirits.'

'Oh, please.' Tricia groaned again. 'They're just cakes, right? How can they protect against evil spirits?'

'They're hardly just cakes,' argued Luca. 'They're crisp, light crusts, and when you bite into them, the flavour of orange-flower-infused ricotta bursts into your mouth along with the texture of crushed pistachios. There are good cannoli and bad. I'm very fussy and will only eat at places where they fill the shells the moment you order them so they don't go the slightest bit soggy.'

'At home the cannoli we buy are great, fat, sickly things,' Valerie put in.

'Yes, so I've heard. Here they are slim and delicate and nowhere near as sweet. Of course, there are different versions depending on where you go. Some include chocolate or honey, Marsala or rosewater, candied lemon peel, or even *zucca*, a preserved watermelon rind. There are family recipes that have been handed down through the generations and never put in writing, just as there are for other specialities like *arancini,* or the spiced fig nut cookies we call *cuccidati.*'

'You make it sound so romantic,' said Poppy.

Tricia snorted this time. 'It's cake! It's not romantic.'

Luca laughed again. 'You taste the cannoli at Il Capriccio then tell me you haven't fallen in love.'

Moll had been taking notes as he spoke, thinking all this would be useful for her blog. 'How do you make your cannoli?' she asked him.

'To be honest, I don't make them. I buy them like everyone else does. Usually they are thinner and crisper than I would ever manage. And at places like Il Capriccio, they fry the shells around a piece of cane instead of doing it the modern way with a stainless-steel tube. Some say the finest cannoli are to be found in Palermo, but in my opinion nothing beats the ones here.'

Moll made a careful note of everything he said, then stuffed her notebook back into her scuffed leather satchel. It was full of other things she thought she might need – a shell-pink muslin scarf to cover her bare shoulders in case they visited a church, a spare memory card for her camera, glasses for reading the small type on restaurant menus – but even so, it was only half the size of the vast bag Tricia was toting. Even Moll recognised the logo on it as Gucci. A thing like that would cost a month's wages, and all it did was carry stuff just as Moll's old satchel did. She couldn't begin to understand the silliness.

They parked close to the seafront, walking in the sunshine past yachts and fishing boats bobbing in the marina and up towards a large piazza with some fenced-off historic ruins at its centre.

'This is the Temple of Apollo,' Luca explained. 'It dates back to the sixth or seventh century and has an interesting past. The Greeks built it, then the Muslims took it over, and later on the Normans turned it into a church.'

Moll saw that all that was left were stubs of columns, a few stone steps and tumbling walls with mown lawns stretching between them. She wasn't one of those people who could feel the history in places like this. There was never any sense of the people who had walked there before her. Still, she fired off a couple of shots in case she could use them later.

Tricia seemed equally as unexcited. After a brief glance at the ancient stones, she asked, 'Where are the shops you told us about, Luca?'

He pointed up towards a wide boulevard lined with plate-glass windows where Moll glimpsed mannequins sporting summer fashions in bright colours (and, inevitably, the tiniest of sizes).

'Actually there's a shop I'd like to visit,' she told Luca. 'I read about it in the guidebook back at the house. It's called Il Gusto di Sicilia.'

'Yes, yes, I know it well. You'll have to walk to the other end of the island, but it's not so far. They sell many locally made artisan foods there, and some wine too.'

'Sounds great.'

'They'll press lots of samples on you,' Luca warned. 'Be careful not to eat too much.'

'I'll leave room for swordfish and cannoli, I promise.'

'In that case, I'll mark it on your map,' he offered. 'Let's meet back at the Temple of Apollo at midday, then go for lunch. Don't be late; they won't keep our table.'

The group broke apart; Val followed Tricia for the shopping while Moll continued with Poppy and Luca towards the old town. Walking briskly, they turned down a narrow side street and reached a set of buildings that curved into a long piazza dominated by another great baroque cathedral.

'This is Ortygia's Duomo,' Luca told them. 'It was once a Greek temple, and if you go inside, you can still see the original Doric columns.'

Poppy craned her neck, staring up at the grand facade. 'I wonder if my grandfather came here when he was a boy. He was born on Ortygia but never spoke of its history, just the food and the weather.'

'This is where most of the island's big weddings and christenings are held,' Luca told her. 'I expect he'd have come here at some point, even if his family worshipped in another church. Shall we go in?'

'Yes, I'd love to,' Poppy agreed.

Moll wasn't tempted. Churches, no matter how beautiful, weren't the real reason she was here.

'I'm going to press on,' she said. 'I may come back later if there's time.'

No one tried to persuade her to change her mind. Poppy accepted the shell-pink scarf to put round her bare shoulders, and as she and Luca walked up the steps of the cathedral, it fluttered between them in the breeze. Moll couldn't resist taking a picture.

Once they'd disappeared through the massive arched doorway, she took a seat at an empty table at the crowded pavement café opposite. Lately she had found that a glass of Coca-Cola gave her an instant lift, and she needed one right now, even if they did charge some exorbitant price for it.

In front of the cathedral there was a middle-aged bride posing for photographs. She didn't have the best of figures and her dress hugged it a little too closely. As she sipped her ice-cold Coke, Moll was reminded of her own wedding. She recalled being zipped into ivory taffeta so tightly she could barely breathe, never mind enjoy any of the wedding supper.

The Sicilian groomsmen in their spivvy suits weren't unlike her ex-husband Keith's friends – especially the one in drain-pipe trousers. Keith was an East End boy and they went in for much the same look those days, particularly at weddings.

Moll finished her drink and paid the bill. It wasn't that she regretted her marriage – she had the girls because of it, after all. What she was sorry for were the years of living life the way Keith wanted it. He controlled everything from the television remote to the way they ate. She recalled years of buying meat off the bone and seasoning it with nothing more than pepper and salt. Frying chips in a big vat of hot fat. Putting bottles of brown sauce and ketchup on the table and seeing it sloshed over everything. Serving cups of tea with dinner and side plates of thickly buttered soft white bread. That was at 6 p.m. sharp every night. Keith ate with the television blaring in the corner and by 7 p.m. was at the pub.

Some of her friends had husbands who were much worse.

At least Keith didn't come home drunk and angry. He had never hit her, not once. He adored Lola and Rae, used to take them to the swings in the local park for an hour every Sunday. Now it was pizza and a movie instead, but Moll suspected not much else had changed.

It had begun with small rebellions: putting dinner on the table half an hour late, jazzing up his stew with garlic she bought ready-minced in a jar, using fresh herbs instead of dried. Moll hadn't understood about food then. Mostly she cooked the same things her mother had. But she knew she had it in her to live life more richly.

Everything changed when she tasted pesto. There had been an article about it in the style supplement of a Sunday newspaper, and Moll thought it sounded lovely so went all the way to Clerkenwell to buy some from an Italian delicatessen. She ate it with a spoon straight from the jar. It was like nothing she had tried before; the sweetness and scent of bruised basil, the bite of fresh garlic, the smoothness of oil and cheese, the slightly resinous taste of pine nuts, all brought together and exploding with flavour in her mouth. She went back to buy more, even though at first she had baulked at the cost.

That small jar of pesto woke up more than her taste buds. Suddenly Moll realised how much she was missing. Her rebellions grew bigger. She bought a book by Elizabeth David and insisted on cooking from it, even though Keith left most of his dinner on the plate and stopped off for fish and chips later. She went back to college to study social work. She grew basil in pots and made her own pesto.

Everyone was shocked when she asked for a divorce, no one more than Keith. Her parents worried about security; friends asked if she really thought she would find someone better.

As she stood to leave the café, Moll watched the Italian bride climbing into her wedding car. She didn't envy her one bit. There was never a moment when she thought of marrying again. Men needed so much bolstering up and listening to. They had moods you had to manage, and physical demands. Moll didn't have the time or energy for it.

Both her mother and grandmother had stayed married to the same men happily enough for decade after decade. But they had never walked medieval streets lined with buildings the colour of pale honey, streets so narrow no car would fit down them. Rather than pasta, they had eaten instant mashed potato; Angel Delight not cannoli. Their lives were measured out in mugs of tea and spoonfuls of sugar (three per cup).

Moll's route took her along the seafront, past restaurants with striped awnings whose waiters called out to her, urging an inspection of their menus. She couldn't see one called Il Capriccio so shook her head firmly and carried on.

Il Gusto di Sicilia was Moll's idea of the perfect shop. Its door lay open to the street, leaking the mustiness of hard cheeses and the smoke of cured meats. Just beside the doorway there was a woman holding a tray of tiny sandwiches to tempt in passers-by. She couldn't resist taking one. It was filled with a hard spicy cheese and fresh basil, so delicious her mouth watered for more.

The place was a temple of food. One entire wall was lined with jars of pickle and preserves and Moll walked along it, examining them carefully. That one contained a cream of artichokes, this a pesto of wild fennel, and this a sweet-sour caponata.

Above the counter hung gourds of local cheese, and within it were firm cakes of baked ricotta. There was a display of salami and sides of prosciutto, there were shelves of vinegars and oils, glass cabinets groaning with dishes of antipasti. Moll was greedy for the sight of it all. She hoped they didn't mind her taking pictures.

Despite her promise to Luca, it was impossible to resist the tasting samples. She tried sweet sausage, smoked mozzarella, ricotta with mint and capers. They insisted on opening wine and pouring her a glass to enjoy with the tasty morsels of food.

It was the prices that amazed Moll – everything seemed a fraction of what it would cost in London, even though the quality and variety was better. Still, she chose what she wanted to take home carefully, spending money only on things she was certain she wouldn't find there.

The walk back was much slower, weighed down as she was by her shopping. By the time Moll reached the Duomo, it was too late for her to see inside, so she continued on to their meeting spot.

Valerie and Tricia were there already and clutching shopping bags too, only theirs had names of clothes shops written on them. There was a brief show and tell, pulling things out and rustling through tissue paper, Moll pretending more interest than she felt. Tricia had bought a couple of floaty frocks and a pair of impractical sandals (definitely expensive), Val a couple of cotton T-shirts (certainly less so). Moll expected they found her purchases just as mystifying.

'Hey, where's Luca?' Tricia glanced at her watch. 'He was the one who told us to be on time. He's ten minutes behind schedule.'

'I hope we don't lose our table,' said Moll. 'He said there was a risk if we turned up late.'

'I hope not too,' agreed Val. 'I'm desperate for a sit-down and a cold drink.'

Tricia scooped up her shopping bags. 'Why don't I go back to that last shop? They spoke pretty good English there. If they can tell me where Il Capriccio is, then I'll head over and secure our table while you two wait here for the others.'

Moll had to admire her decisiveness. 'I can't think where they've got to. I left them at the Duomo and that's only five minutes' walk away.'

It was at least another ten minutes before they caught sight of Luca and Poppy weaving through the crowds shoulder to shoulder. Was it Moll's imagination, or were they holding hands? Still several metres away, they broke apart and Luca began to wave.

'I'm so sorry,' he said, reaching them. 'We were wandering around and completely lost track of time. But I called the restaurant and they said Tricia had saved our table so there's no need to rush.'

Il Capriccio wasn't right beside the sea like the more touristy places but a couple of streets back and hidden inside a crumbling baroque house with an overgrown garden. A waiter ushered them into a low-ceilinged room where roughcast walls were covered in cheaply framed black-and-white photographs of the island as it once was. Recalling how the best food was often found in the least pretentious surroundings, Moll was reassured.

It was a moment or two before she recognised the young man sitting beside Tricia at a table near the window; and then she realised where she had seen him before.

'Isn't that the chef from the vineyard we went to? What was his name? Santo something? I wonder what he's doing here.'

'Yes, I think you're right, it is him,' Valerie agreed.

Out of his chef's whites he looked even younger: dark fringe flopping into brown eyes fringed by long glossy lashes, smoothly shaved olive skin. Moll wasn't surprised to see that Tricia seemed delighted. She had already called for an extra place to be set at the table.

'It's Santo's day off so he's come to sample another restaurant's cooking,' she explained. 'I thought no one would mind if we squeezed him on to our table. After all, the bigger the group, the more dishes we can try.'

Almost as soon as they took their seats, a waiter brought out small plates of ricotta sprinkled with pistachios to graze on while Luca and Santo gave their attention to the menu.

After a spirited discussion they agreed to begin with slices of smoked swordfish, a platter of razor clams dressed with hot flakes of dried chilli, and tiny red shrimps in a salad of oranges, spring onions and parsley.

The dishes came out randomly. Since she hated taking notes at the table, Moll photographed each one before tasting it. Knowing there would be more to come, she tried only a couple of forkfuls and hoped the pictures would be enough to jog her memory.

Conferring over the menu again, Luca and Santo ordered more food to be brought to them. Moll would never forget the *arancini*, little fried balls of rice paddling in a sauce of red mullet and wild fennel. Or the two platters of pasta; one piled with spaghetti dressed in fresh sardines and fennel; the other with macaroni and clams in a sauce made creamy with ground pistachios.

To follow there was more swordfish, this time served with a sauce of briny green olives and a dish of sweet Tunisian aubergines baked with caciocavallo cheese.

Moll hardly bothered to join with the conversation, so focused was she on singling out the flavours on each plate. Santo seemed the same. He was taking his food seriously, looking, smelling and eating with quiet concentration, and giving his attention to Tricia only in the gaps between courses.

Moll wished she were sitting next to him. She would like to talk about the food they were enjoying, to ask how highly he rated Il Capriccio's menu, if he thought the chef here cared as much as he did, if the dishes he tried would influence his own. She recalled how beautifully the meals had been presented at his vineyard restaurant, while here they were served up family style on chipped platters. Did Santo think that mattered?

There was so much to learn about cooking, and that was what excited Moll. She might have liked to train as a chef rather than a social worker, but she'd had the girls by then and needed a job that fitted in with school hours.

At last there was a break in the bringing out of dishes. Luca ordered coffee and suggested they take a few minutes before the final course of cannoli.

'A few minutes?' Tricia patted her flat stomach. 'It'll take longer than that for me to be ready for dessert. Perhaps someone will split a cannoli with me? All these calories and carbs ... I'm not going to fit into the dresses I just bought.'

Moll couldn't have been less interested in people's body issues. Thinking of food as calories, fat content and carbohydrate levels, as nothing but numbers to tot up; what could be more boring? To do it in the course of a meal they were all enjoying ... well, she thought that was plain bad manners.

In her experience, groups of women could talk for hours about what they had or hadn't eaten, and how they felt about it. Fortunately, aside from murmuring about how very full they felt, Valerie and Poppy didn't seem inclined to make a big deal of it.

Moll steered the conversation onwards in case they changed their minds, turning to Poppy to ask, 'So tell us, what did you and Luca get up to this morning? Where were you both for all that time?'

'Sightseeing ... kind of ... I'll show you.' Poppy rummaged in her bag. 'I wanted to find the house where my grandfather was born. The trouble is, I don't have an address because he emigrated to Australia when he was a young boy and doesn't remember much about Ortygia. All he had was an old family photo I came across in an album. I took it without telling him and brought it along hoping it might help.'

Poppy produced a creased black-and-white photograph she had tucked into a clear plastic case for protection. It showed a solemn woman with dark hair and a smiling boy in a sailor suit standing together in a doorway beneath a balcony decorated with baroque swirls of stone.

'I'd hoped that since the island is so small I might be able to spot it. The trouble is, there are so many houses that look very like this one,' explained Poppy, ruefully. 'Luca and I walked for ages round a maze of narrow lanes. Every now and then we'd find a place that seemed right, but then we'd notice a difference in the stonework or the arch of the doorway. Finally we saw this building ... I took some pictures. Here, have a look and tell me what you think.'

Poppy passed round her camera so they could see the images she had shot from several different angles.

The house was on a narrow lane with walls that were scuffed and scarred. 'Its balcony does seem to match the one in your photo,' agreed Moll, examining it closely. 'What are the chances of another place having exactly the same stonework?'

'I'm not sure. But the building next to it seems right too.' Poppy held up her camera and the old photograph side by side. 'I suppose I was being romantic. I hoped to feel some affinity with the place, a sense of belonging ... but no.'

'Has your grandfather never been back to Sicily?' wondered Moll.

'No, never. I guess for that generation it was such a long, expensive trip; and now his health isn't great. So I have no idea if I still have relatives on the island. My grandfather lost touch with all but one branch of the family that went to America. Growing up I never felt very Italian. We didn't speak the language at home. Grandad was our only link to the past, and he thinks of himself as Australian now.'

'Did you knock on the door of that house?' asked Tricia.

'Yes, but there was no one home.'

'You should go back again after lunch. Perhaps there'll be someone there who can help you.'

'I suppose I could ... Is it silly, though? I mean, what am I going to say to them, even if we are related?'

'Surely it's not unusual for people to want to trace their Sicilian roots?' Tricia turned to Santo and Luca. 'Is it?'

'Not at all,' agreed Santo. 'Foreigners come here all the

time for that ... from England, America, Australia; all the many places Sicilians end up. I think there are even some websites for immigrants who want to reconnect with distant relatives here. For a fee they'll write to everyone in your home town who shares your family name.'

'Imagine how thrilling it would be if you found a second cousin or one of his great-nephews,' Tricia said. 'You have to try. I'll come with you if you like.'

Poppy looked at Luca. 'Is there time?'

'Of course, if it's what you want. I should be the one who comes, though, in case you need a translator. But you know, it's possible your family scattered to different parts of the world years ago and no one is left here. Those were tough times. Most people thought the future was better elsewhere.'

'If she doesn't knock, she won't know,' pointed out Tricia.

Moll found herself agreeing. 'Yes, life's too short to worry about what you'll find on the other side of every door.' (She was quoting a self-help book she had read.)

Valerie gave a half-smile. 'Now you're sounding like Jean-Pierre. Still, I think you're right. Even if they're not related, whoever lives there may have some clues to offer.'

Since they were to spend a few more hours on the island, Tricia suggested a power walk to burn off the lunchtime calories.

'I'm much more inclined towards a gentle amble myself,' Valerie admitted.

'Me too,' agreed Moll. 'But don't let that stop you if you want to race off. We'll stroll along behind at our own pace.'

Santo offered to accompany Tricia on a circuit round the waterfront, and she seemed pleased. They set off together fast, long legs striding, with little care for crowded pavements, and Moll was happy to be left behind. No matter how much of an effort she made, it felt more relaxing when Tricia wasn't around.

She checked her map. 'Shall we go just as far as the Arethusa fountain?' she suggested to Val. 'There may be a spot where we can sit by the sea and have a coffee.'

'Sounds perfect.'

'Who knows how long Luca and Poppy will be. I suppose it depends if they find anyone at home this time. Still, I suppose we're not in any hurry.'

'I do hope Poppy traces someone,' said Valerie, 'and that they welcome her. She seems a little lost to me. Or am I imagining that, do you think?'

'No, I agree with you. Although I rather suspect she might have found someone already.'

Valerie looked at her quizzically. 'I'm sorry?'

'Not a relative, though,' Moll teased.

'Oh, now you're being cryptic.'

Moll laughed. 'I think I might have seen her and Luca holding hands earlier. It certainly looked like it.'

'Really? How lovely.' Valerie said it warmly. 'How exciting.'

'I guess so,' said Moll.

'Don't you remember how it feels, the thrill of first attraction and wondering if you'll ever find a way to get together, and then how it is when it happens?'

'Not really,' Moll admitted. 'It wasn't like that with my ex, Keith. He lived two streets away and our parents knew each other. I can't recall exactly how we got together. I think we went to the cinema, and then he kissed me after that. All my friends had boyfriends and I felt left out, so ... Well, you know ... it just kind of happened.'

'And you ended up marrying him.'

'Yes, when I was pregnant with Rae. We'd been together five years by then, and getting married seemed the thing to do. We split up eight years later.'

'I've made my share of mistakes too,' Val told her. 'My first husband drank, and I mean proper drinking, from morning to night, bottles hidden all over the house. Not that I realised it when I met him; he just seemed a fun guy, one who knew how to have a good time. And my second husband ... well, let's just say he was worse.'

'Then at long last there was Jean-Pierre.'

'Yes, I found a good one in the end. Hopefully you will too.'

'No, I don't think so,' Moll said. 'Not me.'

Reaching the fountain, they peered over the high wall surrounding it to find a sad-looking semicircular pool with a few ducks and a clump of papyrus.

'Not very exciting,' said Moll, digging around in her satchel for the guidebook. 'I wonder what all the fuss is about.'

Valerie was reading from a brass plaque on the wall. 'It says here that it's a freshwater spring and that the ancient Greeks believed it to be the embodiment of the nymph Arethusa. She was transformed into it to escape the attentions of an unwanted suitor.'

'That seems extreme.'

'Yes, particularly as the cad then went and had himself turned into a river so he could mingle his waters with hers.'

Moll laughed. 'Men ... how typical!'

'Even my ex-husbands wouldn't have gone that far.' Valerie was laughing too.

They took a table shaded by an awning in a row of bars and restaurants that stretched along the sea wall. It was a beautiful spot and well worth paying for a couple of drinks they didn't really want so they could rest and enjoy it.

Moll asked for sparkling mineral water, Valerie ordered an espresso. For a while they sat quietly, Moll checking the photographs she had taken and making notes about their lunch at Il Capriccio for her blog.

'Ah, this is nice.' Valerie stretched out her legs so her calves were in the sun. 'So relaxing.'

Moll looked up. 'Poor frantic Tricia, I expect she's almost completed her first lap by now. Speeding round the island in the heat of the day like a mad thing.'

'Probably,' Valerie agreed. 'You two do seem to be getting on much better today, though.'

Moll wrinkled her nose. 'I'm not going to pretend to like her. I think she's dangerous.'

'Dangerous?' Valerie laughed. 'How?'

'It's the way she is with men – with Santo today, and Vincenzo Mazzara last night.'

'She's flirting, there's nothing wrong with that.'

'It's a way of saying she can have everything she wants, even them.'

'Gosh, you really don't like her, do you?'

'Not at all.'

'Well I think she's an interesting lady, funny and smart. You're right about one thing, though.' Valerie pointed. 'Here they come, look.'

Tricia was loping along the seaside promenade, swigging from a plastic bottle of water and talking to Santo, who was keeping pace with her stride. Neither glanced across and noticed them. Whatever their conversation, it held their attention.

'Dear God, they really are doing laps. How many do you think they're planning?'

'I wish I had that kind of energy.' Valerie looked wistful.

'Really? I'm too full to move. I'd rather take it easy.'

They had been sitting at their waterfront table for another half-hour (and two more drinks), people-watching and chatting about nothing in particular, by the time they spotted Luca and Poppy strolling along beside the sea wall.

Valerie waved to attract their attention. 'We're over here,' she called. 'How did things go?'

Moll hadn't expected them to have much success so was unsurprised to see Poppy giving an emphatic thumbs-down as they approached the café.

'It was a waste of time really,' she told them, sounding disappointed. 'Not worth keeping you waiting for half the afternoon, I'm sorry.'

'What a pity.' Valerie was sympathetic. 'Still, we've been having a perfectly nice time here, so don't feel bad about us.'

'Was there anyone at home this time?' asked Moll.

'Yes, a mother and two young children,' said Poppy. 'She was lovely and insisted on offering us coffee and little biscuits, then showing us around the place, which is tiny, of course. But she wasn't a relative. It seems the house has changed hands several times over the years. The signora had no idea where my grandfather's family might have ended up.'

'What about trying the city hall?' Valerie suggested. 'Would there be a registry of births, deaths and marriages? You might find some useful information there.'

'Perhaps, but do I really want to spend my whole time chasing round after ghosts when there seems such a tiny chance I'll get anywhere?' Poppy sounded wistful. 'I only have a few more days here, after all, and it's a pity to waste them, as who knows when I'll be able to take another holiday.'

Moll thought it more of a pity to give in so easily. Either Poppy wanted to find her relatives or she didn't.

'Anyone on this island could be related to you and you wouldn't know it,' she said. 'The waiter, those people walking over there.'

'Only distantly,' responded Poppy.

'But still.'

'At least I got a look inside the house and imagined my grandfather's childhood there. That's something, isn't it?'

Moll knew for certain that generations of her own family stretched back through English history, barely putting a foot anywhere more exotic. They were working-class stock, as her mother always said (staunchly proud of it). Being ordinary was enough for her. She didn't envy Poppy her drops of Italian blood. Yet still, if there had been a chance that she herself was connected to someone on this tiny island, she would have done her homework properly before getting on the plane.

'I could try some stuff online for you,' she offered. 'It wouldn't take long to post a few threads on message boards and Facebook anyone with the right surname.'

'Really?'

'You are on Facebook, aren't you?'

'Yes, but only because Brendan thought it would be a good idea for work,' admitted Poppy. 'It seems such a waste of time otherwise. I'd rather have real friends and catch up with them face to face.'

'Me too,' agreed Luca. 'I have a page for the cookery school, of course, but that's it. My friends are the people I see every day.'

Moll didn't understand their attitude. Here was this miracle of technology and they couldn't see its potential.

'Why don't I have a go when we get back? It can't do any harm.'

(ii) A cup of hot chocolate & a plot

It was early evening by the time they arrived back in Favio. Tricia wasn't with them. She had sent the briefest of texts to say she was accepting an invitation to spend the evening with Santo and they weren't to worry or wait up.

Moll raised her eyebrows but said nothing.

Her room was as she had left it, belongings strewn everywhere, bed rumpled. Dropping her shopping bags in the middle of the floor, Moll grabbed her laptop and logged on. There were a few messages to respond to. Lola and Rae had e-mailed a photo of the cat asleep on a sunny windowsill and another of the lasagne they had reheated for last night's dinner. Moll was relieved to see proof that they were eating properly, and fired back a shot she had taken of the view from the terrace along with a description of their lunch at Il Capriccio.

She spent half an hour or so putting the word out about Poppy's grandfather, whose surname – Planeta – seemed reasonably common. Even if she failed to rustle up a lead, at least she had tried. You never knew with the Internet. It was a matter of the right person seeing something you had written. Things might happen very quickly after that.

It would have been easy to spend the whole evening roaming round websites and message boards. Often it was how Moll passed her free hours at home. But here it felt as if she was squandering the potential the time might hold, so she quit the Internet, powered down her laptop and went to see what the others were up to. No one would want to eat a proper dinner after such a long lunch, but perhaps it might be time for a drink.

Valerie was sitting on the terrace. She had changed into smarter clothes and seemed to have applied a little more make-up than usual.

'Are you going out?' Moll asked.

'We both are, remember? Vincenzo is coming by to take us for a hot chocolate.'

'Oh no, I think he meant just you.'

'Don't be silly. He was talking to both of us.'

'Even so, I think he might prefer it if it were the two of you,' insisted Moll.

Valerie seemed flustered. 'No, really, you must come.'

Moll didn't want to play gooseberry, but she was keen to taste this hot chocolate everyone said was so amazing.

'All right, if you insist … at least for a little while,' she offered. 'But I'm not going to get all dolled up. I won't be the one whose outfit he notices.'

Val brushed her fingers over her black silk dress, as if smoothing out wrinkles (there weren't any). 'Oh, this is an old thing. I've had it for ever.'

'Well you look very lovely,' Moll told her. 'Let's have a drink first, shall we? I was just thinking about making a gin and tonic. I'll shout up to Poppy and see if she wants one too.'

'Poppy went out five minutes ago. Didn't say where.'

'Running?'

'No, I don't think so – she wasn't dressed for that.'

'Oh well, I guess everyone is coming and going this evening. Maybe we'll catch up with her later.'

Moll prided herself on making a killer gin and tonic. The secret was tall glasses, loads of ice, a big squeeze of fresh lemon and a heavy hand with the gin. They drank them out on the terrace.

Valerie reeled at the first sip. 'Wow, that packs a punch.'

'I know, perfect, isn't it? My talents are wasted in social work. I should be running a cocktail bar somewhere.'

'Or a restaurant, you're such a good cook.'

'I've missed out on that, unfortunately.'

'You've got twenty-five years of work ahead of you. Maybe more at the rate the world is going. You could retrain if you wanted to, I'm sure.' Valerie took another tentative sip of gin. 'Still, I guess restaurant work is a young person's game.'

'It's too late for me,' Moll said. 'I don't think I'm going to be making any fresh starts at this point in my life.'

From their position at the far end of the terrace they had a partial view of the steps below. Valerie kept glancing down. She seemed jittery, fiddling with the silver pendant round her neck, clinking the ice against her glass, smoothing the fabric of her dress again and again. Moll supposed this was what you were meant to feel like on a first date, although she never had herself.

The light had almost faded by the time Vincenzo Mazzara came into view climbing the steps. 'Ah, ladies, good evening,' he called up to them. 'I hope you are ready to come and share some of Favio's best hot chocolate with me.'

He was wearing a white linen shirt, open slightly at the neck to show a hint of gold round his throat. It seemed he had made just as much of an effort with his appearance as Valerie.

'Absolutely,' replied Moll. 'We'll be right with you, won't we, Val?'

The hot chocolate was so creamy and rich they needed teaspoons to taste it. This was nothing like the mild, milky cocoa served up in English cafés (thankfully). It was proper chocolate, dark and bittersweet, melted into a cup and the consistency of custard.

'It is a drink for winter really,' admitted Vincenzo. 'After you have had it you feel as if your blood is flowing more freely.'

'I can't imagine Favio in the wintertime. Is it bleak?' wondered Moll, scooping up another luscious spoonful.

'It is quiet without the tourists and the skies are greyer, but we have our consolations. Not only this hot chocolate, but our sweet-sour rabbit stews, our dense soups of chickpeas and squid, and our pasta al forno. All the heavy foods we avoid over the long hot months are our reward in winter.'

'I didn't think I'd be hungry again this evening after that huge lunch, but you're making my mouth water,' Moll admitted.

'You are a real food-lover, I think.' Vincenzo sounded approving.

'It's my passion,' Moll agreed. 'My house is full of cookbooks; every window ledge and shelf is crammed with them. I keep swearing I won't buy any more, but then I see another I can't resist. My daughters tell me I'm obsessed.'

'How can one not be obsessed?' said Vincenzo. 'Food is a kind of miracle really, isn't it? You take the raw ingredients, transform them in endless ways, put them in your body and eventually they become your skin, your hair, your blood. What could be more magical than that?'

'Lots of people don't care what they eat,' remarked Moll. 'All those women who are too concerned with their figures to enjoy good food. Tricia, for example – I don't expect she drank much of her hot chocolate last night, did she?'

'Tricia?' Vincenzo considered it. 'She is different, I think. She takes her energy from other things besides food. And her pleasure, too.'

Moll had nearly emptied her cup. The inside of her mouth was slick with chocolate; her teeth felt coated with it.

'I don't like waste,' she remarked. 'In my house we finish our food. No crust of bread or fatty end of meat is thrown away. Bones are made into stock. Rinds of Parmesan are melted into soups. I buy the best ingredients I can afford and use up every bit of them.'

'That is the Italian way too,' agreed Vincenzo.

'Is it dying out, though? Will everyone end up living off things that come from supermarkets in sachets and cartons? Even here in Italy?'

'I very much hope not,' said Vincenzo. 'That is one of the reasons I want to compile my food guide – to help people recognise quality and learn to steer clear of junk. It is my mission, in a way. A thing I can do to stop the Italian love of eating well dying out so quickly.'

Valerie was drinking more slowly. Her cup of chocolate was still half full.

'People are so odd about food,' she observed, toying with her spoon. 'Bossy and judgemental. Women I know are always going on the latest diets: dairy-free, gluten-free, low-carb, macrobiotic, whatever the current craze is. They become almost evangelical. There have been times I've felt my love of cheese and meat has threatened friendships. But surely there's no correct way to eat?'

'So long as you use fresh ingredients and cook them properly, then no,' Vincenzo agreed.

'What if I enjoy junk food?' Valerie asked. 'There's that

orange cheese that comes wrapped in individual slices and tastes a bit like plastic. I can eat a whole pack as a snack and I love it melted on to white bread. I rather like that cream you spray from a can; it's such fun. And I have to confess I've been known to eat at Dunkin' Donuts.'

Vincenzo put his hands over his ears. 'No, no, stop, I cannot listen to this,' he said, laughing.

'But it's true. Worse still, I'm not sure I really care if the olive oil is extra virgin or not, so long as it tastes OK.'

'You are saying this to torment me,' Vincenzo complained.

Valerie smiled. 'I enjoy food, good and bad. When we were in New York together, Jean-Pierre and I used to have movie nights with popcorn, packets of chips and deep-dish pizza from a box. I liked it just as much as going out for dinner.'

'It's fake food,' objected Moll.

'Yes, and delicious.'

'I have never eaten a deep-dish pizza,' Vincenzo admitted. 'How is it?'

'Mmm, it's good,' insisted Valerie. 'Pepperoni, three types of cheese, jalapenos, maybe a few bell peppers, ham, meatballs.'

'*Madonna mia*, all of that on one pizza?'

'More sometimes,' Valerie laughed. 'At one place in my neighbourhood they do unlimited toppings for ten bucks.'

'Next you're going to say you like McDonald's,' said Moll.

'Well ... I can't pretend I haven't eaten it from time to time. Although I prefer Wendy's; they do decent chilli cheese fries.'

'My girls eat that sort of food even though they know I hate it,' said Moll. 'And my ex-husband was a fish-and-chip man. Actually, it's true chips can be rather delicious eaten piping hot out of newspaper on a chilly evening, with your fingers all salty and greasy. I'm not opposed to that.'

Vincenzo looked thoughtful. 'The way we eat says a lot about the people we are,' he said. 'Myself, I am a curious man. I am prepared to try your deep-dish pizza or your fish and chips. I will keep an open mind. But if these things are not good, I won't take a second bite. I never eat for the sake of eating.'

'I don't need to try the chilli cheese fries,' insisted Moll. 'I can imagine what they taste like. I hate to waste my hunger as much as I dislike wasting food.'

Vincenzo nodded. 'So we're all different.'

'I guess we are,' agreed Moll.

'Still, there is no reason why we shouldn't get on; like each other; enjoy spending time together; even fall in love. Our differences are what make us interesting to one another.'

'They do say opposites attract, don't they?' said Valerie.

Moll decided this was her cue. She faked a yawn and began fishing in her purse for some euros. 'I'm a little tired,' she said. 'But you two should stay here and have a nightcap. It's such a lovely evening.'

Valerie was clutching at her handbag. She seemed uncertain. 'Well, I ...'

'A glass of Amaro, perhaps,' suggested Vincenzo. 'They have a local one here that is very good. We drink it as a tonic. It is wonderful for the digestion.'

'OK, then,' Valerie agreed, putting down her bag. 'Yes, that does sound a nice idea.'

As she walked away from the table, Moll was followed by the murmur of their conversation. She heard Valerie laughing at something Vincenzo was saying. Glancing back at her sitting in a pool of soft light, her hair swept up from her face, elegant in her black silk, Moll thought she looked years younger and very happy.

The night was warm, and Moll felt heavy with hot chocolate, so she took her time heading along the main street, finding the atmosphere in Favio after dark rather pleasant. Tricia had been disparaging, of course, but Moll thought it lovely to see groups of young people gathering to eat gelato and couples arm in arm taking a stroll in the coolest part of the day.

She walked on well beyond the flight of steps that would have taken her back to the house, hearing snatches of music from a crowded pizzeria and stopping to admire the lighted facade of a church. She felt safe here, much more so than in London, where the shadows held threats for women out on their own after nightfall. There were no gangs of drunken youths, no angry young men, no beggars even. If there was crime and ugliness, it was kept well hidden in Favio.

Moll heard Orsolina's voice before she saw her emerge from the doorway of the pizzeria, talking loudly in Italian to an older man, kissing him lightly on both cheeks to say goodbye.

From the first she had marked Orsolina down as beautiful but shallow. Watching her now did nothing to change that opinion. Even the way she turned smoothly from her companion on one slender heel, tossed her silvery-blue pashmina over her shoulder and carried on down the street seemed deliberately elegant.

She might have swung right past without noticing Moll if she hadn't stopped her with a polite '*Buona sera*.'

'Oh, hello,' Orsolina replied. 'You're out late this evening. Where are your friends?'

'They've all gone off in separate directions.'

'Leaving you alone, poor thing.' Her voice was laced with wine and husky with cigarettes.

'I'm fine, really,' Moll told her.

'Why don't you join me? I'm heading to the bar up above for a last drink. They make a good hot chocolate there ... although my father might not agree.'

'Thanks, but I've had some already this evening.'

Orsolina shrugged. 'Why not come anyway? I expect to meet up with some friends. It will be fun.'

Moll hesitated. On the one hand, this was a chance to

experience more of local life. But she had never been confident walking into a roomful of strangers. She found small talk unbearable and knew she made a bad first impression. Easier to return to her room and catch up with the friends she had on Facebook and Twitter instead.

'Luca will be there,' Orsolina encouraged her. 'Come for one drink.'

Moll was keener if people she knew might be there. And, after all, she wasn't in any real hurry to return to the house. 'All right then, thanks, I'll come.'

Together they headed up the flight of steps that led to the cathedral, Orsolina wobbling over the uneven ground once or twice and stopping to remove her high heels, sinking to below Moll's shoulder without them. She was the daintiest of creatures, the kind of woman that made Moll feel clumsy and instantly more aware of the loose threads hanging from her clothing and the folds of flesh round her middle.

It was quiet in this part of town. Aside from the chirping of crickets in the trees, all Moll could hear was the thump of her own cork wedges on the stone steps and the softer glance of Orsolina's bare footfalls.

It was Orsolina who broke the silence. 'So tell me, are you having a good time at the cookery school?' she asked.

'Oh yes, it's great. Luca's an excellent teacher.'

'He's enjoying it too. He likes your group a lot.'

'Doesn't he always like his groups?' Moll wondered.

'Not all. Some are demanding and nothing is good enough for them; others are dull to be with day after day. Your group he adores, though; more than any before, I think.'

'Really? What makes you say that?'

'Usually he wouldn't choose to spend his free evenings with the guests. But last night he was with the Australian Poppy, no?'

She said it lightly enough, but still it struck Moll that Orsolina must be jealous. Had she noticed what everyone but her seemed to have missed so far – the flare between Luca and Poppy, the ripples of an attraction? Moll decided to find out.

'You're right, he was,' she replied, just as lightly. 'He went off alone with Poppy on Ortygia today too. They were gone for ages, actually.'

'But she is here only for a few more days, then she will go home surely. Australia is a long way away.'

'Yes, a very long way,' agreed Moll. 'But did you hear that Poppy thinks she has family here? We've been trying to help her track them down. Wouldn't it be interesting if she discovered a permanent connection to the area?'

Orsolina let out a tiny, impatient hiss of breath.

'I've posted some stuff on the Internet,' Moll added. 'It's amazing how far-reaching it is. It wouldn't surprise me at all if we made some progress. And then perhaps she'll stay in Sicily a little longer.'

Orsolina stopped and grabbed at her arm. 'What does he see in her? Tell me. Is she prettier than me? I don't think so. Funnier, more interesting, sexier; what is it?'

Surprised at the strength of her reaction, Moll shook her off. 'I'm sure I don't know.'

She wondered how Orsolina would react if she knew her father was down at the café below flirting with an older woman. Was she equally as possessive of him? Moll stopped short of trying to find out.

'I'm surprised Luca is single at his age,' she remarked instead. 'He's good-looking, smart, charming. Why hasn't some woman snapped him up?'

'They've tried,' Orsolina told her. 'But Luca never gets involved.'

'So do you think he seriously likes Poppy?' Moll found she hoped so.

There was another exasperated hiss from Orsolina. 'She isn't the right person for him. I've known him for years;

understand him better than anyone. He comes to me for advice, spends more time at our home than he does his own, is so close to my father. I can tell it would never work between them.'

That was when it dawned on Moll. There was only one reason for this girl to invite a woman like her for a drink. 'You're worried Luca will be with Poppy again tonight, aren't you?'

'I know he is. The barman up there is a friend – he texted me.'

'And you're hoping I'll be a distraction, that Poppy will feel she has to talk to me instead of Luca.'

'Don't be ridiculous.'

Shaking her head in disbelief, Moll turned away from her. 'Well you'll have to find another way to come between them,' she tossed back. 'You're not going to use me like that. I'm going home.'

'Are you crazy? It's just a drink, that's all,' Orsolina called as Moll began to hurry away. 'You've got the wrong idea entirely.'

Moll didn't bother to reply. Storming back down the steps, she took some satisfaction in knowing she had been right about Orsolina from the start. Shallow, yes, and devious too; a stark contrast to Poppy, that was for sure. Poppy, with her easy smile, who had never been anything but open and friendly with any of them.

Moll knew where her loyalties lay. As soon as she got back to her room, she would check the computer. If there were no replies to her posts about Poppy's long-lost relatives, then she would spread the net wider. She had a lot of contacts; surely someone would have a helpful idea.

A little earlier, she had been only mildly interested in Poppy's search. Now she was determined to get some results.

Food of Love

Luca Amore is thinking about photographs, the way they tell the truth and all the many ways they can be made to lie. He is sorry he has used his camera to tell so many lies. As the years have gone by, he has felt more ashamed of it, not less.

For a long time Luca has been trying a sort of penance of his own invention, a denial of what once drove him. He has led a quieter, simpler life, but it has never changed the way he feels. Now here in this bar with this woman, he wonders if at last he has found what he needed all along.

With his camera he might change her face – shadow its angles, blow out the fine lines beneath her eyes, make her look younger and even more beautiful. Or he could take a candid portrait, show her how she really is, with her nose freckled and a little shiny from the heat, the mascara smudging darkly beneath her eyes, her smile pushing her skin into tiny creases.

He is certain she would choose the honest image of herself. She is much too clear-eyed to be vain. He sees nothing artificial about her. Her skin isn't concealed beneath layers of make-up, her fingernails aren't fake, her hair appears to be the plain brown she was born with. Her beauty doesn't seem to interest her at all.

Luca is pleased to be sitting beside her in this little bar, sipping lazily on limoncello. He likes listening to her voice; how it lilts at the end of every sentence, how she stretches out her vowels. She is talking, telling him things about her life. He is wondering if he can stop her going back to it.

Luca didn't mean to fall for her. It crept up on him. He recalls how tentative she was on that first day, nervous almost of the pasta dough as they made their cavatelli, anxious for his help. He remembers how he touched her too-warm fingers and took her by surprise. He thinks about the very first time they were alone. Preserving capers together; moving round each other as they sorted through them to pinch off the long stems, brushing shoulders as they layered the tender green buds in jars with fine sea salt.

Even once he understood what was happening, Luca couldn't seem to show her how he felt. He settled for staying close. It was enough to set eyes on her each morning, to see the glossy swing of her ponytail, her peachy skin and her easy smile.

In Ortygia he risked taking her hand and she didn't pull away. He cradled her fingers so gently in his and they walked the narrow streets linked this way. Their skin warmed and moistened, it rubbed together. He tightened his hold on her.

Still no words have been spoken. Luca is afraid words might crush this delicate thing between them. But he has only four more days. Four days to change the course of two lives. Will it be enough?

Poppy

Brendan has texted me at least three times every day since I've been here. It's been about work things mostly but none of it important enough to interrupt my holiday. It's like he won't let go of me completely. We're divorced, have separate homes now, but he has to keep that connection.

I had thought things were working out OK, but now can see I'll have to make some big changes when I get home. Selling real estate together, it wasn't such a good idea. It gives him an excuse to call me, even drop round at my house from time to time. He always has some comment to make. Why did I choose to paint the walls that particular shade of duck-egg blue? Plain white would be better. You can't go wrong with white, he tells me.

I love having my own place. It's a tiny terrace in Paddington, so narrow you feel as if you could very nearly touch the walls on either side. I have a galley kitchen with steps down to a courtyard where I've planted things in pots. And upstairs there's the tiniest balcony off my bedroom. On summer mornings I like to sit out there for a few minutes while I drink my coffee.

I had to scale down my stuff before moving in, but it was good getting rid of clothes I don't wear and boxes full of things I hardly look at. My life feels less cluttered now. And it doesn't matter that the house is tiny, as there's only me in it.

I can't believe the number of friends who've tried to set me up with another man. What's the rush? When I tell them I'm not ready, they go on about my biological clock ticking. As if I'm going to settle for someone because my ovaries are getting older. Yes, of course I'd like kids one day, but if it doesn't happen, then life won't be over. There are other ways to feel fulfilled, aren't there?

This limoncello is so good. I tasted it once at home and thought it was like washing-up liquid. Maybe it's being here and on holiday that makes it so delicious. Nothing is the same as usual on holiday, is it? Everything feels, looks and tastes so much nicer. I bet if I took a bottle of this home then it wouldn't be half as good when I opened it.

I can't believe there are only four more days left here. I should have booked for longer but didn't know how I would get on on my own. I didn't realise how good a time I was going to have.

I so wish I were staying in Sicily. I'd like to see more of it; go to Taormina, Cefalu, Stromboli. And maybe have the chance to find out more about my grandfather's family. Still, I guess I can come back some day. Or do some research from home like Moll suggested.

You know, this trip has exceeded all my expectations. You've done something wonderful with your cookery school, Luca. I really can feel the love when we all cook together; and I almost sense your nonna watching us and approving of what's happening in her kitchen.

What a shame you can't find that recipe book of hers. To have that link with the past would be so special. I come from a new country and a family that remade itself. That can be an exciting thing, and yet in some ways I envy you having such deep roots here. It must give you a sense of belonging, to know that generations of your family have walked the same streets, climbed the same steps, eaten food grown in the same earth.

Do I want a coffee? No, no, I can't drink it at night. The caffeine keeps me awake and buzzing. I'd love one of those amazing hot chocolates, though.

Oh look, there's your friend Orsolina. She might want to join us for a cup of chocolate too. There's a spare stool right here. Let me shift over and make a space for her between us.

Day Five

(i) Silver scabbard fish & a disappearance

It was such a joy to wake to the light rather than the ringing of her alarm clock. Poppy had taken to lying in bed and letting her mind wander for ten, twenty minutes or more. With nothing immediate to worry about, and the day ahead mostly arranged, it seemed so much easier to think clearly.

The time, the space, the calm, that was what holidays were meant to be about. Brendan always liked to describe himself as an 'active relaxer'. He had to be doing things: surfing, cycling, endless DIY projects involving power tools. He wore his busyness like a badge of honour, as if slowing down was some sort of failing.

Poppy was beginning to understand that she didn't want to be a busy person. It was a revelation, one that shocked her. These days the world ran on full diaries and ringing phones, didn't it? Schedules were crammed fuller and fuller. 'So busy, so busy,' everyone chanted like a mantra. How was it possible to step back from that? It was the modern way of life, after all. Yet Poppy was becoming convinced the best route was to try.

At last she felt ready to push back the sheets, swing out of bed and set her bare feet on the ground. There would be no going out running this morning; it was already far too hot. She was surprised to find she didn't much care.

She wondered what Luca would bring for breakfast today. More of the strawberries, perhaps – they were sweeter than any she had eaten before – and some of those feather-light cornetti to dip into a cup of milky coffee.

Poppy checked her phone. She had switched it on to silent mode before falling asleep, as she had expected Brendan to contact her. Sure enough, there were three messages waiting. One to say he had a new listing that would go to market the week she arrived home; one to ask her opinion on an offer; and a final text wondering how her holiday was going.

She wished he would stop it. Whatever made him think she cared about work when she was so far away from it? 'Stay connected' was how Brendan signed off his final text. But why? What was wrong with disappearing from your own life for a few short days? Let the e-mails and phone messages pile up, let the pages of her diary stay empty and houses go to auction without her. She was here in Italy having new experiences and meeting new people. Surely that was more important.

Her mood less buoyant, Poppy showered and dressed. Without bothering to return any of Brendan's messages, she left her phone on silent and went downstairs.

No one else was up and Luca hadn't arrived. Most likely he was tired, as last night they had stayed out late, talking and talking. Orsolina had joined them, and she too had seemed in no hurry to go home. The town was entirely still when they left the bar; there were no people or cars on the streets and their voices seemed to echo from the old stone buildings.

After saying goodbye to Poppy at the bottom of the steps, Luca and Orsolina had continued on together, still talking loudly, but switching from English to Italian. They were at ease together, so affectionate, surely they must be a couple just as Tricia had suspected.

Still, Poppy had noticed that Luca seemed at ease with everyone. She recalled how he had taken her hand that afternoon in Ortygia, gently and without any warning. At first she had been startled, but then remembered how very tactile

Italians could be. She had seen how even the men hugged and touched each other all the time; it was about warmth and friendliness, that was all. Even so, it had been lovely walking through the streets linked together like that, and when he let her go she was a little sorry. Brendan had never been one for hand-holding. Poppy realised she had been missing out.

She poured a glass of orange juice from the fridge and went to sit out on the terrace, scaring a couple of feral cats as she opened the French doors. This was the nicest part of the house; its selling point. It was no more than a stretch of terracotta tiles wrapped round with a wrought-iron railing, but there was a view of the jumble of honey-gold buildings opposite and on most days it caught a cool breeze. Poppy could imagine Luca's grandmother coming out here for respite from the heat of the kitchen, pegging up laundry to dry, watering her pots of oregano and basil, calling a greeting to her neighbours, writing in her recipe book. It was the perfect place to entertain friends or sit alone and clear your mind. Poppy felt at home here.

'Oh, good morning, you're up nice and early.' It was Moll, her voice bright. 'Shall I make coffee?'

'Sorry, I was just about to do it.'

'No, no, stay there. I know where everything is. I'll make it.'

Poppy heard her bustling about the kitchen. There was a hint of fresh coffee beans on the breeze and, several minutes later, the hiss of the moka pot.

'Here you go,' said Moll, bringing out a tray. 'There's no milk so you'll have to have an espresso. It's one sugar, isn't it?'

'That's right.'

'Ah, there's nothing like the first coffee of the morning.' Moll settled in a chair beside her. 'You don't mind if I join you?'

'No, of course not,' said Poppy, although she had been enjoying the solitude.

'I came back here fairly early last night and did some more research about your family. It turns out there are lots of people with the surname Planeta but none I could find in Ortygia.'

Poppy was disappointed. 'They must have all moved away like Luca said.'

'It's not all bad news – I did find some Planetas not too far away in the town of Noto. Most likely they're not related to you, but you never know. And since we're scheduled to visit Noto tomorrow, maybe you and Luca could check them out?'

Moll had written down three sets of names and contact details on a page torn from her notebook. 'This one's a lawyer,' she said, pointing to the top of the list. 'And this one runs a hairdresser's. I'm not sure about the other.'

'Thanks so much.' Poppy took the sheet of paper gratefully. 'I can't believe how much you've managed to find out in so short a time.'

'Well, it wasn't terribly difficult,' Moll told her. 'And if you don't get anywhere with these, then I've got some feelers out on message boards.'

Poppy sipped her coffee. It was strong and sweet, lifting her energy. 'Do you think I should ask Luca to call them before we go to Noto? See if there's any chance they're linked to my family?'

'Yes, that's a good idea,' Moll agreed.

'I don't know, though … how would you feel if some stranger contacted you claiming to be a relative? They might think I'm after money or something.'

'You're in two minds about this, aren't you? Why is that?'

'I guess I am,' agreed Poppy. 'It's because of my grandfather, really. He's always said the past isn't important; it's the future that matters. He left Ortygia not long after that photograph was taken. Imagine cutting yourself off from everything familiar and starting a new life on the other side of the world. It might be difficult at his age to rediscover the people you had lost.'

'But you're doing this for yourself, not him,' Moll pointed out. 'And it's reasonable to want to know where you came from. I reckon your grandfather is wrong; the past does matter.'

'Do you really think so?'

'Yes, of course. It's part of what makes us who we are. I like to imagine that something of me will be passed down through my girls to their children and beyond. That's one of the reasons to have kids, isn't it? To leave a little of yourself behind; to matter.'

'My ex-husband Brendan always says the only point in having kids is so there's someone to look after you when you get old and infirm,' Poppy admitted.

Moll laughed. 'He sounds charming.'

'Oh, he's not so bad. But babies aren't his thing at all.'

'I can't imagine how my life would have been without the girls,' Moll said, thoughtfully. 'Pointless, I expect. We're all part of a chain really, aren't we? Stretching from the past into the future. I think there's something comforting about it.'

'And what if you don't have a child?'

'Then the chain breaks,' Moll told her.

'Hello. Good morning. What has broken?' It was Valerie. She looked different today. Less tired; peppy even. She'd let down her hair, and it fell in loose silvery waves on to her shoulders.

'Nothing's broken, not yet,' Moll told her. 'Can I get you a coffee? Then I want to hear all about your evening.'

'There's not much to tell,' Valerie promised. 'We had a couple of nightcaps, then took a stroll up the main street while we talked.'

'Who is we?' Poppy wondered.

'Just Vincenzo and I.'

'Really?' Poppy was pleased for her. 'Did you go on a date?'

'Oh stop it,' Valerie said, almost girlishly.

'So Tricia was right after all. There really is a romance brewing with the chocolate-maker,' Poppy teased.

'Of course there isn't, just a lovely friendship,' Valerie insisted. 'Where is Tricia anyway?'

'Probably still upstairs straightening her hair into submission.' Moll was tart.

'Really? It's very quiet up there. I assumed she'd come down already.'

'No, there hasn't been any sign of her at all,' said Poppy.

'That's odd. You know, I didn't hear her come in last night either.' Valerie sounded concerned. 'Did either of you? I hope she made it back OK.'

'Shall I go upstairs and check?' Poppy wondered.

'Yes, take her up a coffee,' Moll suggested. 'There's enough left in the moka pot.'

In Tricia's room, there was only the faintest breath of her perfume on the air; the shutters were open, the bed made, the hair straighteners cold. Poppy realised she hadn't come back last night. Her guess was that she must still be with Santo.

Closing the door, she went back downstairs. Moll would get some mileage from this. Her dislike of Tricia hadn't shown any sign of easing.

'Oh, the silly girl,' sighed Valerie, when she heard. 'You don't think she's really ...'

'I'm not sure,' admitted Poppy.

'Of course she has,' said Moll, briskly. 'It was obvious she would the moment she went off with him. Still, it's her business and it's not as if her husband needs to find out. None of us are likely to tell him, are we?'

'No, I suppose not,' agreed Valerie. 'And if it's just a holiday fling, then no harm done perhaps.'

'I'm sure she's got up to this kind of thing before,' said Moll.

Poppy wasn't convinced – Tricia was a divorce lawyer, after all, and knew the damage caused by reckless behaviour. Would she be prepared to take that sort of risk?

'I wonder when she'll be back. We have a cooking session this morning, don't we?'

'She won't care if she misses that,' said Moll. 'She's more interested in the chefs than what they cook. Actually, at one point I thought she was going to get her hooks into Vincenzo Mazzara. I'm glad she left him for you, Val.'

'Moll, you've got quite the wrong idea about—' Valerie began, but they heard the front door open and she broke off.

It was Luca, weighed down with shopping. He had a bag of fresh fish, another overflowing with vegetables, some bottles of wine and a large box of pastries.

'Good morning, good morning,' he called, letting the door slam shut behind him.

He didn't seem the least bit concerned when he heard of Tricia's absence.

'Actually, I had a text from her first thing,' he said, unpacking their breakfast. 'She's going to spend the day at the vineyard with Santo. I think she's planning on joining us again tomorrow.'

From the first, Poppy had been drawn to Tricia. She thought her irreverent and amusing, the sort of friend who made everything that little bit more fun. Even so, this was unexpected.

'Does this kind of thing happen here often?' she asked Luca.

'Now and then,' he admitted. 'We've had a few romances. One woman fell for a waiter from the pizzeria down the road. We hardly saw her except when he was working, and later he moved to England to be with her. I think they're still together.'

'But Tricia is married ... she has a family ...'

'I didn't say it was right, just that it happens.' Luca placed the platter of pastries on the table. 'More coffee?'

'I'll make it.' Poppy touched the moka to see if it was cool enough to take apart. 'It's only that I'm surprised. She said she was unhappy in her work, not her marriage. I got the impression her husband is a nice guy. It was him that booked this holiday for her in the first place.'

'Santo is a nice guy too,' Luca remarked. 'But let's forget about them for now. Eat breakfast and then I'll show you how we Sicilians break all the rules and combine cheese and fish in the same dish.'

Moll frowned. 'Years ago my mother used to cover cod in cheddar cheese sauce,' she said. 'I always thought it drowned the flavour of the fish.'

'This will be better,' Luca insisted. 'Surely you trust me by now?'

Poppy ate a couple of pastries, drank another coffee and went to find her apron. The prospect of a cooking lesson no longer made her anxious. In fact, she was looking forward to learning to make something she might be able to recreate in her own kitchen.

Scabbard fish turbanti, carciofi ripieni, caponata di mandorle: Luca was writing on the blackboard menu.

'Today we'll be cooking a light lunch to enjoy on the terrace,' he told them. 'In my nonna's time, there would have been a pasta dish to start, but now even in Italy we are trying to eat a little less of it.'

'I thought pasta was practically a religion here,' said Moll.

'That's true, and it is one thing I would never give up entirely,' agreed Luca. 'But the occasional day without it won't do my soul any harm.'

The four of them stood at the long kitchen bench and Luca laid the long fillets on the clean worktop.

'I really love this fish,' he said with feeling. 'In Sicilian we call it *spatulidda* and eat it baked with herbs or simply grilled. This is the way my nonna used to prepare it for those she loved, so of course it's my favourite. I remember it was the very first dish written down in the recipe book she always used to keep in this kitchen. Of course, that is lost now, but I tasted her version so many times it wasn't too difficult to recreate it.'

He set them all to work: Poppy grating the caciocavallo cheese, Moll making breadcrumbs and Valerie chopping fennel and capers. Once all had been combined and seasoned, Luca showed them how to spread a layer of the mixture on to a long fillet of scabbard fish, roll it up into a turban and fix it with a wooden skewer.

'Sometimes cooking is a lot like playing, isn't it?' said Poppy, mounding the coarse mixture on to her fillet.

'Not too much,' Luca said, watching over her. 'We'll sprinkle any that remains on top, so it won't go to waste.'

The scabbard turbans were put into a lightly oiled dish along with some quartered tomatoes and more olive oil, ready for the oven.

'I wish I could convince my girls that cooking is like playing,' remarked Moll wistfully. 'They definitely don't see it that way.'

'I didn't either, before I came here,' admitted Poppy. 'I always felt pressured when Brendan and I had friends over for dinner; worried the food wouldn't turn out right. Possibly I was cooking the wrong sorts of dishes. Or perhaps it's just that Luca is making everything seem easy and fun, and I won't manage nearly so well when I try this at home on my own.'

Luca glanced at her again, but said nothing.

'Try making another turban to make sure you've got it,' urged Moll. 'It's not so tricky really.'

Once all the scabbard fish had been used up, Luca set the tray to one side and got on with demonstrating how to make the caponata of almonds, green olives and celery. Poppy noticed he was keeping her especially busy. She was the one who toasted the almonds golden, prepared the vegetables, then cooked them until they were tender. He must have noticed how she was the least confident of the group and was doing his best to help her catch up. She wasn't used to such thoughtfulness in men; Brendan had never had a talent for picking up on how she was feeling.

While the caponata was cooling, they made the final part of the meal, loosening the leaves of small, spiny artichokes and stuffing them with chopped anchovy, garlic, parsley and mint, then steaming them on the hob.

Valerie and Moll busied themselves setting the table as the fish turbans cooked in the oven. Poppy lolled against the kitchen counter, enjoying Luca's company, watching as he tidied.

'Are we not making a dessert today?' she asked.

'No, since it's so hot I thought we might go out for a granita after lunch. Tomorrow there is a busy schedule, so today we'll enjoy an easy afternoon and later I'll cook dinner for you all.'

'Really? You won't ask us to help at all?'

'You can help if you like. But if you'd prefer to relax, that's fine too.'

'Don't you ever get sick of cooking and cleaning up?' Poppy wondered, watching him scrub the worktop.

'Not so far. Sometimes I find cooking a playful thing, just as you said earlier. Other days it's an adventure, since I don't know quite how a dish will turn out; or a challenge if it's a complex one.'

'You should do a Food of Love cookbook,' she suggested.

'I've thought about that. Perhaps one day.'

'You could even take the photographs yourself.'

Luca frowned. 'Food photography is very different to the work I used to do. I'm not sure I'd be much good at it.'

'I'd buy your book,' Poppy told him. 'You've really helped me discover food in the past few days and opened my eyes to all sorts of things.'

'I have?' Luca sounded pleased. 'Such as?'

'The importance of ingredients, how there's no need to get hung up on perfection, how interesting food can be. Before, I just ate food; I never thought about the history of a dish or why it might have been created.'

'So your trip has been worthwhile. And it isn't over yet.' Luca smiled at her. 'You never know, perhaps the best is yet to come.'

Poppy helped him slide the turbans of silver fish on to the plates, spooning their juices over the top. As she carried the dishes out on to the terrace, Luca uncorked a bottle of chilled *rosato* wine.

'Another wonderful meal,' Valerie sighed, taking a seat at the table. 'Aren't we lucky?'

'Yes, poor old Tricia doesn't know what she's missing,' said Moll.

Poppy ate with relish, allowing the flavours to infuse before swallowing, a feeling of well-being flooding through her with each mouthful. The marriage of fish, breadcrumbs and cheese was a perfect one. The vegetable dishes were good too; the caponata had that sweet-sourness she was learning to love about Sicilian food, the artichokes a salty kick of anchovies.

When they had finished, Luca topped up their glasses and brought out the remainder of the cheese along with a plate of thinly sliced crisp fennel and a serpentine-shaped loaf with a crust of sesame seeds.

'If we're going to continue to drink, then we must continue to eat,' he told them.

The wine had brought a slight flush to his cheeks and his eyes seemed to sparkle. 'Cheers,' he said, raising his glass. 'To your good health.'

They sat out on the terrace until the sun shifted and the

umbrella over the table no longer provided much shade. By then, a second bottle of wine had been finished and Poppy felt the pleasant fuzz of afternoon tipsiness. Listening to her new friends laughing and chatting as they basked in the heat of the afternoon, she had a momentary sense of everything being right in her world. It was strange to think she had met these people only a few days ago. She was so at ease with them already, so much lighter and more carefree than she had felt in ages – it was as if she was relaxing into being herself in a way that seemed impossible at home. Holidays did that to you, she supposed.

'I think it's time for a granita,' Luca declared. 'The café in the piazza makes a beautiful one with lemon and mint. Very refreshing. Who will come and join me?'

Moll said yes straight away, of course – Poppy had never met anyone so prepared to try every new flavour that came her way. Valerie had to be talked into it, mainly because she couldn't face the walk back up the steps.

'I'll grab my bag,' said Poppy eagerly. 'Then I'll follow you all down.'

Back in her room, she glanced at her phone to find another flurry of annoying texts from Brendan. This time he was concerned because she hadn't responded to his previous messages. Was everything all right? Did he need to call out Interpol?

It would be the middle of the night in Australia by now. Still Poppy flicked back a quick 'All good thanks', and, with guilty satisfaction, imagined its arrival jolting him awake.

By the time she had unearthed her sunscreen, found her hat, and chucked a lip gloss, her key and phone into her leather tote, the others had left without her. She reminded herself that she was on holiday and in no rush. Once she had got over her flash of irritation with Brendan, she would catch them up.

She let her mind wander as she strolled down the steps and turned towards the piazza. She was thinking about Moll and how kind she had been to trawl the Internet on her behalf. Thinking about Tricia too, and wondering what she thought she was doing spending the night with Santo. She was so busy thinking, she didn't see Orsolina hurrying out of the narrow lane that led to the Mazzara *dolceria*.

'Oh my God, I'm so sorry,' she said, as they barrelled into one another.

'No, no, my fault,' Orsolina gasped, holding on to her arm. 'I wasn't looking where I was going. And now I've turned my ankle in these silly heels.'

'Are you all right?'

'I'm not sure.' Wincing, Orsolina tried to rest her weight back on her injured foot. 'I think it's only a bad sprain. Would you mind helping me back to my house? I may need to rest it for a little while.'

'Yes, of course,' agreed Poppy, mortified to have hurt her.

Limping down the lane, Orsolina leaned heavily on her arm, gasping once or twice in pain but otherwise saying nothing. Step by slow step they continued past the *dolceria* and on towards an old wooden door set into the rock of the hillside.

'Here we are at last,' said Orsolina, sounding relieved.

Poppy was amazed to find the Mazzara house entirely hewn into the rock of the hill, with a few shuttered windows and the low doorway the only sign it was a dwelling at all. The door opened to reveal a cool, dim interior. Once her eyes had adjusted, she saw roughcast walls painted white, cream church candles waiting to be lit, and an old burled walnut sideboard covered in framed photographs.

'What an extraordinary place,' she said.

'It's been my family home for hundreds of years. Be careful, the ceiling is low in parts.'

Poppy helped her through the arched doorway and into

a surprisingly large living chamber, where Orsolina lowered herself gingerly on to a worn leather couch and rubbed at her sore ankle.

'Would you mind fetching some ice? It might help stop the swelling. The kitchen is through there ...' She pointed towards a series of open archways.

The place was like something out of a fairy tale; each room scooped out of rock. From habit, Poppy began composing real-estate copy in her head.

'My job is to sell houses,' she told Orsolina, returning with the bag of ice she had found in the bottom of the freezer. 'But I've never come across a place like this before.'

'At one time, many people in Favio dwelled in grotto houses. They were very basic, mostly hovels, not like this one. My family has expanded it over the years, with each generation adding their own touch. Have a look around if you want.'

Poppy didn't wait for a second invitation. She had always liked seeing inside other people's houses; glimpsing lives different to her own. 'I would love to.'

'Please be my guest. I would take you on a tour, but I think I'd better stay here and nurse my ankle for a while.'

Poppy peeped through every doorway, finding Vincenzo's tidy office and an old playroom. Upstairs were several bedrooms, linked by dark passageways and excavated round pillars of rock, with pocked stone ceilings and doors leading out on to a small terrace. It was obvious which room belonged to Orsolina; clothes and jewellery covered every surface. The others were far less cluttered, decorated only with simple crosses above the beds and candles set into alcoves.

Back downstairs, Poppy looked more closely at the photographs on the sideboard. Many featured Luca. Here he was on a boat with Vincenzo; there at a table in a pizzeria, and here was a more recent shot of him bare-chested on a beach beside Orsolina, who was looking lithe in her bikini. They made an attractive couple, she thought. It was difficult for her not to envy the bond they seemed to have ... and the history too. Poppy had walked away from all that in her own life, and while she knew for sure that it had been the right move, still there was a sense of having failed at something important.

'What an incredible place,' she said to Orsolina, returning to find her with the bag of ice still clamped to her ankle. 'So unusual.'

'I was born in this house. My children will be too.' She sounded very certain. 'We would never sell it.'

Poppy saw it then – this girl had what she lacked, a link with her past. She was part of a long chain that would stretch into the future; and this strange house was what connected every piece of it.

'Isn't it dark and damp in the winter, though?' she asked. 'Doesn't it ever get oppressive?'

'That's what Luca always says. But it has many advantages. In winter we are shielded from the bad weather; in the summer it is very cool. The walls are thick so it is quiet. And at night, with all the candles lit, it is very romantic. Even Luca has to admit that.'

'Have the two of you been together long?' Poppy asked.

Orsolina widened her eyes. 'Together?'

'Oh, I'm sorry.' Poppy wondered if she had it wrong. 'I assumed from all those photographs of the pair of you ...'

Orsolina laughed. 'Together. Not together. You know Luca. Nothing is simple.'

'Well I don't know him really.' Poppy felt awkward. 'I mean, I've only spent a few days in Favio, so how could I? But you seem like a couple ...'

'I'm sure we will be eventually. It's taking him a while to realise it, that's all. You know how men can be.'

'I guess,' agreed Poppy.

'And Luca is especially troubled,' Orsolina confided. 'His

past has been ... well he's not the person he first seems, that's for sure.'

'He isn't?' Poppy was surprised.

'People don't talk of it much these days,' she dropped her voice, 'but there was a big disgrace, a scandal when he lived in London. After that, Luca went off the rails for a while. My father was the one who saved him. They spent hours out on his boat, fishing and talking. Without Papa, I'm not sure Luca would have got through it.'

Now Poppy was completely astonished. 'What happened that was so awful?' she asked.

'I can't really say – that is his story to tell, not mine. But we all tread carefully with him, even today. So you see why I haven't forced the issue. We care for each other, of course, but we have to take our time.'

'Gosh, I hope it works out for you both.' Poppy meant it.

Orsolina gave a brave smile. 'Thank you, you're very sweet,' she said softly. 'It will, some day.'

(ii) Ice & heat

Leaving the grotto house and hurrying towards the piazza, Poppy tried to imagine what on earth Luca might have done. For him to be so deeply affected, it must have been something serious. Made a girl pregnant, perhaps? Surely there was little shame in that these days. Harmed someone? She found it difficult to believe.

As she neared the piazza, she spotted him at the café with the others. He was laughing, looking handsome as always. After what she had just heard, though, Poppy wasn't sure she trusted this view of him any more.

There was no reason for her to doubt Orsolina's words. Now that she thought of it, Poppy remembered odd moments when Luca's usual brightness had dimmed. That day at the olive estate, for instance, when Tricia asked about his photography and he turned so cagey. Maybe that had been a glimpse of the man he really was. Poppy wished she knew. If only Tricia were there. She was the one to talk this through with.

'*Ciao*, Poppy,' Luca called to her, waving. 'We thought you were lost.'

'I bumped into Orsolina,' she told him, noticing the empty granita glasses on the table. 'Am I too late?'

'We've finished, but I wouldn't mind another.' He looked at Valerie and Moll. 'Ladies, can I tempt you?'

They both made their excuses. Moll was off to update her blog with details of the morning's cooking session; Valerie was drowsy and wanted to relax.

'I'll stay with you,' Luca offered. 'What would you like? Coffee granita? Lemon and mint? Today they also have one with almonds.'

'Coffee,' Poppy decided, wishing they weren't to be left alone. All the questions she had, ready to trip off her tongue, none of them appropriate. She remembered how steamed up Moll had become about Luca's right to privacy. Really, there was no way to ask him without being intrusive.

Luca hailed the waiter, ordering two coffee granitas.

'Did Orsolina keep you talking for ages?' he asked as they waited for them to arrive.

'She showed me her grotto house,' Poppy explained. 'That's what took so long.'

'Ah, and what did you think of it?'

'Weird … dramatic … I don't know that I'd want to live there. If it were mine, I'd turn it into tourist accommodation.'

Luca barked a laugh. 'Don't let Vincenzo hear you say that.'

'Would he be offended?'

'Myself, I think you're right – it's not my idea of a home really. But Vincenzo is a traditionalist in every way. It pleases him to live where his ancestors did.'

'I can understand that. It must feel comfortable and safe.

But is it limiting too? Living life the same way your father did, and your grandfather, and however many there were before him.'

Luca looked thoughtful. 'Don't you think happiness can come from being limited? Or contentment at least?'

Poppy found she was listening more carefully to his words now, holding on to them. Everything he said seemed to have a deeper meaning.

'I wonder what made my Sicilian great-grandparents decide not to settle for their limits,' she said. 'Why travel to the other side of the world for a new life?'

'Poverty,' Luca said, his tone certain. 'Restlessness. The hope of something bigger and better.'

'Perhaps they couldn't stand the thought of staying in the same village for the rest of their days.'

'If you create a good life, then surely it doesn't matter where you spend it,' argued Luca. 'For myself, I have no desire to live anywhere but Favio. It offers all I need. Lots of people I know are the same – Orsolina, for instance. I expect she'll spend her days in the house she was born in.'

'Hasn't she ever been restless; wanted to live in a city, have a bigger life, at least for a while?'

Luca shrugged. 'Her friends are people she went to school with, her life is comfortable and she has every material thing she could want. This is her home and she is happy here. Why change?'

The granitas arrived, and Poppy dipped in her spoon to take a taste. The shaved ice crystals froze her tongue and the sweet espresso flavour was rousing.

'What about you?' she risked. 'Are you content with your limits?'

Luca poked holes in his granita with the end of his spoon, shifting the ice around. 'Perhaps it would be good to see them widen a little ... but not too much. I like a life I can depend on.'

Now Poppy was even more curious. 'Have you always been that way?' she wondered.

'Not at all, I was young and restless once, always thinking there was something bigger and better out there for me. Then I discovered I was wrong. And I was lucky; it was possible to come back here and start again.'

This was the time for Poppy to ask. She shaped the questions in her head. *What happened in London? What terrible thing did you do?* But she found she couldn't speak them aloud.

'Most people's lives have boundaries,' Luca continued. 'We all have to earn a living, clean our houses, eat three times a day, sleep eight hours. It doesn't matter where you live or what you do, there has to be some sort of dull routine underpinning everything. The trick is to make it seem not so dull.'

Poppy realised she had lost the moment. 'I suppose so,' she said instead.

'What happened to your great-grandparents in the end anyway?'

'Oh, they had a little bakery in Darlinghurst, worked long hours, I think. My grandad took over from them, and later my parents ran it for a while. So I guess you're right: they travelled all that way, but their lives were about week after week of hard work, just as they would have been here.'

'Perhaps there were enough small things in every day that brought them joy,' Luca suggested. 'They may have preferred knowing what they were going to be doing for the rest of the week, or the year.'

'Well maybe ... I hope so.' Poppy liked that idea. 'They died long before I was born, so I've never known if they regretted leaving Sicily or not. But my grandfather always seemed content baking bread. He had his regular customers and he and Nan lived in an apartment above the shop. They used to close up now and then to go to the races at Randwick. Grandad still likes his flutter on the horses.'

Luca began on his granita, small mouthfuls he sucked from the spoon. His face was in full sun, so he was wearing dark glasses. Often when she was selling real estate, Poppy tried to read her clients. It was easy enough to tell if someone liked a property and could imagine living there. The nervous first-timers, the bolshie ones who thought everyone was out to cheat them, those who said one thing but meant another, she recognised them all. This man was more of a challenge. Every time she thought she saw him clearly, the picture seemed to change. Now it seemed he was letting down his guard a little. If this was the real Luca, he was far more sensitive than most of the men Poppy had known; softer and more thoughtful, too.

'So your grandparents had a good life, even if it was a small one,' he was saying now.

'They did,' she agreed. 'It seems as if I don't take after them much. I wasn't content to settle for the good life I had, or else I'd have stayed married to Brendan.'

'But you weren't happy?'

'I wasn't unhappy ... I was somewhere between the two, and that didn't seem enough.'

Luca pushed aside his empty granita glass. His eyes met hers, and for a moment he held the glance. 'What do you think it would take to make you happy?' he asked.

'I'm not sure. Some people stay restless all their lives. I'm beginning to wonder if perhaps that's me. I hope not.'

Luca touched her hand. His fingers were still cool from the icy glass. 'Don't worry, Poppy, I think you'll know when you find the limits you're prepared to live with.' He said it gently, then smiled. 'How did we end up having this conversation anyhow? It's too serious for a sunny afternoon. We're meant to be relaxing.'

Poppy supposed she might never find out the truth about Luca now. Not that it really mattered. In a few days she would be leaving, and so however much she was growing to like him, however good it felt to have his hand resting lightly over hers, how could it be important to learn his secrets?

'You're right,' she agreed. 'Maybe being in Orsolina's gloomy cave house has affected my mood somehow.'

'Ah, in that case, I have an idea to cheer you up. Something I've been wanting to show you. Finish your granita and we'll go.'

Yes, Luca was far more sensitive than she had imagined, Poppy decided. A surprise of a man in many ways, it seemed.

Luca left some cash on the table to cover the bill and they headed across the piazza together. Folding her arm in his, he steered her up a narrow lane, towards a church with a plain marble facade.

'Often the priest here locks up because he isn't keen on tourists,' he told her. 'Hopefully today we'll be lucky.'

At his push, the door opened with a loud creak. Poppy felt the coolness of the air inside and smelt the holy trinity of incense, candle wax and dust. Their footsteps echoed as they walked up the plain nave of the empty church, and Luca led her between the pews to a darkened window that filled a long stretch of one wall.

'Now watch this,' he said, slipping a coin into a slot machine beside the window. Instantly the scene behind it lit up, and Poppy saw a vast and rambling Nativity set in a steep town that looked very like Favio, complete with twinkling stars, donkeys, grotesque-looking wise men, shepherds and awed villagers. There were sound effects too, the lowing of cattle, the cry of a baby, the music of a lute player up on the hill. Some of the figures twitched and moved; others stared towards the manger, frozen in adoration of the little Jesus. It was the most fabulously kitsch thing Poppy had ever laid eyes on. She began to giggle.

'That is unreal … too awful.'

'No, no.' Luca was laughing too. 'If the priest finds us

making fun of his famous Nativity, we will be in trouble. There will be a terrible scene, I promise you. No laughing, Poppy.'

'I can't help it, the thing is so outrageous.'

'Yes, I know, but you mustn't giggle in church ...'

Somehow one of Luca's arms found its way round her waist; his other hand touched her cheek. She turned towards him, still half laughing, and he stopped her laughter with his lips. The lights of the Nativity clicked off, the figures stopped jerking, the music finished; he kissed her.

Poppy was dizzied with the suddenness of it. Dimly she recognised that they ought to stop, but she still couldn't pull away. Instead she held on to Luca, fleetingly shutting out everything but the touch of his lips and the heat of his skin.

When at last they broke apart, they stood together in the silent church, leaning in, breathing. It was Luca who spoke first. 'We would be in just as much trouble for this as for laughing,' he said gravely. 'It's very fortunate that the priest doesn't seem to be around.'

'Yes, it is,' Poppy replied shakily.

He rubbed his cheek against hers, breathed the smell of her hair. 'Did you realise how I felt about you?' he asked, his arm a tight band round her waist. 'I've taken you by surprise, haven't I?'

'Yes, you could say that.' Her voice sounded strange to her, whispery and awkward.

'So is it OK?' He watched her face, carefully.

For a moment, all she wanted was for Luca to kiss her again, so that there would be no time for her thoughts to gather and crowd out all the wonder of knowing he was attracted to her.

She glanced at the darkened window of the Nativity, then back at Luca, unsure how to respond.

'Poppy, you're too quiet. Tell me what you're thinking,' he said, relaxing his hold a little.

'It's just that I'm puzzled,' she said softly. 'Until today, I'd assumed you and Orsolina were together. And now, this … It's a lot to take in.'

'Orsolina is my good friend – an old friend – that's all,' he promised.

'It's none of my business, but I think she expects more than that.'

'Unfortunately, I can't do anything about her expectations,' Luca said, flatly. 'Believe me, I've tried. And anyway, they have nothing to do with you and me.'

'When we talked this afternoon, she told me she's sure things will work out with you two eventually. She said other things too.'

Luca frowned. 'What things?'

Everything had been changed by that kiss. There seemed no reason for Poppy not to say it now. 'She mentioned something that happened when you were living in London. A scandal. She wouldn't say more than that.'

For a few seconds Luca considered her words, then he nodded his head. 'Yes, I see. So would you like to know more?'

'I don't have any right to,' she said in a small voice.

'I'm the man who just kissed you; I would hope you want to know more about me.'

Poppy tried to steady herself. 'Luca, I'm only just divorced. I like you a lot, but this is unexpected and—'

'Stop or I'll have to kiss you again,' he warned. 'Then you won't be able to say any of the things I'd prefer not to hear.'

'No, not here, we shouldn't …' She pushed back against the circle he had made with his arms.

'Really?' He smiled, and suddenly there he was, the carefree, charming Luca she'd first imagined him to be. 'I'll tell you anything you want to know. Much more than Orsolina has ever heard. More even than her father, who is the only person I've ever spoken to about any of it.'

Poppy wasn't sure she wanted to hear his secrets now. If she listened, would it seem like a promise to him?

'You don't have to.'

'I know. This is a part of my life I have spoken about to so few people. But I find I want to tell you, even though you will think differently about me. You may not like me very much once you hear what I have to say, Poppy. Perhaps you'll hate me.'

He was staring at her, his eyes burning.

'You know, Luca, this has got a bit too intense for me,' she told him.

'Yes, I see that, I'm sorry.' He let his arms fall.

'I think I'm going to head back up to the house now.'

'No, please don't do that. Come with me instead. Just to my mother's place. Remember how you wanted to see my photography? That's where I keep it. Come on,' he urged. 'It will explain everything.'

Poppy had never met this kind of passion in a man before. She was entirely unbalanced by it. 'OK then,' she said, uncertainly. 'I'll come for a little while, I guess.' She hoped she wasn't going to regret it.

The priest appeared as they walked back down the nave, bustling towards them, a large key in his hand.

'The church is closed – *chiuso*,' he called, his voice hostile. 'What are you doing here?'

'Sorry, Padre, we were just leaving,' Luca replied. 'We came to see the Nativity.'

'The Nativity is closed too,' he barked at them. '*Chiuso, chiuso*, it is all closed.'

As they walked through the door, he slammed it hard behind them and they heard a final muffled cry: '*Chiuso, chiuso*.'

Poppy couldn't help smiling. 'Oh God, imagine if he'd caught us kissing in there. He'd have gone crazy. What were you thinking?'

Luca squeezed her hand. 'I couldn't help it. I've wanted to kiss you for days. It seemed the only place to get you alone.'

Luca's mother lived in the highest reaches of Favio. Her house lay behind a high iron gate and had sweeping views over the clifftop to the town below.

'Don't worry, Mamma isn't here at the moment,' he told her. 'My family has a house near the beach, like lots of people in Favio. When the weather gets warm, she prefers to stay there.'

He showed her into the kitchen and poured a glass of mineral water. 'I'll be just a moment,' he promised.

As she waited, Poppy tried to make sense of what had happened. She had enjoyed being kissed by Luca, liked it a lot. It felt urgent and wayward, like the kissing of her teenage years. Married life didn't lend itself to that kind of intensity, and the feel of lips bruising lips, stubble rough against her skin; she had almost forgotten how exciting that could be.

But none of that was why she had come to Sicily. This trip was about independence and adventure, finding out who she really was without Brendan always there at her side. Luca didn't figure into any of that. A troubled, secretive man was hardly what she needed right now – particularly a man being claimed by another woman.

And yet Poppy couldn't help touching her lips, remembering the taste of him. She wondered what he was about to tell her. She couldn't imagine hating him.

'Here we are.' Luca returned holding a lidded carton covered in dust. 'I haven't looked at any of these for a long, long time.'

Upending the carton, he tipped a pile of photographs on to the kitchen table. All were A4 prints, some colour, others black and white, and all showed the same woman. Poppy recognised her face straight away, knew the slim figure, the cropped blonde hair, the black-kohled eyes.

'Why do you have a big box full of pictures of Princess Diana?' she asked, puzzled.

'I thought I'd have an exhibition some day, do a book or a portfolio. I kept on printing up the damn things.'

'You took these shots?' She was still confused.

'Yes, every one.'

Amazed, Poppy began sifting through them. 'This one of her is famous, isn't it? And this one. I've seen them in magazines.'

'Pretty much everyone has, I expect.'

'And you took them,' she repeated stupidly.

'Those and thousands more. That was my job back then.'

At last her mind cleared. 'You were a paparazzi photographer?'

'Yes.'

'And you followed Princess Diana around?'

'Other famous people too, but mostly her. I know how that must seem to you. Paparazzi don't exactly have the best reputation. All I can say is that at the time it was easy to justify. And you know, she didn't always mind being photographed. Some of the tip-offs came directly from her. She used us from time to time.' He picked up one of the prints. 'It's funny how you can know a face so intimately and yet not the person at all.'

Poppy was having trouble with this new version of Luca. It was the most difficult yet to come to terms with.

'How did you even get into a job like that?' she asked.

'By accident.'

'And you enjoyed it?'

He shrugged. 'It seemed a life without limits. No limit to the money we could earn, the places we could travel, to what we could do and have. It was exciting.'

Poppy supposed she could understand the attraction of that. 'So what went wrong?'

'You know the answer to that question; she died.' He grimaced. 'She died, and I was there.'

'In that tunnel ... in Paris?' She stumbled over the words, thinking of the news bulletins she had watched at the time, and so very shocked that Luca could have been a part of it.

'Yes, I was on one of the motorbikes ... chasing her.'

'So what happened exactly?' Poppy had to know.

Luca couldn't quite meet her eye. His gaze shifted from the photographs on the table to the family portraits lining the wall. 'It was all so fast,' he said hesitantly. 'And so crazy. One moment my partner Harry was screaming at me to speed up or we'd lose her; the next there was this terrible sound and I saw her Mercedes turning towards us, a mass of twisted metal with smoke pouring from its engine and the horn blaring.'

His words brought the scene to life. Poppy was mesmerised. 'What did you do?'

Luca paused again, as if regretting ever starting on his story.

'Did you try to help her?' she pressed him.

He hung his head. 'No, I did nothing at first. It was Harry who jumped off the bike. He ran to the car with some of the others and I thought he was going to help her, but he had his camera and started pushing his way in to try to take pictures. Someone was yelling at him to get back and I heard him swearing. Then other people came, a doctor I think, a policeman. Everyone was taking shots, flashes were strobing, sirens were wailing. I picked up my camera and started shooting with the rest of them.'

He sounded so ashamed. Poppy could find nothing to say.

'I didn't know she would die,' he promised her. 'The others, yes, the driver, Dodi, they were pretty messed up. But she still looked like herself; beautiful. Harry got us out of there just in time. Some of the others were rounded up by the police and taken off in a van. We were free, which meant we could keep on working. It meant we were at the hospital shooting pictures when her coffin left, with the crowd spitting on us and yelling insults.'

'How could you do it?' Poppy felt herself drawing away from him.

Luca stared down at his hands. 'How could any of us do it? I guess it was partly the adrenalin, that single focus when you're on a story. And there's something about having a camera up at your eye; it's a barrier between you and the world, it gives you distance. Today I see the whole thing from a different perspective, of course; the way you must view it, or the way my nonna certainly would have. Now I feel entirely different, but that changes nothing.'

He began throwing the prints back into their box, roughly enough to do them damage. 'I never looked at the images I captured that night. They were all destroyed. I can still see them in my head, though, frame by frame.'

Poppy had been a teenager at the time. She recalled being a little obsessed by all the press articles and TV news shows that had covered the story of the royal tragedy. 'The paparazzi were blamed for the crash, weren't they?'

'We were blamed by the public, yes, and some of the media too, even though they had always been happy to run our pictures. In the end I blamed us just as much as they did.'

'But your motorbike wasn't involved?'

'No, we were way back. Still, the Mercedes was speeding to get away from all of us. I don't know why really; we only wanted to take pictures, and that never killed anyone. All the same, if we hadn't been chasing them, they'd have driven more slowly. There would have been no crash and she would still be alive. So in that way it was our fault: mine, Harry's and the other guys who were hunting her that summer.'

He rubbed his eyes tiredly. 'The game was over after that. I went back to London, but I didn't shoot any pictures of the people leaving bouquets outside the gates of Kensington

Palace or stand in the crowds watching her coffin pass. I mourned her in my own way and on my own. If I left the apartment, it was only because I'd run out of whisky. I didn't answer the phone; saw no one day after day. The more I thought about what had happened to her, the guiltier I felt. She'd been so much a part of my life, it was difficult to know what to do without her.'

'You had a sort of breakdown?' Poppy guessed.

Again Luca hesitated. 'No, that came later,' he admitted. 'That came after I discovered that some of the phone calls I'd been ignoring were from my mother. She was phoning to say Nonna was sick. In the end she wrote a letter, and by the time I got round to opening it, it was too late. Nonna was dead and buried; I had missed my chance to say goodbye. That's when I understood what grief was. That's when I fell apart.'

Poppy could tell from the tautness of his face the pain he still felt. How very hard this story must be to tell. How totally overwhelming it was to be chosen to hear it. She wanted to touch him. Instead she sat across the kitchen table, the carton of photographs between them.

'And that's when you came back to Favio?' she said.

'Eventually, yes. For a long time I didn't know what to do. People were kind to me; Mamma, Vincenzo, Orsolina too. They gave me time, little tasks to do, a job behind the counter of the *dolceria* when I was ready to work. But my nonna had left her house to me and I wanted to honour her memory in some way. With the help of my friends and family I began to restore it; replacing cracked tiles, rotten wood and crumbling stone. Then one day I came up with the idea of the cookery school.'

'And that's what you've been doing ever since.'

Luca nodded. 'I wanted a life with limits. Most of all I wanted to be the person my nonna had believed me to be.'

Poppy knew she wasn't going to repeat any of this to the

others. It might make a sensational story, something to gossip about. But now she agreed with Moll: everyone had a right to secrets.

'I ought to throw these pictures away.' Luca stood and picked up the carton. 'I have no use for them any more.'

'They're a big part of your past. Isn't that important?'

'Not this piece of it; not to me.'

'Why talk of it, then? Why tell me now when it would be so much easier to keep your secrets?'

'Because Orsolina dropped all those hints and I didn't want them to be the thing that stood between us.' Luca held the box against his chest, his eyes burning into hers. 'I like you, Poppy. I have to be straight and true with you. There isn't time for anything less.'

While he went to return the carton to wherever it was kept hidden, Poppy sat at the kitchen table, struggling to come to terms with the confession she had heard, to sort through the mess of her thoughts and decide how she felt about Luca now. To distract herself she examined the rows of framed portraits covering the kitchen wall. Many featured a grey-haired woman with a broad, handsome face; she guessed this was Luca's nonna. There were pictures of Luca as a boy with his mother, smart in his school uniform, on the beach with friends, growing up into a striking teenager and then as a handsome young man. Poppy felt as if she was seeing his whole life laid out for her ... or almost all of it.

'There are no photographs of your father here,' she remarked as he returned to the kitchen.

'Things didn't work out between him and my mother. He left Sicily when I was still very young and I was brought up by women.' He gestured to the wall of framed pictures. 'Most of them are gone now.'

'That's sad.'

Luca shrugged. 'It's life. You love people, you lose them.'

He was standing right beside her, this sweet, sad man.

She felt a rush of feeling for him. How could she not reach out? How could she do anything but hang her arms round his shoulders and squeeze him tight? There in his mother's kitchen, with the clock ticking on the wall, they kissed for a second time. But this time it was different, tentative and tender.

They stayed there kissing for what might have been an hour or only ten minutes. For a while Poppy lost herself completely. She let her hands fall down his back, slipping them beneath his T-shirt. She felt him do the same. Carefully at first, they touched each other. Before long clothes were being unbuttoned, skin pressing against skin. Everything felt delicious and new: his body, how he smelt and tasted, the way he felt beneath her hands, the way she felt about him.

'Luca ... thank you for telling me everything,' she whispered. 'I understand how important it is, how you feel ... I want you to—'

'Shh, not now.' He stopped her. 'Come upstairs, Poppy. Will you? Let's be together, you and I, while we have the time.'

'Yes,' she agreed. There was nothing else to say.

Later, wound up in old linen sheets and each other's bodies, they dozed for a while, and when they woke up, Luca fed her chocolate square by gritty sweet square and it felt as decadent as anything they had done together.

'I've never met a man who keeps a supply by his bed,' she told him.

'Then you've never met a man who was educated by Vincenzo. This is his chocolate, of course. Often I'll eat a couple of squares first thing in the morning to wake myself up. That's it – you've heard all my secrets now.' Luca laughed awkwardly, then, feeding her the final square of chocolate, crumpled the wrapper and tossed it on the floor.

She closed her eyes for a moment, enjoying the texture of

it as it melted in her mouth, and its hint of spice; the comfort of the bed and his closeness.

'Let's stay here for ever living on chocolate,' she suggested, pushing her face into his chest.

'If only we could.'

'I suppose the others would miss us.'

Luca sighed. 'Sooner rather than later, I fear. I promised to cook dinner, remember. They will be waiting.'

'Oh damn yes, of course.' Poppy would have preferred not to face up to anyone yet. She thought about what would come next. Would Moll, Tricia and Val guess what had happened between them?

'Just ten more minutes.' His fingers played in her long river of hair. 'Or maybe twenty.'

'Luca.' She rolled away from him. 'I didn't expect this to happen.'

'Neither did I.' He reached over to pull her back. 'I'm happy that it has.'

'In a few days' time I'll be leaving Favio.'

'You don't have to,' he said quickly. 'You could extend your holiday, stay here with me longer. I'll look after you, I promise.'

Poppy thought of what was waiting at home: her house, friends, her job, and, of course, Brendan. Was there really a big rush to return to any of it? Could she prolong her stretch of freedom? Spend more time with this Sicilian man she found so complicated and compelling?

'I guess I could change my flight.' She was tentative. 'Perhaps I'll look into it.'

'I'll call the airline for you if you like.' Luca sounded pleased. He shifted his weight until he was almost on top of her. 'Still, just in case we only have a few days, let's make the most of them, shall we?'

He began kissing her again. Poppy tasted the last traces of chocolate on his lips, and kissed him back greedily.

*

She smelt of his bed, Poppy realised as they walked together down the several flights of steps that led back towards the cookery school. It was a musky fragrance and seemed to be in her hair as well as on her skin. She liked it better than any scent she'd ever put on. She thought it suited her.

The pavements were crowded, but his hand was in hers, holding them together. Every now and then he greeted someone he knew, and she saw faces register surprise. They must expect to see him with Orsolina, she decided, wondering with a sudden jolt how long it might be before word found its way to her.

He dropped her hand when they reached the food shops on the main street, ducking into the butcher's to buy thin slices of veal and stopping at a roadside stall for vegetables. Here he seemed liked the old Luca, choosing his cuts of meat with confidence, arguing about the freshness of broccoli and the ripeness of tomatoes. But Poppy knew this was only the first layer of him, the part he let the world see. She never would have guessed how much lay beneath it.

Food of Love

Luca Amore is making *carne murata* in his nonna's wide terracotta dish, layering thin slices of veal with onions and potatoes, tomatoes and herbs.

He feels her eyes on him as he moves around the kitchen. He wonders what she is thinking.

Everything he does is flavoured by the way he feels. He makes a pesto of almonds, plum tomatoes, shredded mint and garlic, pounding and working it into an oily paste with his pestle and mortar. He kneads pasta dough by hand, dividing it into strips and twisting them into shape. He has done the same for every guest who has stayed here; this time, though, it feels different.

Usually preparing food is soothing for him. Following familiar routines, occupying his hands while freeing his mind to wander, and then the reward when the smell of baking meat or the sweetness of simmering tomatoes seeps into the room. This evening Luca feels clumsy. He is struggling to perform one task after another in the correct order. He wants this dinner to be over and the drinks on the terrace finished. He needs to be alone with her.

He wonders if she is regretting the afternoon they have spent together. From her face, it is impossible to know. Her cheeks are slightly flushed, her skin a little shiny, her lips raw from kissing. Her beauty is all about slight flaws. That was one of the things that drew him to her.

She is perched up on a stool now at the kitchen counter, talking to the others, who are sitting at the table. Their conversation tells him nothing at all. It is just women filling the silence with words. He listens to it like music.

The *pesto trapanese* is a little salty; the pasta water should be boiling by now. Luca tries to concentrate. This is a simple enough meal, but he is losing control. He is rushing.

One thing Luca's nonna taught him is that a dish deserves the time it needs. The flavours in a sauce must be allowed to bubble and blend; the sinews in meat need hours to braise and soften. Food that is hurried has no depth; it fails to satisfy. Luca wonders if a love affair is exactly the same.

There should be a hundred more dishes of granita shared at the café in the piazza, more afternoons eating chocolate between his mother's old linen sheets. They need to learn how their flavours will mingle over time; they need hours to talk and hours more to be silent together.

Luca can think of so many things he would cook for her if he had the chance. Zucchini *agrodolce* with fresh mint and hot chilli flakes, spaghetti black with cuttlefish ink, aubergines smoked and doused with garlic and lemon. The desserts he would feed her. Tarts of pistachio and ricotta, prickly pear sorbet if she were here in late summer, golden croquettes of deep-fried rice coated in honey for comfort over winter. He worries that those meals may never happen.

Luca polishes glasses and cutlery, finds plates and sets the table. He checks the pasta and pulls the dish of baked veal from the oven. This meal is ready. That is the only thing he is sure of.

Tricia

Don't look at me like that. I know exactly what you're thinking, but what you don't understand is that I needed this. I'm not going to feel guilty. I refuse to.

My life is so prescribed. Day after day I taxi from home to work, then back again. The inside of my office or a courtroom, the inside of my house; I'm in control, in charge. I'm the one that makes sure the cleaner is paid and there's food in the fridge. It's me that books the dental appointments, organises play dates and takes care of all those other things that keep a family running. Meanwhile most of my mind is worrying away at whatever case I'm working on. I can never switch it off, not unless I sink a bottle of wine, and even then it's there, crackling away in the background, like having the radio on.

There are times I want to scream or cry, or both. Of course I don't, because what would everyone think if suddenly I fell apart? I can't afford to let go; there are too many people counting on me. The only thing to do is keep going.

For a while there with Santo I got out of my own head; lost control, was someone other than myself, and God it was good. Val was right about men who can cook – they are better in bed. I wish I'd known that before.

Yes, there have been other times ... not a lot ... just enough snatched from everyday life to keep me going. Paul has never found out, my children aren't affected, I keep it separate always; I'm rigorous about that. I wait and take my chances where I can. And Santo was good at it, really excellent. He took me to a place I needed to be.

When you go to bed with a man who isn't your husband, it's like every nerve is exposed; all those senses that have dulled over the years of sameness, they sharpen up instantly. There's the thrill and the risk; there is so much newness, but most of all there's the knowing that it will end and you'll never need to see each other again. That lowers the stakes – it means nothing, so you can let yourself go completely.

The morning after was perfect. Santo lent me an old shirt and a wide-brimmed hat and sent me out into the vineyard gardens. I weeded and hacked like a maniac; got covered in sweat and dirt, and by the time I'd finished, everything looked tidier except me.

My dad used to say his garden was the only place he could think clearly. When he got home from work, he'd take his torch and spend half an hour in our narrow strip, no matter how late it was. He grew flowers mostly – zinnias, asters and dahlias; anything with nectar that attracted butterflies and bees. That was his escape. While his hands were busy in the soil, he could sort through the strands of his mind; uncoil them and see everything properly. At least that's what he told me.

These days it's all lawn where Dad's flower beds used to be, and my mother pays a man to come and mow it. She won't hear of having annuals dying back untidily at the end of the season, flower heads that droop and drop, or anything that straggles and needs to be pruned. In her opinion, a garden should be like a photograph, and look the same every day.

Santo allowed me to do whatever I wanted in his garden. When I'd finished, he helped me build a fire to burn the waste, and later he cooked what I'd harvested and there was nothing to do but eat, drink wine, and watch him work, until the kitchen closed and it was time for us to go to bed again.

Just like Moll said, all of us have a right to privacy, don't we? We're allowed a few secrets. Well this one is mine, and I trust you'll help me keep it.

Day Six

(i) Gelato & white lies

Tricia never, ever felt guilty while it was happening. Guilt was for the morning, particularly this one, as she crept up the steps to the cookery school and let herself in to find Poppy in the kitchen. There was no need to explain herself – it was her business, after all – yet she found herself trying. It was quite clear Poppy didn't have a clue what she was talking about. There was nothing in her life to help her understand it, after all.

Faced with her disapproval, Tricia almost regretted taking off with Santo, but if not him, then it would have been someone else: Luca, Vincenzo Mazzara, a random waiter or bartender. She had been on course for it the moment she arrived in Italy with no one to hold her back. It had taken a few days to adjust; to become the version of herself she might have been without a husband and children. Then, on the island of Ortygia, walking fast and freely with that beautiful young chef, she had felt something inside her wake up. A hungry, demanding and impatient thing she recognised.

She had been the one to suggest spending the evening together, expressed an interest in dining at the vineyard again, hinted at her willingness to be seduced. There had been a chance he would turn her down; he was much younger than her, after all, and possibly there was a girlfriend somewhere. But Tricia could handle rejection. It was one of the risks she took every time.

She thought of it as a holiday within a holiday, and it wasn't difficult to justify. In a way, even her family would benefit, for she would return home refreshed enough to bed back into her life, at least until the next time.

How could Poppy, with her neat divorce from her dull husband, understand the truth of it – sometimes urges were safer satisfied. This morning Tricia felt defused, and yes, a little guilty too, but only temporarily while Poppy's eyes were on her and she could read the thoughts going through the girl's mind.

'Of course, I wouldn't say anything,' she was promising now. 'I don't even know your husband, so how could I? But even if I did, your secret would be safe, don't worry.'

'Let's not mention it again, hey,' Tricia suggested.

'What about Val and Moll? And Luca? They'll have guessed.'

'Val's too well bred to say anything. And Moll ... well, after her outburst at me the other day, it would be ironic if she did. As for Luca, I'm sure he's seen it all before.'

'And you won't be seeing Santo again?'

'I shouldn't think so. Not unless we bump into each other a second time, and that's unlikely. Now, how about some coffee?' Tricia rummaged in the cupboard for the moka pot. 'I'm desperate for a cup.'

'Yes please.' Poppy still sounded cool. 'I was about to make some when you came in.'

Tricia hoped she would thaw. The coming days would be boring if she didn't.

'Remind me what's on the agenda today,' she said, filling the moka with water. 'Are we meant to be going out?'

'Yes, to Noto to taste artisan gelato and explore.'

'That's right ... sounds good.'

'Moll thinks she's found some people there with my grandfather's surname,' Poppy told her. 'I was planning to get Luca to call them last night, but then we ... we ran out of time.'

'Will you look them up anyway?'

'If I'm there, I may as well.'

'And what about yesterday, did I miss anything important?'

'We cooked fish for lunch, tasted granita and then Luca made dinner.'

'That's it?'

'Um ... quiet day,' said Poppy, fiddling with the corner of the coffee packet. 'Nice, though.'

'I expect Luca will be here with breakfast in a moment.'

'Expect so.'

Without bothering to wait for her coffee, Poppy declared she was heading upstairs to change. She was wearing jeans and a creased floaty top; her hair was rumpled and there were smudges of mascara beneath her eyes; it looked like she had dressed straight out of bed. Tricia had done the same. The dresses and sandals she had bought on Ortygia had seen her through the past couple of days, but this morning was shaping up to be a hot one, and she needed a fresh outfit to suit it.

Up in her room, she put her phone on for a quick charge and considered Skyping the kids. They didn't expect her to be in touch every day, but they might be wondering where she had got to by now. Before that she would shower, organise her clothes and hair, bring herself back into line completely. It wouldn't matter if she missed breakfast. She had allowed herself to eat far more than usual in the past few days, so a few skipped meals were in order.

Tricia let herself think about Santo one last time – how he had looked when she had unsheathed him from his chef's whites, the tautness of his skin and the muscles that flexed beneath it, the burnt-butter smell of him – and then she turned on her laptop and logged on to her Skype account.

It wasn't a problem to smile for Paul or put on her Mummy voice for the children. She could slip back into it easily enough no matter what. She teased the kids with promises of presents, said she loved them all and couldn't wait to see them (which was true), reminded them about Zara's dental appointment, told Charlie where to find his cricket kit, and then they said goodbye and the screen went blank.

There had been moments when Tricia wondered what exactly Paul did in his times away from her. There were medical conferences he attended alone, social engagements too, so it was entirely possible he went with other women. Tricia had never asked, and wouldn't. Why shake up their lives? They both worked hard and deserved a release; the least said the better.

By the time she got downstairs, the others had finished their breakfast. They tried to make her eat a leftover pastry, but Tricia was adamant she wasn't hungry.

'There'll be a gelato tasting soon, and I expect there are feasts planned for lunch and dinner, aren't there, Luca?'

'Actually, tonight was supposed to be a free evening,' he replied. 'But we've had a dinner invitation and – I hope you don't mind – I accepted it on everyone's behalf.'

'Really, who from?' Tricia hoped it wasn't Santo.

'Vincenzo and Orsolina have asked us to join them. He's an excellent cook and their home is an interesting setting for a dinner.'

'That sounds great.' She was relieved.

'How lovely … so generous,' Valerie and Poppy both murmured.

Only Moll seemed less than enthusiastic, which was odd, as usually she was the first to put up her hand for any new food experience. 'Was it Vincenzo who invited us? Or Orsolina?' she asked.

'Both of them, of course,' Luca replied. 'Why?'

'Just wondering,' Moll muttered, before going off to cram even more junk into her overstuffed satchel and get ready for the outing.

*

The drive to Noto took them past the same scenery as every other trip, alongside vineyards and olive groves, mountains and ravines, dusty farmhouses and fields of dry grass. Barely bothering to glance out the window, Tricia used the time to make notes on her iPhone. She listed all the things she had to do when she got home. There were bills to be paid; Zara needed a birthday gift to take to a school friend's party, Paul to be reminded the car was due for a service. Being organised was the only way to cope with the onslaught of her real life. It was time to make a start on it.

Nearing Noto, the conversation in the car turned to gelato. Tricia had never had an especially sweet tooth, but on a hot day like this, she did enjoy an ice cream, and she said so.

'This is artisan gelato,' Moll was quick to remind her. 'Quite different from your Haagen Dazs or your Baskin Robbins.'

'Yes, I know that.' Tricia struggled not to sound testy. 'Although to be honest, I'm not sure why it's different.'

'It's about the milk-to-cream ratio and the speed it's churned, isn't it?' Val piped up. 'Jean-Pierre was a big gelato fan. He always said it was lower in fat than ice cream so he could have an extra scoop.'

Luca laughed. 'Jean-Pierre was right, but, as with all the Italian specialities you've tried, there's good gelato and there's bad, and you're about to discover the difference.'

'I'm glad I didn't eat breakfast,' Tricia said to no one in particular.

As they drew into Noto, the traffic grew thicker and the driving more frantic. What were all these people doing? Tricia wondered. Some might be tourists, true, but even so, there seemed to be enormous numbers out on the streets for an ordinary work day. She thought of the long hours spent at her desk and how, even then, it was difficult to get through her workload. Did everyone else have so much more freedom from Monday to Friday?

'We'll stop here and walk to the centre of town,' Luca said, pulling into a car park. 'Caffe Sicilia is near to the cathedral and other sights worth seeing. It's renowned for its pastries and granita as well as the gelato.'

They walked in a straggle (Tricia striding ahead, Poppy beside Luca, Valerie with Moll at the rear) past pink-stone buildings and on into a piazza filled with old men on benches, mothers with spoilt sons and pretty girls in short skirts. Every Italian town appeared to have its quota, Tricia had noticed.

Caffe Sicilia was the sort of place she might have walked straight past; it looked quite humble, just a dark doorway with an awning over it and a few chrome tables outside, very like any other bar or café. Inside was a narrow room blooming with cakes and pastries, and at the very back a small cabinet freezer filled with stainless-steel containers of gelato.

'I expected to see lavish mounds,' Tricia remarked, 'and lots more flavour options.'

'When you see gelato piled up high like that, it's a sign it's not the real thing,' Luca explained. 'It's the fake stuff.'

'Fake gelato? Really?'

'Yes indeed. They say that in Rome, up to ninety per cent of the gelato sold is made from a powdered mix rather than fresh ingredients.'

'If it tastes good, does it really matter?' Tricia could predict what the answer would be, but Luca seemed to expect her to ask so she went along with it.

'For me, yes. I want real food, not something that has been turned into a powder then transformed back into a thing I can eat.'

'I agree,' said Moll. 'That's exactly my philosophy.'

'In that case, you should know about the other sign that gives away the fake gelato,' Luca said. 'The colours are too bright. The mint should be white, not bright green, the pistachio an earthy tone. If it's real gelato, it looks dull and the pay-off is in the taste. Here at Caffe Sicilia the chef is famous for trying all sorts of unusual combinations. He is not afraid to experiment with strong sweet and savoury elements. My favourite is the orange salad with sea salt and olive oil. I also love the one he does sometimes with black olives.'

Tricia glanced at Moll. Her face was alight with excitement as she pushed close to the freezer cabinet to choose her flavours. 'Is that tomato and basil?' she asked. 'How extraordinary. The chef here must be the Heston Blumenthal of ice cream.'

'I guess he is in his own quiet way,' agreed Luca. 'This café has been in his family since 1892. It is one of the places no one would argue should be in Vincenzo Mazzara's food guide, because the gelato here is incomparable.'

'I've no idea what to choose.' Moll looked bewildered.

'Yes, that's always the problem.'

Tricia wasn't going to waste half a morning deliberating, no matter how unique the flavours. She ordered a scoop of what seemed the simplest (almond and cinnamon) and sat outside, shaded by a parasol, to eat. She had to admit it was beyond delicious: not too sweet, with a gentle nuttiness and a hint of spice.

Moll appeared clutching a two-scoop cone, with plans to go back for more. Poppy had chosen a rich chocolate, lively with orange and lemon zest, Val a scoop of *torrone*. There was much sharing to taste each other's choices and a lengthy discussion of which was the best. Tricia held on to her cone. Leaning back in her chair, she licked the milky almond drips before they ran down into her lap.

Luca was talking about Noto, how the old palazzos had been allowed to crumble and the roof of the cathedral had fallen in. 'It was a tragedy,' he told them. 'The art world went into shock.'

'How extraordinary; so much care is taken over food here, so little over everything else,' Tricia observed.

'Food nourishes your whole body, architecture only your

eyes,' Luca pointed out. 'When people are struggling, there isn't the means to care for both. But for Sicilians there is beauty in stone that's scarred and worn. We don't love our buildings any the less for it.'

Once Moll had ordered her second cone, he led them on a walk past churches with graceful facades and beneath buttressed balconies covered in cherubs and nymphs. He was a dutiful tour guide, reciting facts and dates, but Tricia only half listened as he talked about the earthquake that had flattened the place centuries ago and the baroque town that rose to replace it.

She took a few photographs to show Paul (he enjoyed architecture), but felt disengaged otherwise. Perhaps she was tired after two nights with so little time for sleeping; or maybe this holiday had gone on long enough and she had lost her taste for it.

'Are you going to hunt down your relatives while we're here in Noto?' she asked Poppy, hoping for a distraction.

'I think so, yes.'

'Oh good, can I come?'

Poppy looked sideways at Luca, leaving him to reply.

'The trouble is, we have a lot of ground to cover,' he explained. 'I was going to suggest you go and check out the restoration of the cathedral in the meantime.'

Tricia had seen the inside of enough churches over the years. 'Really I'd much prefer—' she began.

Moll interrupted. 'No, do come with us. I read in the guidebook that there are some interesting shops tucked away. We could explore them afterwards.'

Taken aback by this sudden warmth, Tricia said, 'Oh … OK then. I hate to miss a chance to shop.'

'Perhaps we should wander over that way now,' Moll suggested. 'Val, you ready?'

'Yes, count me in.'

Resting a hand on Poppy's shoulder, Luca smiled. 'We'll

meet up with you later for lunch, then. Say in about two hours on the steps of the cathedral?'

'Do you really think we'll want lunch after so much gelato?' Moll shook her head. 'No, I'm sure I can't manage it. Don't rush. If anyone does get peckish, we'll find somewhere that sells pizza or *arancini*.'

Tricia thought Moll seemed to be acting out of character. First refusing a meal, and now, as they turned to retrace their steps, walking quickly instead of stopping every few paces to take photographs, opening a good distance between them and the others, a smile on her plump face and her brow sheened with sweat.

'Oh well done you,' Valerie said to her when they were out of earshot.

'What's going on?' Tricia glanced back at Luca and Poppy, who were shoulder to shoulder, rounding a bend.

'Has Poppy not told you?' Moll sounded surprised. 'Put it this way, you're not the only one who didn't make it back to the house last night.'

'You're kidding.' Tricia recalled finding Poppy in the kitchen earlier that morning in yesterday's crumpled clothes and smudged eye make-up. She had been so caught up in her own affairs, it hadn't struck her when it ought to have been obvious. Poppy too had only just got home.

'So how did you know?' she asked Moll.

'Well I didn't say anything ... obviously ... but it's been pretty clear for a while there's an attraction there. Then last night Luca was all over the place cooking dinner, and Poppy was on her toes. It was a strange sort of evening and they both disappeared off to the bar without asking if we'd care to join them. Val says she didn't hear the front door slam again until first thing this morning.'

'Wow ...' Tricia hadn't realised sweet little Poppy had it in her.

'I thought it would be nice for them to have some time

alone today,' said Moll. 'It can't be easy trailing round as part of a group. And tonight, well, who knows what that dreadful Orsolina has in store.'

It was obvious Tricia had missed a few things in her absence. 'What do you mean ... what's wrong with Orsolina?' she asked.

'Let's go and find somewhere to have a cool drink, and I'll tell you.'

Over glasses of iced limonata at a café shaded by leafy trees, Moll poured out her story about Orsolina. 'Her friendliness that night was all show,' she told them. 'The only reason she wanted me in that bar was to sideline Poppy. Of course she tried to deny it, but she's so possessive over Luca. And I don't trust her ... or like her for that matter. Generally I'm right about these sorts of things.'

Tricia couldn't condemn Orsolina for trying to fight her corner. 'Poor thing, there she is making all that effort with designer clothes, and it turns out Luca's type is natural girls. Still, this is just a holiday romance with Poppy. She'll be going home soon, then Orsolina can have another shot at him.'

'I'm not so sure about that. The world is such a small place now,' Moll mused. 'It will be easy enough for them to keep in touch, even when Poppy is back in Australia. Things might develop.'

Generally Tricia tried not to think too much about the shrinking of the world, and all the ways it was getting easier to find each other ... and be found out.

'Poppy's only just divorced,' she pointed out. 'She won't be looking for commitment. And for all we know, Luca makes a habit of this kind of thing.'

'I don't think so,' Moll said. 'At least that wasn't Orsolina's story.'

Tricia wondered if Moll was overstating things. It was possible her imagination was more active than you would think to look at her. She might have got the wrong idea about whatever was going on with Poppy and Luca. And her grudge against Orsolina seemed a little excessive (Tricia suspected that Moll was prone to grudges).

'Oh well, I guess it's none of our business anyway,' she said lightly, unable to resist a tiny dig.

Moll must have been telling a white lie about the shops. Beyond a few souvenir places and stores selling the local honey and olive oil, Tricia couldn't see many. She bought a map and tourist guide, but found it was nunneries, churches and old stone all the way.

At the far end of the main street there was an arid-looking garden with palm trees, pine and oleander. She sat beside a fountain and waited for the others to catch her up. She had walked out on them in a shop where Moll had been staring at sealed jars of food as though they were jewellery or shoes.

From her bench she could see a playground and a child with an ice-cream-plastered face watching the bigger kids on the swings. There was something about him that reminded her of her son Charlie, a gravity and patience odd in a small boy. She felt the urge to chase the older ones off so he could have his turn.

Poor Charlie, she hoped he wasn't going to find life too hard. Zara was more like her: bold and certain, unafraid to ask for what she wanted, one of the popular girls. But Charlie worried her. He was timid about so many things: large dogs, high slides, dark rooms. His tears came easily and he tended to cling.

Paul was always so sweet with him. He never tried to push Charlie to be braver, like she had seen other men do with their sensitive sons. On weekends they spent hours building Lego towers or curled up on the sofa with piles of books and DVDs. Charlie was one of the reasons Tricia still loved her husband. How could she watch them together and not love him?

Now she looked at the poor ice-cream-covered kid. Where was his mother with a wet wipe? Where were his friends? Surely close by, yet she couldn't see anyone.

Tricia might have gone through life without children happily enough, if not for a drunken night and sloppy use of contraception. Even then she had considered an abortion, talked it through with friends. The impact of a baby on her career and her body, the way her freedom might be curtailed; they had discussed it late into the night over bottles of Chardonnay. Tellingly, Tricia had only managed a few sips. She must have suspected even then that she would go ahead with the pregnancy, just like Paul wanted. As soon as the baby was born and she saw her tiny shells of fingernails and nubs of fat feet, she had known it was the right thing.

Paul was the one who had argued for a second child. Didn't Tricia own a wardrobe of smocks, a cupboard full of bottles and a breast pump? Wasn't her conversation all about how to find a decent nanny and the best brand of organic baby food? Life had changed already; what difference would one more make?

It had made a big difference, huge. Charlie had grabbed her heart and squeezed it in a way Zara never did. He was a bad feeder, more prone to being sickly, a crier through the night. Paul had walked up and down the stairs with him on his shoulder, so she could get some rest. However, instead of resting, Tricia had worried. What if Paul stumbled and let go? What if something was wrong with Charlie? Was it normal for a baby to cry like this? Zara never had.

Whenever she thought about peeling her life apart from Paul's, she considered Charlie. She could change, but was it fair to ask him to? Other women might be able to tell themselves fairy tales about amicable divorces, but Tricia knew better. Someone always got hurt. And in their case, she knew it would be her son.

She watched the dirty-faced Italian kid. He was still waiting, trusting that sooner or later he would get his turn, even though the bigger kids were swinging higher and higher. It broke her heart.

Getting up from the bench, she turned to walk back towards the cathedral. She might as well go inside and take a look. The others would catch up with her, one way or another.

The interior of the cathedral was blessedly cool and unexpectedly restful. There wasn't the usual surfeit of religious frescoes (they'd been damaged beyond repair when the roof fell in); instead, most of the walls were painted plain white and all the drama was in the soaring arches and thick corniced pillars.

Tricia slid into a pew and bowed her head as if praying. She wasn't, of course. She couldn't even remember the Lord's Prayer, although she had recited it before bedtime with her father as a child. Maybe the words would still be there if she hadn't been so young when she lost him.

Someone slipped into the pew beside her and she heard Valerie ask softly, 'Are you OK?'

'Yes, why?'

'You looked very contemplative.'

'I was thinking about Poppy and Luca,' Tricia lied. 'Do you reckon Moll is right at all?'

Valerie didn't respond. Tipping back her head, she looked at the ceiling. 'It must have been dramatic when it fell in. I hope no one was hurt.'

'It says in my tourist guide that rain seeped into cracks formed by an earthquake and it took eleven years to clear the rubble and rebuild.'

'Do you suppose if there were another earthquake right now, it might all come down and land on our heads?'

'Possibly. You can't go through life worrying about stuff like that, though, can you?'

'Sometimes the sky does fall in,' Val said, a catch in her voice. 'And then what?'

Tricia looked at her. 'Then you rebuild it, I suppose.'

They found Moll sitting in the full glare of the sun out on the cathedral steps, munching on something bready.

'*Scacce*,' she told them. 'I came across a tiny hole-in-the-wall place selling them, and they smelt so good I couldn't resist. Help yourself.'

Tricia realised she was hungry. Crouching down beside Moll, she took one of the layered breads stuffed with spiced meat and broccoli.

'Thanks.'

'You're welcome.'

Tricia dug her teeth in and tore off a chunk; it was oily, and still warm. Next to her, Valerie was doing the same.

'No sign of Luca and Poppy, then?' she asked between mouthfuls.

'None at all,' Moll told her. 'I guess if they're trying to track down all the names on the list I gave her, then it might take some time.'

'No rush, I suppose,' Valerie said. 'We can sit here and people-watch for a while.'

'There's nothing else to do.' Tricia was beginning to feel bored. 'Although on a boiling hot day like this, I'd prefer to do my people-watching on a beach.'

'I'd love a swim,' agreed Moll. 'I wonder if there would be time.'

'If Poppy and Luca hurry up, there might be.'

'I did tell them not to rush,' Moll reminded her.

Moll wasn't such a bad stick really, Tricia decided, good-hearted in her way, even if she did look as if she'd dressed from a jumble sale, and at least a decade older with that short grey hair and skin so sunburnt it would probably soon seem pickled. Did she mind being the only one not to have had any male attention on this holiday? Would she like a flirtation? Or did she really have no passion in her except for food?

She was reaching for another folded bread now; this one filled with black olives, hot flakes of chilli and cooked cheese. The fat she must consume on a daily basis, the calories and carbs … yet she didn't seem to give a second thought to her health or weight. If she lost a few kilos, coloured her hair, went shopping, maybe some man would show an interest. Tricia thought it wouldn't take much to give her a makeover.

'I thought you said there were shops,' she said, trying to rub the oiliness from her fingers without much success.

'There probably are, but I don't know where,' admitted Moll. 'Perhaps we could go back to Caffe Sicilia and have some of the little almond cakes.'

Tricia frowned at the idea of more sugar. 'Or a coffee?' she suggested. 'They might even have somewhere I could wash my hands.'

'Can I ask you something?' began Moll, and when Tricia nodded, she continued, 'Why come on a cooking holiday if you have no real interest in it?'

Tricia thought about it. 'It was something I'd never tried before. Paul is all about us having experiences. We've been cycling in the Dordogne, skiing in Val d'Isere, sailing in the Greek islands, hiking in New Zealand. He says it's pointless going back to the same place year after year; everything becomes a blur if you do that; there are no distinct memories. He likes to find something new.'

'Fair enough … but do you think this holiday has changed your attitude to food at all?'

'It's been interesting, but if I don't cook another thing this year, I don't suppose I'll care,' Tricia admitted.

Moll stopped eating and began licking her fingers clean. 'If I don't cook, I feel antsy. I spend so much time thinking about it, reading books and magazines, planning meals. There's a thrill in identifying the one ingredient that will make a difference, and turn an ordinary dish into a delicacy. I can't paint or play music, so this is my way of being creative, I suppose.'

'At home, our nanny cooks the kids their tea, and sometimes Paul and I will eat the leftovers for supper while we're sitting on the sofa with our laptops,' Tricia confessed.

'You're missing out on something so exciting.'

Tricia laughed. 'I guess that depends on what you consider exciting.'

Moll didn't respond, and Tricia thought perhaps she had offended her again; it seemed easy enough to do.

'Shall we go and check out the cakes, then?' she said to compensate. 'I might be able to fit in a little one before I reach my limit.'

At Caffe Sicilia, there was no one who spoke fluent English, so ordering was a process of mime and laughter. Moll overdid things (naturally) and they ended up with a platter of small cakes and miniature puddings in jewel and pastel colours.

'This will be a challenge,' she said, as they sat down at one of the chrome tables outside. 'We'll see if we can guess the flavours.'

She began cutting slivers from each cake and tasting them, finding traces of jasmine and saffron, bergamot and basil, black tea and mint, as well as the expected honey and almonds, and urging the others to try them too.

'I don't want to spoil my appetite for Vincenzo's cooking tonight,' said Valerie.

'But we won't get another chance,' Moll countered, dipping her spoon into what looked like a mini cassata. 'Have a little, at least.'

Giving in to the lure, Tricia tried a tart of fruits in a sweet-sour marmalade with a flavour she couldn't recognise (fennel, Moll thought); and another topped with pink grapefruit and roasted red pepper that was oddly delicious.

The platter was soon a mess of smears and half-eaten sweet things; and all of them were full.

'What a pity to waste so much,' said Moll. 'If only Poppy and Luca would come soon.'

'If only,' Tricia agreed.

'I guess it's a good sign if it's taking them so long,' said Valerie. 'Perhaps it means they've made some progress.'

It occurred to Tricia that the pair of them might not be searching very hard. 'Do you think Poppy really cares about finding her relatives, or is it just a ruse to get away with Luca for a while?'

'I did wonder that too,' admitted Moll. 'She seems so half-hearted about it; there's nothing I found out that she couldn't have learned for herself.'

Valerie shaved a wedge from a wobbly milk pudding. 'Poor Poppy. Divorce is so disorienting, isn't it? Even if you're the one pushing for it, there's still that moment when you realise the life you'd been banking on isn't going to happen. I expect she feels lost, like she doesn't know quite what she wants or who she is any more. I've been divorced twice and felt much the same.' Swallowing the pudding, she frowned. 'This has got some sort of herb in it. Thyme? Fresh oregano? I'm not sure.'

Moll took a spoonful. 'I'm divorced too, but I never, ever felt lost. I knew exactly what I wanted; my only problem was I couldn't get it all quickly enough.' She licked the spoon. 'Oregano. I like it, it works.'

'Well I've got more experience of divorce than either of you, even though I've never been through it myself,' Tricia told them. 'It shows people's true colours. That's all I know.'

As she spoke, Luca and Poppy came into sight. Unaware of being watched, they were loosely holding hands, walking quite slowly and deep in conversation. Tricia saw straight away what she had managed to miss so far. They were crazy about each other, right in the middle of that first attraction where nothing they did together seemed old or boring, and no one else mattered. She remembered it as the best part, the fizzy bit, and found herself envious even though she knew it never lasted.

Moll called out, waving to attract attention. Seeing them, Luca dropped Poppy's hand. He said something to her and she looked pink-cheeked, although from too much sun or embarrassment, Tricia wasn't certain.

No one else remarked on it, or even seemed tempted to. Instead, keen for details of their morning, they peppered Luca and Poppy with questions as soon as they sat down at the table: 'What happened, did you find anyone, what did they say?'

'We thought it was going to be another waste of time, didn't we?' Poppy glanced at Luca. 'The lawyer's place was all shut up, the other Planeta we couldn't find at all, but then we tried the hairdresser, who turned out to be interesting. She didn't know much herself, but she was sure some of her family had emigrated to Australia and thought her father would be able to help. She showed us a photo of him, and he does look a little like my grandad. The only thing is, he won't be there until this evening, and we can't hang around until then. Perhaps we could phone him.'

'You should come back,' said Tricia. 'Better to see him in person if you have the chance.'

'Yes,' agreed Moll. 'Vincenzo and Orsolina won't mind if you're a little late for their dinner. We'll hold the fort till you arrive.'

'Are you sure?' Luca asked. 'I feel guilty neglecting you.'

'It was supposed to be a free night anyway,' Tricia pointed out.

'Yes, there's no need to feel guilty, it doesn't bother us,' added Moll.

'In that case, I think I'd like to come back,' decided Poppy. 'I've got a feeling we might be getting somewhere this time.'

(ii) A dinner of surprises

Tricia had never realised how many savoury dishes could be made using chocolate. Vincenzo was reciting them: rabbit stews thickened with it, chicken sauced, soup laced and pork rubbed. According to him, a shaving of dark, unsweetened chocolate lent an ordinary chilli con carne a bitter note, or added depth and richness to a braise. To Tricia's ears this speech sounded well practised. Still, it was good that he was talking, fixing them with his bright eyes and filling the silence with words.

At first Moll's exclamations had covered any awkwardness; this was her first visit to the grotto house and she was beguiled. Soon enough Orsolina had interrupted. Where was Luca? Poppy? She pressed her lips together when she heard they were in Noto together and after that said very little.

The other thing Tricia couldn't miss was that the framed photographs on the sideboard in the hallway had been changed; there were fewer of Orsolina as a child and far more of her with Luca. If this was staged, then it wasn't very subtle. Tricia wondered what she was playing at.

They had arrived right on time, despite Valerie deciding to change her outfit at the last minute. The dress she was wearing now was flimsier than any Tricia had seen her in before, its neckline lower and its fabric a gauzy rose gold. Vincenzo, of course, was enchanted, remarking on how beautiful she looked, taking her hands and kissing her cheeks, ladling on charm as rich as his chocolate. Then he returned to the kitchen to prepare the appetisers, leaving Orsolina to welcome the rest of them properly, taking their handbags and wraps to put in a small anteroom off the hallway, where she fussed about for a while hanging things up.

Now they were all out on the terrace in the evening sun, drinking chilled Prosecco and eating warm crostini daubed with molten chocolate, a drizzle of peppery olive oil and a sprinkling of briny sea salt. Tricia found the blend of flavours unexpectedly compelling, but still shook her head at the offer of a second.

As it grew darker, they moved to the dining room, a cavern lit by candles with a rough-hewn wooden table at its centre that might have seated twenty people. At one end Orsolina had spread a white cloth and laid out crystal and cutlery.

'We have too many place settings now,' she complained. 'Will I clear them or shall we hold on for Luca and the Australian girl to arrive?'

'Oh, Luca said not to wait,' Moll told her breezily. 'He didn't want the meal to spoil.'

Orsolina bit her lip. 'Papa?'

'Let us take our seats at the table and relax,' decided Vincenzo. 'I have an *amuse-bouche* for you to try, an experiment. I will save some for Luca and his friend.'

This time from the kitchen he brought out truffles made from goat's cheese mixed with powdered chocolate and rolled in crushed almonds.

'I have included chocolate in this dinner where I can without overwhelming the menu,' he explained, taking a seat next to Valerie and smiling at her. 'I will be very interested to see if you can find it in each dish.'

Moll seemed entranced; she was trying to take a photograph and murmuring something about the light. Meanwhile Vincenzo was busy twinkling at Valerie while his daughter sat opposite, glowering and silent.

'Well, hasn't this been a day of experimental eating?' Tricia remarked. She was good at small talk.

Valerie bit into her truffle. 'Tonight is the best part yet, though, isn't it?'

Vincenzo gave a quick shake of his head. 'Do not speak too soon; the evening has barely begun.'

'I feel sure you wouldn't serve us anything that wasn't perfect,' said Valerie, almost coquettish.

'Perfection? I would never promise that. What I will give you is interesting food that respects tradition but still surprises, a blend of the old ways and modern knowledge. All I ask is that you keep an open mind about what you eat.'

This time he disappeared into the kitchen for far longer, and Tricia laboured to keep the conversation going. Moll was distracted, scribbling in her notebook, Valerie appeared half dazed and Orsolina had abandoned her hostess duties altogether and was looking bored. Still, she leapt out of her seat fast enough when she heard a knocking at the front door.

'This must be Luca now.' Her fingers fell into her hair to tidy it. 'How lucky; he's here in time for the pasta course. Can someone let Papa know?'

Tricia jumped to her feet before Valerie could beat her to it. 'I'll go and tell him. I need to use the loo anyway.'

She found the kitchen and Vincenzo, an apron round his waist, a pan of water foaming, a sauce simmering. He looked up as she walked in. 'Is everything OK?' he asked.

'Orsolina said to tell you the others have arrived.'

He grunted, reached for a tray of pasta and began to pile it into the pan with his hands. 'Luca likes to cut things fine, eh?'

'Can I help?'

'You could get the pasta bowls out. They are over there.' He nodded in the direction of an antique china cabinet that almost filled one wall. 'I also need spoons, the silver ones with the ridged handles.'

The cabinet was a trove of old ceramics and oddities; Tricia didn't recognise some of the things she found there. Assuming Vincenzo meant the plain white restaurant-style bowls, she pulled them out and placed them on the counter.

'Those spoons might need a quick polish,' he told her, tossing over a cloth.

Paul would laugh if he could see her now, rubbing the tarnish from antique cutlery. This wasn't behaviour he expected from a wife who would rather eat with plastic forks than waste time washing up. Tricia peered at a spoon, and was forced to admit she wasn't doing an especially good job of it.

'Do not worry; they are too old and worn to ever look shiny,' Vincenzo told her.

'I guess the advantage of a candlelit dining room is that no one will notice.'

'Being worn makes them even lovelier to me,' he insisted. 'I like objects with history. Things that had a life before I came along. Many Sicilians my age are the same way, I think. The young people, though, they are different.'

Tricia shrugged. 'I must be young still, then. I prefer new, not shabby.'

'But there is beauty in age and imperfection; newness can be sterile.'

Tricia was cynical. 'Luca said something similar earlier. Do you men really believe it, or is it just something you like to say to charm women my age?'

He looked surprised. 'I believe it wholeheartedly or else I wouldn't say it. Look at the patina on the metal of these old spoons that have touched a hundred mouths or more. Or the scars on the walls of the baroque palazzi on the main street, even the dents in the Piaggio Ape trucks of the vegetable sellers at the market – all have a beauty to me beyond anything perfect and new. They are more interesting.'

'So perfection is boring, then?' Tricia wondered if the man felt he had to flirt with every single woman he met.

'Yes, very boring ... so you can stop polishing my great-aunt's spoons. I need them now anyway.'

Tricia watched him mix the macaroni with a light tomato sauce and spoon it into the bowls, adding to each a couple of black olives and a sprig of rosemary. Then he took the spoons, filled them with a mixture of something crumbly and nested them artfully amid the pasta.

'Breadcrumbs, the cheese of the poor,' he told her. 'We will sprinkle them over the macaroni at the table.'

'Just breadcrumbs?' Tricia asked. 'Or have you added something else?'

'Salt, of course, and pepper, a few minced herbs.' His yellow eyes locked on to hers. 'And yes, chocolate, bittersweet and grated very finely so it becomes part of the flavour of the whole dish and you would never guess it is there.'

As he passed two full plates for her to carry, Vincenzo managed to brush his body against hers in a way Tricia knew was neither accidental nor necessary. She didn't bother to respond. Her time with Santo had been all that she needed. It was almost a relief to have it over and done with.

In the dining room the mood had shifted, thanks in the main to Poppy, who was bubbling with excitement.

This time it seemed they had got somewhere. The hairdresser's father came from a big family, many of whom had left Sicily over the years. He was almost certain that one of his uncles, who couldn't get into America, had ended up settling in Australia instead, and was going to talk to his sister, who had a better memory for these things.

'She has all the old family photograph albums too. He's going to arrange for us to meet her. He was lovely, wasn't he, Luca?' Face shining, she flicked a glance at him. 'No English, of course, and sadly he didn't seem to understand when I tried to speak a little Italian.'

Tricia watched Orsolina as the story was repeated. Her expression was guarded and it was quite impossible to tell what was going through her mind. Forking up a piece of macaroni and absent-mindedly putting it in her mouth, Tricia forgot to look out for the flavour of chocolate. Orsolina held her attention. She was making a pretty picture of herself, hair caught behind her neck and tumbling down one shoulder, the silver of her bracelets gently singing as she moved her hands to emphasise what she was saying.

'You mustn't get your hopes up,' she was advising Poppy now. 'Check anything these people tell you. Be very careful. The world is full of con artists, and the thing about them is they always seem so nice.'

'But this family have nothing to gain from being related to me,' Poppy pointed out.

'They don't know that,' said Orsolina. 'Take care, that's all. People aren't necessarily what they seem and the best of us can be hoodwinked.'

Vincenzo brought out the main course, cheeks of beef braised with rosemary and served with wilted chicory. The meat fell apart at the touch of a knife, unctuous with chocolate-spiked sauce, smoky with pancetta; still Tricia struggled to find the appetite to do it justice. She was caught up in the theatre round the table: the gradual unfolding of something between Vincenzo and Valerie, his charm at full force now, and then this tense triangle of people beside her, with Luca's expression darkening.

'There's no need to be dramatic,' he was saying to Orsolina now. 'Anyway, what would you know about con artists?'

'I've met some people who appear one way but are actually another.' She shrugged. 'I'm sure we all have.'

'That's not the case here,' Luca told her.

'Are you certain? You've only just met these people; they're strangers. Do you trust your instincts? Are they really so reliable?'

Tricia suspected they weren't talking about Poppy's potential family any more.

'Is this any of your business?' asked Luca, a little sharply.

'I'm concerned. Do I have no right to be?' Orsolina widened her eyes.

Poppy interrupted. 'Really, it's fine. I'm just going to see an old lady and look at her photo albums. There doesn't seem much risk there.'

Orsolina looked away, playing with the bracelets on her arm, sliding them up and down, saying softly, 'I guess we'll have to wait and see how things turn out.'

'I guess we will,' Luca agreed.

Tricia took a last mouthful of the beef dish and lined up her knife and fork to show she had finished. 'What an extraordinary dinner,' she said. 'In more ways than one.'

Moll must have assumed she meant the setting. 'Oh yes, this wonderful dining room. And the food ... do you think you might share the recipe for the beef, or is it a family secret?'

'I do not believe in secrets when it comes to recipes,' Vincenzo said.

'So I can put it on my blog?'

'Of course, I would be devastated if you didn't.' Vincenzo smiled at her, his pale eyes glittering in the candlelight.

Moll giggled and her cheeks coloured. So even she wasn't entirely immune to the man's appeal, Tricia observed.

He was clearing the dinner plates now, Moll standing up to help and peppering him with questions about chocolate and meat, the best ways to bring them together and balance out their flavours. He focused on her (that stare that singled you out), nodding as he replied, making her laugh and blush again.

Tricia supposed flirting was his way of being, as much a part of him as his passion for chocolate. She glanced at Valerie. How much store was she setting by this man? She hoped not much at all.

The meal ended with balls of candied citrus peel dipped in powdered sugar. Vincenzo served them with cups of strong black coffee spiced with cardamom and glasses of sticky, dark gold dessert wine.

'No chocolate for dessert?' Tricia was surprised.

'No, because you expected it.' Vincenzo looked smug. 'And why would I do what is expected of me?'

As the evening seemed to be coming to its end, Vincenzo suggested they take a *passeggiata* along Favio's main street and perhaps stop at the bar in the piazza for a final drink.

'After a meal like this, I enjoy a glass of whisky on ice,' he said. 'If I have worked hard in the kitchen, I think I deserve it.'

Orsolina fetched their handbags and wraps from the anteroom in the hallway. She made a game of trying to remember which bag belonged to which woman. Moll's scuffed satchel proved no challenge, neither did Tricia's Marc Jacobs clutch. But she struggled to decide who matched with the slightly worn caramel-coloured leather tote

'Now whose is this? I don't recall. Let's see if I can guess. It's stylish, so it may belong to Valerie. But it's practical too, like Poppy. Hmm, I may have to look for a clue.' Orsolina peered inside playfully. 'There's a book in it. That may help.'

What she pulled out of the bag wasn't really a book but a mess of cobbled-together pages, covered in neat slanted writing and caught with an elastic band.

'But that's not mine,' Poppy said, confused.

'What the hell ...' Luca exclaimed at the same time. He snatched the book. 'What the hell,' he repeated.

'I didn't put that in my bag,' Poppy insisted. 'What is it anyway?'

'This is my nonna's recipe book,' said Luca. 'The one I told you about that has been lost for all this time. Why do you have it?'

'This woman must have found your book and taken it,' Orsolina said quickly. 'That's the only explanation. She's a thief.'

Luca held the bundle to his nose, inhaling the smell of its musty paper. Sliding off the elastic band, he turned the pages.

Some of the recipes were scrawled on the backs of old pasta packets, some on waxed paper saved from meat wrappings; all were in the same handwriting. 'Where did you find it?' he asked Poppy.

'I didn't find it,' she exclaimed. 'I've no idea what it's doing there. Someone must have put it in my bag.'

Tricia glanced at Moll and Valerie and, seeing they were stunned too, struggled to gather her wits. Someone had to speak up for Poppy.

'It's quite obvious what has happened here,' she said, coolly enough, she thought.

'It is?' Poppy still looked confused.

'That book was planted in your bag by a person who doesn't want Luca to trust you. Someone who is jealous.'

Angrily, Vincenzo interrupted. 'What are you saying?'

'Well, it would have to be someone who is close to Luca, wouldn't it, who has had access to his house over the years,' Tricia continued. 'Perhaps this person helped with the renovations, advised on the decor, and found this book ... and has kept it until now ... for some reason.'

'Orsolina?' Luca's voice was quiet and low.

'Don't be ridiculous. This woman took your book, not me.'

He shook his head at her.

'Which of us do you trust?' Orsolina demanded. 'The woman you have known all her life or the one who was a stranger until a few days ago?'

Vincenzo attempted to take charge. 'There must have been a misunderstanding,' he said, taking his daughter's arm. 'Perhaps it is time to say *buona notte*. Tomorrow when heads are cooler we can talk about this again.'

'No!' Orsolina shook off his hand.

'*Cara*, *cara*, no,' Vincenzo spoke to her quickly and quietly in Italian.

'I'm trying to stop Luca making a mistake,' Orsolina cried back at him in English.

Tricia watched as Valerie opened the front door and slipped out quietly. Moll followed, but there was no way she was going to do the same. This drama held her.

Luca turned to Orsolina. 'I thought you were my friend,' he said, sadly. 'I thought we cared about each other. Why did you take my nonna's book? You knew what it meant to me.'

'It was in *her* bag,' she argued.

Tricia intervened again. 'Yes, because you put it there. Come on, this is silly. Why would Poppy want to steal a tatty old recipe book that means nothing to anyone but Luca?'

'I can't imagine what her motives were,' Orsolina snapped.

'But I think we all know what yours are,' Tricia countered. 'And it seems a pretty tragic attempt to me. I'd have expected something smarter from you.'

'Me too,' Luca said, his face a mask of disappointment. 'I've always thought better of you than this, Orsolina. What can have possessed you, when you knew I was turning the house upside down in search of Nonna's book?'

'I was trying to help you,' Orsolina burst out. 'The builders were making such a terrible mess and the book would have been destroyed, so I took it for safe keeping. I meant to give it back. Then life got busy and it slipped my mind.'

'Until now,' said Tricia.

She lifted her chin. 'I was trying to stop my friend, who I love a great deal, from making another big mistake with his life. Maybe it was the wrong thing to do, but I couldn't think of another.'

Luca shook his head. 'Orsolina, have you gone crazy?'

'You know better than anyone the lengths people will go to, the things they'll do,' she said, harshly. 'Haven't you tricked and lied just to get a picture ... just for money? What I did was for love, not greed, and that doesn't seem crazy to me.'

'*Basta!* Enough!' Vincenzo thundered.

'I agree, it is enough, and we are leaving.' Luca took

Poppy's arm. 'That was a wonderful dinner, my friend; it's a shame it had to end so badly.'

Tricia followed them out of the door, unable to resist stealing a look back. She glimpsed Orsolina tight in her father's arms, her head tucked into the folds of his shirt. It sounded like she was crying.

Out in the dark lane, the others were waiting. They walked back to the cookery school briskly and without a word. Only once they were inside, still puffing from the climb up the steps, did Poppy put her hand to her mouth and say, 'Oh my God.'

'I'm so sorry,' Luca apologised.

'It's not your fault.'

'She's my friend, I took you there.'

'Well at least you got your nonna's book back,' said Poppy. 'Would you let us have a proper look at it?'

Luca placed the worn old book on the kitchen table and leafed through its scuffed pages slowly and carefully, reading the names of the recipes aloud and translating here and there. 'This is her recipe for salami. I remember how the whole family would get together to make it, all my aunts and cousins too, always in winter so the salami didn't spoil while it was hanging. It was like a sort of festival.'

He flicked further into the book. 'Here is how she made her fried fava beans, and here's a recipe to use up the wild fennel we found growing at the roadside. These are instructions on how to peel a prickly pear and turn it into a jelly. Some of these recipes I thought I'd forgotten, but seeing them now is almost like tasting them again.'

'And all this time Orsolina has had it,' Tricia said.

Luca nodded bleakly. 'All this time.'

Food of Love

It is that point in the night where if you wake you worry, and Luca Amore is awake. His body is curled round hers; their skin pressed together, his heart thudding into her back. He would like to fall from this moment quickly into sleep, but his mind is too noisy to let him.

He listens to her breathing and wonders how it will end. Will he drive her to the airport in Catania and see her for the last time on a crowded concourse? Will she promise to come back again? Or will she find it too difficult to tell a lie simply to make him feel better?

Luca imagines how it will feel to know she is somewhere in the world but not in his. Perhaps they will Skype and e-mail until one day they don't. Maybe she will be his Facebook friend and he will follow her life on his news feed. The thought depresses him. He wants to discuss it with her, to find some way to be together. But she is dreaming, her breath slow and steady, every limb relaxed, and Luca can't disturb her.

He opens his eyes, wondering how many hours there are left until dawn. If he rolls away from her, then he might check the clock that is on the nightstand beside the book he wants to keep close so he never loses it again. He is struggling to believe his friend has had it hidden all this time. He wonders why. At first he was angry, but now he only feels sad.

Was the book a part of him for Orsolina to keep? Did she

hope *so* badly for more? Luca is stunned. He thought he had made himself clear years ago. He wasn't for her. She was a sister, a lifelong friend; he thought she understood this. From time to time he saw her in the company of other men and assumed she had moved on. But she has wasted years and years. She has held on to his nonna's book and schemed.

Now Luca must do some scheming of his own. He closes his eyes and rests his face against the nape of Poppy's neck, softly, so the movement doesn't wake her. Outside he hears a dog barking and the rumble of a truck driving past. Favio is beginning to stir. He tightens his arm round her belly, feels its rise and fall, the warmth of her skin and the blood beneath it. He knows she is embarking on a new phase of her life; he wants to be part of it.

Valerie

Oh poor Vincenzo, to have gone to all that trouble and then have the evening end so badly. What a hare-brained idea of Orsolina's that was. I guess there was a chance Luca might have been taken in ... at least for a while ... but it wasn't going to make him fall in love with her, was it? That's something you can't force, no matter how much you plot and plan.

Yes, sure, a cup of coffee would be lovely if you're making it ... I'm dying for one.

Imagine how embarrassed Orsolina must feel this morning, and how sad. I'd love to go and talk to her. Haven't we all made fools of ourselves over a man at some point? When you fall so hard, it's difficult not to. It would be nice to have the chance to tell her that.

I can remember years ago, when I was silly and young ... no, not trying to trick anyone, but having a lapse of pride when it came to certain men. Turning up in places where I thought they might be in the hope they'd ask me out. Making phone calls long after they had stopped, failing to take hints, being a little too persistent – that sort of thing.

Suddenly you meet someone and it all seems to click together for reasons you never really understand. At least you tell yourself it's clicked.

Both my husbands pursued me. They were men who could have had any woman they wanted – smart and handsome, so much fun – and they chose me, just an ordinary Manhattan girl who worked behind the accessories counter in Henri Bendel. Looking back, perhaps I was flattered rather than properly in love.

With Jean-Pierre, it was different. To begin with, I wasn't sure. I liked him, we had great times together, but I'd been bitten twice so was cautious. Something smouldered and flamed between us. It burned hotter and hotter all the years we were together. If he had been someplace without me, I never set eyes on him again without feeling a flicker of desire. He was the same right to the end ... well, almost.

I loved Jean-Pierre and he loved me back completely. That's a wonderful feeling, the very best. It's trust and passion, security and excitement, all bundled up together. You'd never think it's possible to have it all, but it is.

Still, love isn't like riding a horse or driving a car. Just because you get it right once doesn't mean you will a second time. There are no guarantees for any of us, and perhaps it might make Orsolina feel a little better to know that. To think of her feeling ashamed – and Vincenzo ashamed of her ... I don't want to interfere, but at the same time ...

What do you think? Should I drop by the *dolceria* for a few minutes just to be sure they're OK? Or would that be inappropriate?

Vincenzo's been so kind to me, I'd like to help. It would mean something.

Day Seven

(i) The smell of coffee beans & an awakening

The rose-gold dress was hanging from the door frame. It was the first thing Valerie saw when she opened her eyes. Last night, wearing it, she had felt almost beautiful. There was a moment, at the dining table in the flattering candlelight, with Vincenzo's eyes on her, when the years had slipped away and she forgot her skin wasn't smooth and her hair was no longer thick and glossy.

This morning the dress still looked beautiful, but Valerie was herself again. Staring in the mirror, she wondered how seeing her reflection might make her feel five years from now, or ten. Perhaps she would have stopped caring by then, but she doubted it. Pulling her hair into a low chignon, she made a half-hearted attempt to do her face before going downstairs to find coffee.

Sitting in the kitchen chatting with Moll and Tricia (no sign of the others), all the talk was of the extraordinary evening they'd had.

'Can you believe Orsolina would do such a thing?' Moll was still incredulous. 'I'd realised she was manipulative, but trying to make Poppy look like a thief … I never thought she'd go that far.'

'Put yourself in her shoes; she wants him really, really badly,' said Tricia.

'You don't get everything you want in life. That's a lesson all of us have to learn.' Moll was staunch.

Valerie felt sorry for the girl. What she had done wasn't right, nor was it especially clever. It had spoiled the evening (and her own foolish hopes of it). It had distressed everyone. But love could drive a woman in the wrong direction. Surely it didn't mean Orsolina was a bad person, even if perhaps she deserved to feel that way this morning.

No one could agree if it would be the right thing for Valerie to drop by the *dolceria* if she got a chance.

'Surely it would be good manners?' said Moll. 'After all, we never thanked him properly for that wonderful meal. And if any of us were to go, it should be you, Val.'

'It's awkward, isn't it?' Valerie mused. 'I don't want to pry, but we may not get a chance to see them again and I'd hate this to be the way we left things.'

'Luca will catch up with them both eventually,' Tricia pointed out. 'He can say thanks on our behalf.'

'Yes.' Valerie hesitated. 'But still ...'

Moll made a pot of coffee, and as Valerie sipped on hers, she thought about the chocolate-maker. Would he welcome a visit or prefer to be left alone? She was uncertain, but suspected Jean-Pierre might have told her to stop overthinking things; to go with her gut instinct.

'There may not be enough time anyway,' pointed out Tricia. 'Our schedule today is pretty busy. We're going for a coffee-tasting, then a picnic lunch by the sea.'

'Perhaps there'll be a moment after that,' Moll suggested. 'I think you're right, Val, this is an awful note to leave things on.'

'They won't care. We'll be the last things on their minds.' Tricia sounded certain.

'On Orsolina's mind, perhaps, but not Vincenzo's,' Moll argued. 'He'll be thinking of us ... of Val ... I'm sure.'

'If you ask me, they're peas in a pod, those two.' Tricia shrugged. 'But really, do what you like.'

Valerie resolved to go with her gut instinct, whatever it

was; she wasn't entirely sure yet. After the morning's activities, she might have a clearer idea. 'I think we may have some free time this afternoon before our final cooking lesson,' she said. 'Possibly I'll swing by then. We'll see.'

Hearing the sound of a key turning in the lock, they all looked over at the front door expectantly. Poppy, trying to slip in quietly, seemed startled to see them.

'Oh, hello, I thought you might all be sleeping in,' she said, awkwardly. 'It was a late night, wasn't it?'

'For you, perhaps, but I dropped off the moment my head hit the pillow,' replied Tricia, mischievously.

Her words failed to get a rise out of Poppy. 'I'd better go and change,' was all she said. 'I think Luca will be here in a minute.'

As she disappeared upstairs, Tricia turned to Moll. 'She must know that we know, right?' she said in a low voice. 'I mean, particularly after that scene last night … how could we not?'

'I expect so, but there's no harm in being discreet, is there?'

'So I'm not to ask her about Luca? Is that what you're saying?'

'I wasn't aware you needed my permission.' Moll's tone was chilly.

Valerie hoped they weren't building up to another fight. She put her fingers to her forehead and felt the throb of a coming headache.

'I don't want to get you all riled up,' Tricia told Moll. 'Not after we've managed to be civil to each other for the past few days.'

Moll stared at her. There was an expression on her face almost of pity. 'Ask Poppy whatever you want. Just don't involve me, OK?' she said.

'OK,' said Tricia lightly.

*

The atmosphere was strained, and, arriving with breakfast, Luca didn't do much to improve it. This morning he seemed subdued. He went through the routine of setting the table, laying out pastries and fruit, but when Moll questioned him about the morning's coffee-tasting, his answers were brief.

The same awkward silence stayed with them throughout breakfast and followed them down to the car, where Poppy sat at the back instead of beside Luca, and Tricia and Moll kept their distance.

Fortunately it was a short drive. The coffee-roaster was in a small warehouse in the highest part of town. Luca accompanied them inside, introducing them to an old man wearing a hessian apron and a jaunty hat folded out of a sheet of newspaper.

'This is Enrico Molinari. He speaks excellent English so I'm going to leave you with him for a while to learn about his coffee,' he said.

Valerie watched him go. She thought she detected something defeated in the slump of his shoulders – unless perhaps she was overthinking things again.

The old man gave out newspaper hats for them to wear, smiling at the sight, and insisting on photographs. Her hat made Valerie itch. It was stuffy in the roasting room, the air heady with coffee beans and the noise of the machines that heated and cooled them deafening.

She listened to the spiel about coffee, the different types of beans and the method of processing. The man talked at length about the perfect *crema*, of acidity, density, viscosity. Valerie thought she was paying attention, but at the finish she couldn't have said whether in the north they preferred the flavour of arabica beans and in the south the character of fine robusta, or if it was the other way around.

Moll was at the front of their little group, and scribbling furiously, so she should know. She was asking questions, shouting above the machines, and listening intently as Enrico bellowed something about nuances of honey and liquorice, about lingering mouth feel and middle notes of caramel and chocolate.

Valerie was losing patience with this. The smell of coffee was seeping into her clothes, hair and pores, the noise of the factory worsening her headache. She was sure it wasn't a long walk back to the cookery school, and mostly downhill. If she hurried, there might even be time to stop in at the *dolceria* on the way.

Touching Poppy's arm to attract her attention, she put her other hand to her temple. 'Not feeling great,' she said. 'Going to take a walk, get some fresh air. I'll see you back at the house in a little while.'

'Shall I come with you?' Poppy sounded concerned.

'No need, I'll be fine once I've cleared my head.'

Valerie felt better the instant she was outside and breathing air that wasn't scorched with coffee. She wasn't certain of the way, but so long as she headed steadily downhill, she thought she should find a part of Favio she recognised.

It was more difficult than she'd expected. The narrow lanes curved and twisted, turning back on themselves; the maze of steps seemed to do the same. Valerie was hot and breathless by the time she realised she was on course for the cathedral, and very nearly there. Her pretty coral shirt had fixed itself to her back, her hair was loosening from its pins and she was sure she must look a fright. There was no time to waste worrying, however. She had realised that her gut instinct was to find Vincenzo Mazzara while she had the chance.

She didn't waver, not even when she reached the *dolceria*.

'*Buongiorno*,' she called, pushing open the door, hoping to hear the peal of Orsolina's voice saying good morning in reply. But there was no sign of her, and an unfamiliar woman was in her place manning the till. Despite her English being barely coherent, she managed to convey that neither Mazzara father nor daughter were there.

'Are they at home?' Valerie asked. 'Will I find them there?'

The woman gestured to the shelves behind her. 'You want chocolate?' she asked.

'No, no, not today, thanks.'

Back on the lane, Valerie paused, trying to make up her mind what to do next. Gut instinct, she reminded herself. She continued on, stopping at the door set in the rock wall and hammering on it. When there was no reply, she knocked again.

At long last Vincenzo opened up. She was shocked at the sight of him. He was still wearing the striped shirt he'd had on last night, but now it was crumpled and open to the waist, with the sleeves rolled high. His eyes were red-rimmed and pouchy, his expression weary.

'Now is not a good time, *cara*, I am sorry,' he said, hurriedly buttoning up his shirt.

'I came to see if you're both OK.'

'That is kind of you. But right now we are not OK, no.'

'Could you pass a message to Orsolina?'

He nodded. 'Of course.'

Valerie paused, trying to decide how best to put this.

'Signora?' Vincenzo prompted.

'I wanted her to know she's not alone; to tell her that most of us have done crazy things for the sake of some man we've been in love with ... yes, me included. It feels terrible now, but in time it won't. That's all.'

He opened the door a little wider. 'My daughter does not feel terrible. Not at all. That is the trouble.'

'No?' She was surprised.

'I have spent all night talking to her, but it hasn't helped.' He sighed. 'She needs her mother.'

Valerie felt helpless. 'It must be very hard.'

'It is impossible.' Vincenzo rubbed a hand over his face. 'Perhaps you should come in after all. Talk to her if she will see you ... it cannot do any harm.'

Valerie stepped inside. The air smelt stale and the light was dim, but not so much that she couldn't see last night's dishes littering the dining table.

'She will not eat,' Vincenzo told her, sounding weary. 'I was making some chocolate for her to drink. I do not know what else to do.'

Valerie followed him to the kitchen and watched as he whisked melted chocolate with a dash of liqueur and a grind of cardamom. He used a wooden beater with a worn handle and the muscles in his arm worked as the chocolate foamed.

'Taste,' he instructed, pouring out a little.

Obediently, she took a sip. 'Yes, it's very good.'

Vincenzo filled a cup with thick, steaming chocolate and put it on a tray with a couple of paper serviettes and a plate of sugared biscuits.

'Stay here while I take this up,' he told Valerie. 'Maybe she will see you, but I don't hold out much hope.'

Waiting for him to return, Valerie cast a look round the kitchen. It seemed that Vincenzo had managed to create the most terrible mess last night, as well as a beautiful meal. There were stacks of plates and pans covered in smears and congealing food. There were graters clogged with chocolate, presses, grinders and whisks, so many different pieces of equipment and none of them clean.

She looked for the dishwasher, but they didn't seem to have one. So, pushing up her sleeves, she began to fill the sink with hot soapy water. At least this was one thing she could do to help.

She cleared the table, washed dinnerware and contemplated the pots. Still there was no sign of him, and she wondered how the conversation was going up there in Orsolina's room.

At last she heard Vincenzo's voice. 'Signora, my apologies ...' He paused in the doorway, taken aback. 'You did not have to do this, to clean for me. I am mortified.'

'Please, don't be, it was nothing.'

Sinking into a chair at the kitchen table, Vincenzo said, 'Thank you ... for all this, and for coming ... I appreciate it.'

'She won't see me, will she?'

He shook his head.

'Most likely I wouldn't have been much help anyway. When you're young, you don't think old people understand a thing, do you?'

'But truly I do not understand,' he admitted. 'Yes, I see why Orsolina did what she did last night. I know how she feels about Luca. But why will she not give up? Why not admit she was wrong?'

'She thinks it was justified?'

'She says she is fighting for him; that he is worth it. I have tried to show her he is a man like any other. I have shared details I was told in confidence because I thought they might alter her opinion, but no. She is stubborn and determined. She refuses even to apologise.'

Valerie saw it had been wrong to imagine she knew how the girl was feeling. This was someone very different to her. Still, she tried to offer a little guidance.

'Perhaps you need to leave it for now,' she suggested. 'Things have a way of working themselves out, don't they? Surely this will too.'

He sighed. 'I hope so. There is nothing left for me to say to her.'

'I'm sure you've done everything you can ... all her mother might have done too.' Valerie hoped to comfort him. 'After all, if she's so set in her opinions, words won't change them. She'll have to learn herself, the hard way.'

'I am afraid she will,' he agreed.

'And hopefully soon, before she wastes her best years,' added Valerie with feeling.

Vincenzo tilted his head to one side, his expression keener now. 'You think the best years come in youth, signora? But that is not necessarily true.'

'In my experience it is.'

'Our later years can bring different pleasures with them, gentler ones perhaps, but not necessarily inferior,' he insisted.

Valerie might have come here with advice to hand out, but it seemed the tables were being turned. She stared at Vincenzo. He had tidied his appearance while he was upstairs, changed his shirt for a fresh one, combed his hair and washed his face. He would be handsome at any age; she could see that.

'It's different for men,' she told him.

Getting up from his chair, he came and stood next to her, very close, beside the kitchen counter. 'It need not be.'

Valerie caught her breath. She took a half-step away.

'I ...'

For a moment he only stared at her. Then he reached out a hand and placed two fingers over her mouth, pushing gently until her lips opened around them. His fingers were roughened by work and tasted faintly sweet. Valerie closed her eyes and he moved closer, tilting his hips to hers. He pressed between her shoulder blades and she felt him run his thumb down the length of her spine. She heard herself gasp.

'You want me to kiss you, signora?' he asked.

She swallowed and nodded. 'Yes.'

Vincenzo came so near, she sensed the warmth of his breath on her face.

'Now do you feel the way you did when you were young?' he asked.

'Yes,' she whispered. 'I'm starting to.'

He took both her breasts in his hands. 'Me too.'

Valerie forgot everything when he kissed her; forgot her head had ever ached, forgot to hate the way her body had softened and sagged, forgot his daughter sulking in her room upstairs, forgot even Jean-Pierre. She leaned back against the kitchen counter, feeling his hands all over her now, and not as gentle.

And then she heard a clatter and the sound of something shattering on the stone floor.

'Papa!' Orsolina was standing in the kitchen archway, white-faced and angry, her empty chocolate cup smashed at her feet.

Vincenzo's hands fell away, his lips left Valerie's and his head turned towards his daughter.

'*Vai via*, Orsolina,' he said, shortly. 'Go away.'

'You know how I'm feeling now, how much I need you, and you're down here with this woman all this time, making love to her,' Orsolina spat out furiously in English.

Vincenzo turned to Valerie, his expression regretful. 'She is right: my timing is very bad. Signora, I am sorry.'

Valerie felt shaky. 'I'm sorry too,' she said, looking from father to daughter. 'I should go.'

'*Si, si*, I think so,' agreed Orsolina.

Taking her purse from the kitchen table, Valerie escaped the room. Vincenzo didn't try to follow her, although he might have called out another apology, but his voice was muffled and she couldn't be sure.

Out on the lane, she tried to gather herself, but her face was heated and her hands still trembling. They had come so close. Next Vincenzo might have undressed her; he might have laid her on the leather couch in his living room, taken her to his bed. Valerie couldn't stop her heart from racing, couldn't help imagining it. She felt poisoned with disappointment.

Slowly she trailed down the main street and up the steps to the cookery school, hoping that the others had left for their picnic so she could be alone to finish what Vincenzo had started. But for the second time that day her timing was wrong. Opening the front door, she found Poppy and Luca standing behind it clutching picnic baskets.

Luca seemed relieved. 'I was wondering where you'd got to. The others thought you might be with Vincenzo ...'

Flustered, Valerie was lost for a reply, but he only waited a beat or two before asking, 'How were things there?'

She grimaced. 'Not good.'

'Yes,' he said, regretfully. 'That's what I thought.'

If only she'd had her wits about her, Valerie might have found an excuse not to join them on the picnic. Instead she found herself heading back down the steps, helping Poppy carry one of the picnic baskets (they were heavy) and making small talk.

Luca's mood appeared to have picked up. He stowed the baskets in the back of the car, promising them all sorts of treats for lunch, and radiating enthusiasm for the nature reserve where they would enjoy it.

As he drove, he talked to them about the history of Sicily's food and how precious salt once was, then tuna fish. How in times past, the place they were going to had supplied the area with both.

Valerie drifted in and out. She kept thinking of being touched and how her body had responded. Yes, she was older now, but nothing had changed. Nothing. She might have felt relieved had she not been left so wanting.

There was a heat shimmer over the tarmac on the road ahead. The others were putting on sunscreen and hats, taking bottles of cold water, readying themselves. Valerie wondered if, back at the Mazzara house, they were still sitting in the half-light of a shuttered room, locked in hopeless conversation.

Outside the car there was the faintest of sea breezes, that stiffened as they followed the boardwalk across the marshy coastline. It freshened the air and helped clear Valerie's head a little, and although she lagged behind the others, her pace wasn't too much slower.

The path wound between tall grasses towards a blue band of sea on the horizon. As she walked, Valerie smelt wild fennel and rosemary. With every step her head cleared a little more until finally she began to see how she had been wrong. There *were* other men like Jean-Pierre, men who shimmered and shone, men who could bring more life to everything around them, including her. She must have narrowed down her world to stop seeing them.

Luca was waiting for her to catch up. He wanted to talk about bird life and conservation, about the rare plants that grew on these salty marshes and the tuna fishery out on the far point that they were to visit before eating lunch.

'Do you mind if I stay on the beach?' Valerie asked. 'I could mind the picnic baskets.'

'Is your head still aching?' Poppy sounded sympathetic.

'Just a little,' she lied.

They found a spot, far enough away from other people, and Luca laid down a rug for her to sit on. 'We'll be back soon,' he told her. 'There's only the ruins of the cannery to see, and that won't take long.'

'Be as long as you like, I'll be fine,' Valerie promised.

She watched them walk away, three women and a man she hadn't known a week ago but who now meant something to her. She hoped they would all stay in touch. Perhaps Tricia would vacation in New York and they'd have lunch together; perhaps Poppy might stop over for a few days and stay. She might buy herself a laptop and keep up with Moll's blog. Send e-mails to Luca when she cooked a dish he had taught her.

Vincenzo Mazzara she had no hopes of. She suspected that their moment had passed. Still, now that she had opened her eyes, perhaps she might see others like him. She was beginning to hope so.

Rolling up the legs of her linen pants, she wandered to the tide line to take a wade in the sea. The water chilled her ankles as it lapped them, but she paddled on a little deeper until it reached her calves.

Her next vacation would be on a coastline, she decided.

She might return to the South of France, or explore someplace new. There were apartments that could be rented and friends who might join her; perhaps even one of the new ones she had made here.

Valerie was glad Jean-Pierre could not see what she had become in the year she had been without him. She had grown afraid of herself. She had given herself up. It was long past time for that to change.

Standing now among the waves that foamed towards the beach, her toes sinking into the wet sand, she felt a strength in her body. She raised her arms in the air, stretched her fingertips to the cloudless sky. She breathed.

By the time the others returned, she had managed (by dint of a lot of wriggling beneath a beach towel) to change into her swimsuit.

'I'm going to take a dip before lunch,' she called to Luca. 'Is that OK?'

She heard the others agreeing that they would love to cool off with a swim. Valerie didn't wait for them. Running down the beach, she plunged into the sea, ducking her head beneath the waves and gasping as she came back to the surface.

'Is it cold?' Poppy called to her.

'Yes!' she yelled back. 'But it feels wonderful.'

Valerie had always been a good swimmer, not fast, but once she found her rhythm she felt as if she could keep going for ever. She hadn't dipped a toe into the sea since that last time in France when Jean-Pierre had been so sick and she hadn't wanted to leave him for more than a few moments. Now there was nothing to stop her, and she swam until she was out of her depth, out beyond the breakers, then turned parallel to the shoreline and began an easy crawl, enjoying the kick of her legs and the feel of her arms moving through the water.

She swam the length of the beach (it was a long one), then turned to head back towards the point. By now she was beginning to tire, but she pushed on, switching to breast-stroke. The others were dots on the beach ahead, and she wondered what they were thinking: that she had lost her mind, forgotten her age? Well perhaps she had. She spat out a mouthful of seawater. And so what? It might even be a good thing.

Poppy was down at the water's edge waiting with her beach towel when she hauled herself out of the water, dripping and exhilarated.

'Wow, that was quite a swim,' she said.

Valerie grinned. 'Yes, I know.'

They had opened the picnic baskets already and started eating without her. Valerie was famished. Once she had dried off and a fresh towel was wrapped round her shoulders, Luca passed her a sandwich. It was only a rough hunk of ciabatta filled with shards of cheese, flakes of dried chilli and sliced green olives, the bread softened with a little grassy oil, but it tasted wonderful. She finished every last crumb, then grazed on a cold fritter of prosciutto, parsley and cheese, artichokes that had been preserved in lemony oil, and a salad of beans with sweet shallots, the seawater trickling from her wet hair and down the back of her neck as she gazed out at the stretch of blue she had conquered.

'I didn't know you were such a good swimmer,' said Moll, admiringly.

'I'm out of practice,' she admitted. 'I expect I'll be sore later. Still, it felt good.'

Even once the baskets had been packed up, no one was in a hurry to leave the beach. Luca produced a bottle of Prosecco from a cooler bag and poured them all a little.

'Here's to the best group I've ever had at the Food of Love Cookery School,' he said, raising his glass.

'Are we really?' Moll looked pleased. 'Will you miss us, Luca?'

'Certainly I will. But we have tomorrow still to come,

don't we?' He glanced at Poppy. 'So no need to start worrying about missing each other yet, I guess.'

'It's gone so fast,' said Moll. 'Mind you, sad as I'll be to leave, I'll be glad to see my girls again.'

'I'm ready to go home too,' agreed Tricia. 'Back to normal life again.'

Valerie noticed that Poppy stayed silent. She stared at the sea, swirling the Prosecco in her glass but not taking a sip.

(ii) The flavour of wild fennel & a dilemma

On the way back to the car, Valerie once again helped Poppy with the picnic basket while Luca darted on and off the boardwalk foraging for fronds of wild fennel, careful to remove only a few from each plant. Soon he had collected a couple of feathery handfuls and he stopped to let them smell its fragrance of sweet anise before stowing it in his cooler bag and disappearing to find more.

Poppy seemed to be flagging, walking more and more slowly, until they had fallen well behind the others. Only when she began softly speaking did it occur to Valerie that she was doing it on purpose.

'Do you mind if I ask your advice about something?' she said.

'Sure, if you like, although I can't promise to be much help.'

'You can keep a secret?'

'Yes, I can do that,' Valerie assured her.

'Not now, though.' Poppy lowered her voice further as Luca reappeared. 'Later on, I'll come to your room.'

'OK.'

If the mystery had something to do with Luca, then Valerie suspected she might not be the best one to give advice. Theirs was a romance she wanted to see work out. She liked them both and felt invested in it.

'Give me a moment to have a shower, then come and find me,' she said anyway.

'Thanks.' Poppy smiled. 'I appreciate it.'

Valerie's skin felt sticky with salt and her hair was drying in ringlets. She was drowsy on the drive back, with the afternoon sun pouring in through the windows on her side of the van and the air-conditioning struggling. She drifted off to the sound of Moll's voice and woke minutes later as the van hit a pothole to hear her still talking. No one else seemed inclined to join in. Tricia was punching the keys on her iPhone and Poppy was staring out the window. Valerie wondered if either of them was even listening.

'Sorry, what was that you were saying?' she asked Moll, forcing open her eyes.

'I was talking about foraging for food,' she replied. 'You can find wild fennel in England, you know, and lots of other things too. Nettle tops to cook in soups, seaweeds, mushrooms of course. There's so much free food out there growing wild, and it's much better for you than the stuff you buy.'

'Do you go foraging?' asked Valerie, interested.

'I did a guided walk up on Hampstead Heath,' Moll told her. 'We found all sorts of edible plants growing right there in the middle of London: chickweed, burdock, willowherb, plantain. It made a good post for my blog. Showed there are food adventures to be had even close to home.'

'What do you think your next adventure will be?' Valerie wondered.

Moll frowned. 'I don't know really. I hadn't planned beyond this trip.'

Valerie failed to stifle a yawn. 'I'm sure you'll find something,' she said through it.

She dozed on and off for the rest of the drive, and when Luca finally pulled over, it was an effort to get out of the car. She felt the tug of muscles in her legs and shoulders, the soreness in her arms, and almost took pleasure in it. It was like a reward.

She showered quickly, not wanting Poppy to knock and go unheard above the sound of rushing water. Still, she was barely dressed when she heard her at the door.

'Come in. Where are the others?' she asked, glancing out into the hallway.

'I think they're both in their rooms. We've got a little time before our cooking lesson ...' Poppy hesitated. 'If you'd rather take the chance to rest ...'

'No, not at all. Sit down. Tell me what's on your mind.'

'Before I start, will you promise me again that you won't say a word of this to anyone? I never said I'd keep it a secret ... but I feel as if I ought to.'

'I absolutely promise you, hand on heart,' said Valerie.

Poppy rummaged in her tote, pulling out a plain brown A4 envelope that she gave to Valerie.

'Luca took these,' she said. 'He had them developed and gave them to me this morning before the picnic.'

Valerie examined the photographs she found inside the envelope. There were four of them, all showing Poppy asleep in bed, hair streaming over the pillows, with a sheet up to her shoulders. She looked peaceful and happy.

'I'd guessed about you two, of course,' she said, wondering if this was her secret. 'We all had.'

Poppy nodded. 'I know.'

Valerie slipped the photographs back into their envelope. 'So what's the problem, then?'

Poppy sat down on the bed, curling her legs under her. 'Luca is the most amazing man I've ever met,' she said. 'The way he's made me feel ... it's almost as if I'm struggling to catch up with myself.'

'And?'

'He wants me to stay in Favio for longer so we can get to know each other.'

'You don't want to?'

'No, I do want to ... I'm just not sure if I should.'

'But why?' Valerie didn't understand it at all. 'You're your own boss, aren't you? Surely you can take another couple of weeks' vacation.'

'It's not just that.' Poppy took the envelope back from Valerie, hugging it to her chest. 'What if I've got him wrong? What if he's not the person I think he is?'

'That's a risk you'll have to take with any man you meet.'

'I know that. But with Luca, I don't trust my judgement.'

'Because you got it so wrong with your ex-husband?' Valerie guessed.

'I didn't get Brendan wrong at all; I got myself wrong. He's hard-working, decent, predictable, just like I thought. It turned out I didn't want those things.'

'And Luca?'

'Luca, it seems, is two men.'

And then Poppy spilled out her story and Valerie was astonished, straining to imagine the Luca she knew doing any of the things she described.

'He showed me the pictures,' Poppy told her. 'He must have followed her all day, every day.'

'Weren't there lots of them trailing round after her? The paparazzi?'

'Luca is the only one I've ever met.'

'Yes, I see.'

'He swears it's in the past, that he's a changed man, but I can't be sure which Luca I'll be getting. That's my problem.'

'The only way to know is to risk staying and find out,' pointed out Valerie.

'What if I'm not brave enough?'

Valerie wasn't certain what to say. 'Very often we're braver than we think ...' she began.

Poppy shook her head. 'Not me, I've never done anything especially courageous in my life. And to fall in love with a man who lives on the other side of the world ... is it just holiday madness?'

Valerie might have mentioned gut instinct, except following her own hadn't worked out so well recently. 'We don't choose who we love,' she said instead.

'I do get to make a choice. I can stay or go. That's what it all hinges on.'

Valerie didn't envy her the dilemma. 'What do you really *want*?' she asked.

'I suppose I want Luca to be the person I thought he was at the beginning. The one who was charming and handsome, who looked after us all. He's all of that, of course, but other things too ... and that's the problem.'

'Yes, I see,' Valerie said for a second time.

'There's no easy answer, is there?' Poppy was rueful.

'Why do you think he gave you those photographs?' Valerie wondered.

'He said they're how happiness looks.' She glanced down at the envelope. 'His and mine.'

'Ah.' Valerie was touched by the gesture, as she knew he had expected Poppy to be. 'I guess you have another day to make up your mind.'

'I almost wish I didn't. I can't think of anything else but this. It's exhausting.'

'I don't even know how to begin to advise you,' Valerie admitted.

'Well what do you think you might do in my place?'

Valerie thought of Vincenzo, trying to imagine how she might have reacted if he had asked her to stay with him. But their situations were so different she found it was no help at all. 'I have no idea ... it would depend on so many things. I'm sorry ...'

'That's OK, don't worry, I didn't really think you'd have the answers. It's been helpful just to talk, to have someone to share this with. My brain's been exploding with it.' Poppy stood and went to the door. 'Thanks, Val. I'll see you downstairs in a little while, shall I?'

'Yes, and don't worry, I won't say a word.'

Poppy smiled. 'I know you won't.'

For Valerie, the final cooking class felt different to the others, perhaps because she was aware of the undercurrents, the tensions and attractions, the fact that nothing was resolved.

Luca's blackboard menu promised a feast: pasta with sardines and wild fennel, rabbit in *agrodolce*, and for dessert a cake of chocolate, almonds and Marsala.

This evening he seemed his ordinary self, organising his equipment and ingredients, chatting about the meal, excited that one of the recipes (the cake) came from his nonna's newly rediscovered book and it was the first time he would make it.

'I hope it turns out well,' he said. 'Still, it's how Nonna wrote it down, so I'm sure it will.'

Valerie tried to imagine this Luca behind a telephoto lens, stalking someone. It wasn't impossible exactly, but the thought was unwelcome and she understood how Poppy felt; she too had preferred not knowing.

They began with the cake: creating a paste from chocolate and almonds, making it creamy with butter, sugar and eggs. Then they started on the sweet-sour rabbit stew, and while it was simmering, soaking up the vinegary juices, they prepared the pasta.

'This is the dish that sums up Sicily for me,' said Luca. 'From the Arabs we have sultanas, pine nuts and saffron, from the sea fresh sardines, and from the land the fennel I picked myself.'

He began by having Moll toast breadcrumbs until they were golden. Valerie chopped an onion and rinsed salt from anchovies. Tricia sautéed it all together in a pan. Poppy was left to do nothing but watch, and Valerie could imagine the turmoil she must be in.

In comparison, Luca appeared relaxed as he chopped his wild fennel, filling the kitchen with the scent of sweet liquorice.

'There's something so satisfying about finding food,' he said as he worked. 'You may not even have realised you needed something, but you change your plans ... your menu ... to accommodate it and the meal is usually better for it.'

'If you hadn't found the fennel, what would we have made?' Moll wondered.

'Today I knew it was there,' he admitted. 'Just like I know there are still capers to be found up on the hill opposite. But other times I will chance across food – borage, chicory, wild asparagus, seeds or herbs – and I'll try to find a way to use them. Wild food is unpredictable but worth it.'

Luca added a little home-made tomato paste to the pan, followed by fine feathers of fennel, the sardine fillets and the Arabic flavours. He cooked the pasta al dente, loosening his sauce with a little of the starchy cooking water.

'Now we're ready to eat the final meal we've prepared together,' he told them.

'You did all the work really,' said Moll, sprinkling the finished dish with the breadcrumbs she had toasted.

The table out on the terrace had been covered in a yellow cloth and linen napkins. Gathering round it, they filled their wine glasses, made a toast to good appetites and tasted the pasta. Valerie savoured flavours she knew she could never recreate at home. So much love had gone into this dish; it tasted of Sicily and sunshine.

'I'm going to miss this place,' she said. 'And the food. It's special.'

'Do you think you'll ever come back?' asked Tricia.

Valerie stared out at the view. It was beautiful, but so were the views from many other places.

'Probably not,' she admitted. 'Although I do hope to keep travelling.'

'I might come,' said Tricia. 'Paul would like Sicily, I think. We could go to Taormina, do the beach thing with the kids for a couple of days.'

Moll frowned. 'I'd love to come back,' she said. 'But I'm not likely to get the chance.'

Again Poppy was silent, and Valerie thought she seemed uncomfortable.

Luca served the rabbit with a salad of fresh leaves dressed with lemon and oil. Although Valerie still had an appetite, her limbs felt heavy and she thought that once she had eaten she might go to her room. She longed to turn out the light, curl up and relive those few moments she'd had with Vincenzo. He had reminded her body what it was capable of and she didn't want to forget it again. Not now that she understood there was time left to be loved; that it wasn't too late. Her skin might be lined and looser, her hair no longer a glory, but she was still the same woman deep down. Strong enough to swim through waves, brave enough to travel, foolish enough to risk her feelings. She had Vincenzo to thank for that.

The chocolate cake had turned out dense and moist. Luca declared it worthy of his nonna for certain. He poured a honey-coloured dessert wine for them to drink with it, tilting his glass towards them in another toast.

'To tomorrow, our final day together; may it be our very best yet,' he said.

Valerie raised her glass to her new friends. 'To the best times and the best people,' she added.

Food of Love

Luca Amore is watching her. She spoons ricotta over her cake, scoops up a little on her fork and tastes it, her tongue licking the tines. She takes another mouthful, then another. There is a smudge of chocolate at the corner of her mouth, but she hasn't noticed. The cake is soft as a ganache and rich with chocolate and Marsala. She eats until her slice is finished and then he offers her more.

He loves to see the way she eats. Tonight he has watched her sucking up strands of bucatini, the sauce flying and splattering on her T-shirt, leaving a stain that she dabs with a napkin then forgets about because she is busy wiping the last scraps from her plate with a crust of bread. She doesn't analyse every flavour, take notes, worry at each dish with her mind. Neither does she push food to the side of her plate and waste it. Poppy eats like she breathes, like she runs, like she makes love. She has abandoned herself to every meal he has served. To cook for her would always be a joy, he thinks.

She accepts a second slice of cake, this time eating more slowly, holding on to each bite, letting it melt in her mouth and slip down her throat slowly. Her hair has been released from its ponytail and is falling over her face, half hiding her expression, so he can't guess what she is thinking. All he knows is how much she is enjoying this cake he has made from a recipe no one has used in years.

He wonders what Nonna might have thought of her. There

was a time when her approval was everything to Luca. Before London, before he lost his way, he almost always tried to please her. He imagines her in this kitchen now. In his mind's eye it is the way it was: the old cracked tiles above the tin sink, the jars of preserves lining the wooden shelves, the misshapen pans and mismatched lids hanging from hooks on the wall.

He thinks of Nonna making this cake: grinding the chocolate and almonds by hand in her pestle and mortar, beating the sugar and butter with a wooden spoon, perhaps breathing hard with the effort of it, adding the eggs carefully one by one and reminding Luca that with baking patience is everything.

She was never so patient when it came to eating. Often she would cut a slice from a still-warm cake and she and Luca would share it, standing over the sink. She loved anything with chocolate in it: tarts coarse with hazelnuts, sweet ravioli stuffed with ricotta and cinnamon, the pastries they made with candied fruit for the feast of St Joseph, the milky puddings, ice cream and granita. She bought fat blocks of chocolate from the Mazzara *dolceria* to grate into all of them. They used to make them especially for her, twice as big as those they sold to anyone else.

His nonna had set a lot of store by people's appetites. '*Brava, brava*,' she would say at the sight of clean plates after a long meal. As a boy, if he were sick she spent hours cooking things he could manage, gentle foods like soups of fennel and potatoes, dried chestnuts and broken spaghetti. It had brought her pleasure to see him eat.

Now Luca understands, for he feels that pleasure too. Food for him has always been a way to lose his inhibitions. He watches Poppy running a greedy finger over the streaks of chocolate left on her plate, and sees that for her it is the same.

Moll

I love the way it smells here. There's some plant that seems to release its scent at night. Honeysuckle? Jasmine? I'm not sure. You're a gardener so you might be able to tell me. No? Oh well, it's not as if I'd ever plant any at home. We've got a tiny back yard, only space for a few pots of herbs. I grow lettuce in my window boxes in the summertime and tomato plants in the kitchen near the sunniest window.

If I had a proper garden I'd have those raised beds, and one of them I'd keep just for asparagus. Imagine going out and cutting the first spears in springtime and eating them steamed and dipped in a poached egg or smothered in hollandaise sauce. Having so much of it you have to find ways to use it up: risotto, savoury flans; the girls would probably like it on pizza.

I'll never have an asparagus bed, of course – it's not only a matter of the space but the time. It takes years for the crowns to become established, before there are enough spears to harvest. I read about it somewhere on the Internet. And I'll be lucky to have years.

It was breast cancer, you see. I did everything they told me to and more – a mastectomy, lymph nodes removed, radiation therapy, chemo, drugs. It seemed crazy to take any chances when the girls are still reliant on me.

But breast cancer spreads faster when you get it young, and I had the invasive one. Before I came away I had some blood tests they weren't happy with. I'm booked in for scans when I get back: liver, bones, lungs, the lot.

I feel fine now, better than fine, but whatever is going on inside me … well, who knows how much time I have left of feeling this way? That's why we scraped together the cash for me to come here. Just in case it's my last chance to travel alone.

I'm doing my best to stay positive, of course. They say worrying won't get me anywhere. They say to hope for a good life, if not a long one. They say a lot of things actually. There are endless blogs and books on the subject. I read everything at first, but now I've stopped.

If I can get through the next few years, see the girls through university and independent; well, that would be enough. With the right treatment it might be possible. Still, it gives me a pang to hear you talk about the travel and adventures you hope to have. It reminds me what I'll miss out on. That's when I get sad or angry, and think 'Why me?' no matter how positive I'm trying to be.

Would you mind not saying anything to the others? Poppy is sweet and Valerie so lovely, but I find it exhausting coping with other people's sorrow. It's an extra pressure I don't need. And I knew you wouldn't get tearful; you're not the type are you, and anyway, you don't like me much. No, that's fine, there's no need to apologise. None of us likes everyone we meet, do we?

I don't know why I'm telling you actually. Perhaps it's because all this is coming to an end and I'm heading home to the black hole of my future. Being here, it's been easier to have a positive outlook, to have hope. Soon I'll have to face reality again …

Still, one thing I've vowed is not to get to the end of my life with regrets. The girls are what are important now. I want to make sure they're equipped for their future; that I've passed on everything I can to them. I want to control the way they remember me. I want them to understand who I am … who I was … and for that to help who they become. I need the time to do all that.

I try not to let them see how scared I am about the tests, the treatments, the pain I may have. I try not to lean on them; worry about them; cry in front of them.

Brave? No, I'm not at all. There are hundreds and thousands of women in the same position as me. There isn't a right way to die, is there? We all have to do our best to keep living as long as we can.

I'm sure that scent is jasmine. There must be some climbing up a wall somewhere. Maybe I will find space to plant a sprig or two in a sunny spot. It would be lovely to close my eyes and have my tiny back garden smell like a Mediterranean terrace. And I read somewhere that it grows fast ... I hope it does.

Day 8

(i) Vines & keepsakes

Moll woke with a headache and the feeling she had said more than she meant to. Why decide to confide in Tricia, of all people? Still, she had been unexpectedly great, had taken the news like no one else Moll had shared it with, listening and asking intelligent questions with no show of pity, no 'poor you'. That must be how she was with her legal clients, Moll supposed.

There had been moments on this holiday when Moll had managed to stop thinking about those blood test results and what they might mean. She never forgot them exactly, but managed to push them aside and enjoy the moment she was in. It had helped that no one knew. She could be the old Moll with them, the strong one who felt like she could cope.

Secondary breast cancer. She didn't know for sure if that would be the diagnosis, but if it was, then she knew what it meant – there were enough websites on the subject. It was something to 'manage' not 'cure'. Moll had seen it described as 'a journey', which made her roll her eyes, but still, she got the point.

Soon the scans would tell her one way or another. The girls (and her doctor) might have preferred her to book in for them straight away, but Moll had needed this break, a few days of pretending that life hadn't changed, of being a normal person rather than a cancer patient. Then last night Luca had made that toast to their final day, and it had reminded her that this little piece of time she had taken for herself was running out.

Whenever Moll told someone about it, she felt as if she was ruining their day. She'd had no plans to mention it to anyone here, but out on the terrace, alone with Tricia, it had come rolling out. Without a doubt Tricia had been shocked, but she was tough, a woman who was used to other people's pain, so the telling was easier than usual. Moll hoped she wouldn't blab it to the others now. Surely she understood that some things shouldn't be gossiped about.

Moll climbed out of bed gingerly as usual. She had grown used to testing herself for any sort of new pain, a warning ache in her back or arm, a wheeze in her chest. This morning her body felt friendly. Her legs were perhaps a little stiff, but she put that down to the walking and swimming yesterday and vowed to be better about exercising when she got back home. A walk every day, a swim in Highbury Pool, had to be good for her either way. Look how fit Val had turned out to be.

She had a quick shower, sniffed at some clothes and decided they were clean enough for another day's wear. There was still time left to check her blog for comments, say hello to her Facebook friends and her followers on Twitter. Besides a few actual friends, none of them knew about the cancer. Moll was the person she wanted to be when she opened up her laptop.

She went down to breakfast feeling nostalgic already for the little pastries and strong black coffee she had enjoyed every morning. Luca had arrived and was setting up the table out on the terrace. She saw he had brought *'mpanatigghi*, the little half-moon-shaped biscuits filled with dark chocolate, almonds and the surprise ingredient of minced beef. Moll recalled how intrigued she had been by them that first morning, and felt as if she had come a long way; at least as far as Sicilian food was concerned.

'Good morning, shall I put the moka pot on for coffee?' she asked Luca.

'Ah, Moll, yes please.' He sounded cheery. 'The smell of it might bring the others downstairs.'

'We're off to the biodynamic vineyard today, aren't we? I'm intrigued to see how it differs from the first one we visited.'

'It's interesting. You'll want to blog about it. This afternoon is free, so you'll have time.'

'Are you and Poppy going back to Noto to see those people who might be related to her?' asked Moll.

'Yes, that's right.'

'Oh well, I do hope it works out.'

'Me too,' Luca said with feeling. 'I'm depending on it.'

Perhaps it was the smell of coffee, but the moka pot had only just boiled when Poppy appeared, followed by Tricia and Valerie. They settled round the table and reached for fruit and pastries, as Moll poured out their coffee.

Breakfast conversation was all about the day ahead. Tricia didn't refer to what had been said last night and showed no signs of treating her any differently either. Often people felt they had to tiptoe round her; Moll could sense compassion oozing from them and she hated it. She was relieved to find there was none of that with Tricia.

She bit into an *'mpanatigghi,* observing the way the sweetness mingled with the traces of coffee in her mouth. There was already a packet of them stashed in her suitcase to take home, so she knew this wouldn't be her final taste. She wasn't ready for final anything yet.

'More coffee?' she asked. 'After yesterday, I feel we should be paying so much more attention to the flavours when we drink it.'

'I'll make it,' Poppy offered, getting up. 'And yes, you're right, I always practically breathe in that first cup. I forget to savour it.'

Luca followed Poppy into the kitchen, and briefly Moll wondered what was going on between them. She had noticed the ebb and flow of their moods and sensed some tension, but hadn't commented on it, of course. That was their business, just like her health was hers.

'I'd better go and Skype the kids,' said Tricia, finishing the last of her fruit. 'This afternoon will be my last chance to buy presents for them, and I'm not sure what they'll want.'

Moll frowned. 'Do you suppose I should get something for the girls? I've got loads of food to take back, but might they want some other little trinkets?'

'Of course they will. They're girls, aren't they?' said Tricia. 'Come with me if you want. I'll try and help you find something they'll like.'

'Well, if you don't mind ...'

'Mind shopping? Never! Val, will you come too?'

'I don't have anyone to buy for really except myself, but I'd enjoy another look around. Yes, maybe I will.'

'That's settled then: the vineyard, shopping and our farewell dinner. The day is sorted,' said Tricia.

They were late setting off to the vineyard because Luca and Poppy seemed to have disappeared somewhere together. Moll imagined stolen kisses and fervent conversation, hoping things were working out for them. For Orsolina she spared no sympathy. The more she thought about what she had done with Luca's family recipe book, the crueller it seemed. It was his link with an important part of his past, and she imagined his nonna would have wanted him to have it.

As soon as he and Poppy reappeared (with no explanation for their absence), they all hurried down the steps and piled into the car. Luca drove a little faster than usual, but Moll wasn't nervous; he seemed good and steady, and anyway, other people's driving was just one more thing in life she couldn't control, and she had given up worrying about it.

Moll found she liked this vineyard more than the first one they had visited. Its winery was housed in a simple hacienda-style building on a parched hill with vines stretching out on either side, the ground between them carefully tilled.

At the gates they were met by the young winemaker. Dressed down in dirt-scuffed jeans, his face and arms deeply tanned, he looked like a simple man who worked the land. But his appearance disguised a fierce intelligence, and Moll might have filled an entire notebook with the new things she learned as they toured the rows of vines with him.

It was ingenious how they were using nature to help them at every turn. They grew fava beans to control nitrogen levels in the soil, encouraged lizards to keep the insect numbers down, sprayed vine leaves with quartz and rainwater to boost light, left out water for birds to drink so they didn't need to crush the grapes to slake their thirst. Even Tricia seemed fascinated.

'So you add nothing at all to the wine?' Moll asked. 'It's completely pure.'

The winemaker nodded. 'No filtering, no sulphur and no irrigation, so the vines sink their roots deeper. It means a smaller yield but improved quality.'

'Less but better,' said Moll.

'That's right. It's about deciding what's important.'

There was a hot wind blowing over the hill and Moll was glad to be led down from the rows of vines into the cool winery, past stainless-steel vats of Chardonnay, and musty oak barrels full of Nero d'Avola. As they talked about turning the grapes to wine, she marvelled again at the passion these people brought to the work. They seemed to have found the thing they were meant to do with their lives. Moll was sorry she had never managed it, suspecting that now she never would.

The tasting took place in a room decorated with photographs of the weddings that had taken place there, and in one corner there was an old wooden bridal carriage. Even Moll thought it romantic.

Food was brought out for them to nibble on as they tried each wine: little balls of fresh tuna flavoured with cinnamon, raw prawns dressed with olive oil and salt, a salad of octopus, vegetables battered and fried, crunchy *arancini* filled with seafood.

Moll always ate more than her fair share when plates were shared like this. Still, the food was plentiful, and with Tricia's nervous grazing, there was sure to be enough.

When she was having chemo, everything had tasted so different. Things she once loved became metallic and unpleasant; her mouth was dry and her appetite gone. There were days when the smell of cooking revolted her and all she wanted was to survive on Complan and not even think about eating. That had been as bad as the hair loss as far as she was concerned, worse perhaps.

She dreaded it happening again. She scooped up a fat green olive marinated in aniseed and chilli. While food still tasted the way it was meant to, she was determined to enjoy it.

'Could I get the recipe for the olives?' she asked the winemaker. 'I have a blog I'd like to post it on. I'll mention your wine too, of course.'

'Yes, why not? This is a family recipe. They're always the best.'

'I must look for a book of Sicilian recipes when I get home.' Moll was enthused. 'Maybe I'll head down to Books for Cooks in Notting Hill. They're bound to have something.'

'Or you could wait for Luca to write his book now that he has all his nonna's recipes,' suggested Poppy.

Moll turned to him. 'Oh, will you? That would be marvellous.'

'I'd like to,' he told her. 'That book is a treasure. I'd forgotten how much is in it. And then there are other recipes I could collect from friends like Vincenzo. But it would be a big project. To manage that and run the cookery school by myself … well, I'm not sure.'

'But you must do it, and soon,' Moll urged him. 'Can't you get some help?'

'I'm working on it.' He glanced at Poppy and added, 'Believe me, I am.'

Moll wondered what was standing between the pair of them. If they liked each other, why bother wasting time?

'Your recipe for the marinated olives?' she reminded the winemaker. 'I could just scribble it down now if you like.'

On the drive back, Moll sorted through her notes and thought about her blog. It had brought her so much pleasure to share what she had learned here each day. At home, she might go up to a week without an update if work was very busy and the cases she was handling especially dispiriting. Those nights they ate rushed food – a grilled steak she had failed to marinate, a few boiled potatoes and a bit of salad – well, there was nothing to say about that. She liked her followers to think of her enriching her life with what she ate, not shoving it down with the plate on her knee as she and the girls watched television.

Luca parked the van at the bottom of the steps and everyone got out except Poppy, who was to drive on to Noto with him and meet the old lady she hoped might be family.

'Are those two all right?' Moll asked Valerie as they trudged upwards. 'There seems to be a bit of an atmosphere.'

'Yes, I know.' Valerie screwed up her face. 'Hopefully they'll work things out, but right now who knows? It's good they've got the afternoon more or less to themselves.'

'If they're having issues right at the very beginning, they should just give up,' Tricia said. 'This is meant to be the carefree part; the problems come later. Don't you think?'

Valerie reached the front door first, puffing slightly, and put her key into the lock. 'I couldn't say really.'

Tricia narrowed her eyes. 'You know something, don't you?'

'I do think there's a chance Poppy won't be coming to the airport with us tomorrow,' Valerie admitted. 'I kind of hope so anyway.'

'I do too,' said Moll.

They agreed to meet again in a couple of hours so that Val could rest, Tricia take another shower and Moll spend some time on her laptop. Wine wasn't her thing really, but the biodynamic vineyard was too fascinating not to write about, and she included the olive salad recipe, making it clear that she hadn't had a chance to test it herself. Moll might rose-tint her life for her followers, but food was something she tried not to mess with.

After she had shut down her laptop, she pulled a chair to the window and sat, leaning on the sill, taking in the view. At home, her windows showed small scenes: a patch of garden, a square of the neighbour's wall, a slice of sky. From up here, the outlook seemed limitless in comparison. She could see layers of butter-gold stone buildings where strangers spent lives much like hers, full of love and hope and anguish; at least she imagined so.

When she was given that first diagnosis, Moll had vowed that if she got through it, she would never waste time worrying about trivial things again. She thought of all the hours filled with stress about staying on top of work, running the home, getting it all done. Her cancer resolution had been to break free of all that by lowering her standards. The house might be grubby, bills paid late, cases get a little less attention, but she owed it to herself to focus on what fulfilled her. That was why she had started the blog and planned food adventures to fill it.

The old anxieties did creep back, but she tried to keep them in perspective. There was never enough money or time, and that was unlikely to change. But now she had a real concern, one she couldn't dismiss. Staring at the rows of houses climbing up the hill opposite her window, Moll wondered how many people inside them had worries just like hers. Right now there might be a woman putting a hand to her breast and fearing a lump; or someone facing treatment; or another who had given up. It didn't reassure her to think like that. In fact, it was depressing. But it reminded her that what was happening was just another part of life. One in four women like her had the disease come back, according to a study she had read about. Someone had to draw the short straw.

Closing her shutters against the view, Moll went and lay down on the bed, curling her body into a ball and pushing her face into the pillow. She allowed herself ten minutes of complete despair. And then she sat up, used the corner of her sheet to wipe the wetness from her face and pulled herself together.

A splash of cold water removed the last traces of tears. Moll grabbed her satchel, made sure her credit card was inside and headed downstairs, hoping the others were ready.

Tricia hadn't been kidding about her ability to shop. They had only moved a few paces down the road and she was already holding a carrier bag with a scarf in it she intended to give to her mother.

'There's a place further on that sells jewellery,' she said. 'Could we take a look in there next?'

'You're the boss,' said Moll. 'I'll follow and hope I find something for the girls.'

'What are you looking for exactly?' Tricia asked.

'Oh God, I don't know. I'm useless at buying presents.'

'What sort of girls are they? Do they have the same taste as you, or ...?'

Moll laughed. 'No fear. They love pretty, shiny things and dressing up. I'm not sure who they take after, but it isn't me.'

From a single glance in the window, Moll could tell the jewellery shop was expensive. It was filled with showy necklaces and rings with tiny price tags that held long numbers. This was the kind of place she wouldn't bother entering usually, but Tricia strode in like she owned it, so Moll trailed behind her.

A few strings of glass beads hanging over the counter caught her eye. The colours were pretty pinks and she could imagine the girls might like them as a novelty.

'What do you think of these?' she asked Tricia.

'They're OK, I suppose.' She fingered them.

'Maybe I'll buy them and then it's done.'

'Hang on.' Tricia touched her shoulder. 'I know you don't have lots of cash to chuck round, but really I think you should buy something nicer.'

Moll looked at her. 'You do?'

'Give them pieces they'll keep for ever and always think of you when they wear; that they might pass on to their own daughters one day if they have them.'

Moll swallowed hard. She hoped Tricia wasn't going to bring on more of her tears.

'I suppose I haven't spent that much money while I've been here,' she said. 'Less than I expected, anyway. Everything has been catered for really, hasn't it?'

'There are some beautiful things here,' Tricia encouraged her.

Moll stared round the shop, bewildered. 'Yes, but I wouldn't know where to start.'

'What about these?' Val suggested, pointing at some highly polished silver bangles. 'They look very like the doughnut bangle Elsa Peretti did for Tiffany. I've always wanted one of those myself.'

'Are they nice?' Moll asked dubiously; she couldn't see it herself.

'Yes, they're a classic,' Tricia told her. 'A timeless piece you could wear for years, from a young girl until you were an old, old woman.'

Moll looked at the price tag. 'I don't know … it's more than I've ever spent on them before.'

'I could help out if you like,' Tricia offered.

'No,' she said quickly. 'Let's keep going and I'll think about it. I can always come back if I don't see anything else.'

'OK then,' Tricia agreed. 'We'll keep looking.'

They continued on, walking down one side of the main street until the shops petered out, then crossing over to walk back along the other side, Tricia collecting purchases along the way. She bought a jigsaw for her son, a flowered summer dress for her daughter, tried on some shoes she quite liked but decided against them.

'The last thing I need is another pair of heels,' she admitted. 'Even I can see that. What I really need is a gift for Paul.'

'There were some cufflinks that looked rather nice in that jewellery store,' Valerie suggested. 'If we're going back there anyway …'

'Can we stop for a sit-down and a cold drink first?' Moll pleaded. 'Shopping exhausts me. All this strolling round and browsing; a brisk walk would be less tiring.'

'Let's go to our usual café; the one in the piazza' suggested Valerie. 'I wouldn't mind another granita. And yes, a sit-down as well. My legs are killing me after that big swim I did yesterday.'

Moll was convinced the waiter recognised them and rather liked the idea that already they were weaving into the fabric of the place. She ordered a granita in a different flavour from last time (sweet and sour lemon), then used the calculator on her mobile phone to work out how much she would be spending in pounds if she decided on those silver bracelets.

It seemed a crazy amount, but Moll could imagine how the bangles would look against the smooth skin of her daughters' arms. She thought about how those arms might freckle and pucker as the years passed, but how the bangles would still polish up to a high shine and look pretty on them.

'Bugger it, I'm going to buy them,' she announced.

'Good on you,' said Tricia.

'I might have to get an evening job waitressing at the curry house round the corner to pay for them.'

'Oh no, don't do that. The smell of curry gets into everything,' Tricia told her, laughing. 'There has to be another way.'

'Well I don't know ... but I think you're right. It's time to buy them something they'll love instead of trying to make them like the things I enjoy.'

'Are your daughters really not into food?'

'Not especially. They like eating what I make but don't have much interest in helping ... they're like most teenagers, I expect. If I insist, then they treat it like an awful chore. I'd like to think that will change, but not so far.'

Tricia sat up straighter in her chair. 'Do you know, I've just had the most genius idea for you.'

'To earn extra cash or get the girls involved with the cooking?'

'Both, actually.' Tricia paused as the waiter came to deliver the beer she had ordered and put out the customary plates of salty, crispy snacks. 'Do you ever get the *Telegraph*?'

'No, the *Guardian*.'

'Yes, of course you would ... Anyway, there's this woman who writes about baking—'

Moll interrupted. 'You bake?'

'No, don't be ridiculous. But Paul has this thing about making sourdough bread, and he likes to read her. He was telling me about this clever thing she did. She set up an artisan bakery at home, with her teenagers doing all the work. Just one day a week, selling loaves they'd made, and the kids kept the profits. It taught them about money and work ethic ... food too, I guess. You should have a look on Google; it's called The Pocket Bakery.'

'Wouldn't there be all sorts of tricky food hygiene regulations?'

Tricia shrugged. 'Who knows, but she managed it somehow. I thought you could do the same, but with fresh, unpasteurised pasta like we've been making here.'

Moll was dubious. 'And sell it to who?'

'You could start with your neighbours. Do a leaflet drop and make small amounts at first. I bet it would catch on quickly. Everyone loves fresh pasta but is too busy to make their own.'

'You could do the cavatelli we made in our first lesson here,' encouraged Val. 'And the maltagliati.'

Moll thought the idea held possibilities. The girls would be interested in the money; they always wanted to buy bits of make-up and new clothes. She would like them to learn a new skill, and maybe a love of good food would gradually seep into them.

'The Pocket Bakery, you said? I'll look it up.'

'Well, it's an idea,' said Tricia. 'It may not work out, but …'

'It's a brilliant idea. I may even have to read the *Telegraph* the days she has her column.'

'Don't go crazy,' Tricia teased her.

Moll pulled out her notebook and scribbled the name down to be sure to remember. She made a list of the things she might need: wooden boards to cover the kitchen counters just like the ones Luca had, cards with the recipe on so customers might make pasta themselves if they wanted to.

Already she was feeling the excitement she'd had when she started her blog, that sense of doing something authentic and worthwhile. She could picture her little house a hive of industry as her daughters used their nimble fingers to roll cavatelli instead of sending texts and play computer games. With them taking care of all the hard work, it wouldn't matter if she were feeling below par. She made a couple more notes about places that might supply semolina flour, then put away her notebook.

'Are you finished?' she asked the others, impatient all of a sudden. 'Shall we pay the bill and head back to get those bangles?'

It took a few moments for Tricia to reapply her lipstick and organise her shopping bags. They were getting up from the table, laughing together at something she was saying, when Moll saw Valerie's expression change. She turned to check what she had seen, and spied Vincenzo Mazzara walking along the main street, wearing a pair of wraparound sunglasses and a pale T-shirt tight enough to show off the squareness of his shoulders.

Moll glanced at Valerie. Her face had arranged itself in a smile and she was raising a hand to wave.

Seeing them, Vincenzo changed tack, coming towards the café. It was as he greeted Valerie with a light kiss on both cheeks that Moll realised why he was wearing the unflattering dark glasses. The redness of a new bruise was spreading out from behind them and down beneath his cheekbone.

Tricia had noticed it too. 'Ouch ... what have you done to your face?' she asked.

Vincenzo touched it lightly. 'A little knock, but nothing serious,' he told her. 'These things happen.'

'Really? It's going to look spectacular once it goes black and blue. You may need bigger sunglasses.'

Vincenzo's fingers stayed on his face to cover the bruise and he was quick to change the subject. 'I am glad I bumped into you. I was wondering, will you be at Luca's place this evening?'

'We're going to the Inn of Lost Flavours for our farewell dinner,' Moll told him.

'Ah yes, such a pity you are leaving tomorrow. But there will be a chance this evening for me to catch you all at home, before dinner perhaps, or afterwards?'

'I'm sure either would be fine,' said Moll. 'We should be there.'

'That is settled then. I will see you later.'

After kissing their cheeks once more, Vincenzo moved on, all eyes following him as he walked away.

'So who do you think thumped him?' asked Tricia.

'It may have been an accident,' pointed out Moll. 'Perhaps he walked into something.'

'Yeah, into the fist of some man whose wife he's been sleeping with,' said Tricia drily.

Moll was surprised. 'He's not that kind of guy, is he?'

'I'd say he's exactly that kind of guy. Val, what do you think?'

Valerie was staring down the street after him. 'I don't know ... Perhaps it has something to do with his food guide. He did say there was a risk of offending people.'

'You don't really believe that, do you?' asked Tricia.

'No, not really,' Valerie admitted, smiling ruefully. 'You're right, of course, he's a desperate flirt. Still, that's not such a bad thing, is it? Flirting can be fun. It can make you feel young again.'

Tricia laughed. 'I wouldn't say Vincenzo is feeling very wonderful just at the moment. But yes, I agree with you about flirting.' She looked at Valerie, head tilted. 'So long as you both know that's all you're doing ... so long as you don't have other expectations.'

Valerie's expression didn't change. 'Yes, of course,' she replied lightly. 'So long as no one gets too terribly hurt and you're still friends at the finish.'

(ii) A feast of lost flavours

Tonight they were to order dinner for themselves, armed with all the knowledge gleaned over the last eight days. Moll didn't want to take any chances. While the others returned to their rooms, she walked on alone to the Inn of Lost Flavours to study the menu that was pinned up on a board outside. Although it was written in Italian, there were photographs of each dish so she could have a decent stab at guessing what they were. She was tempted by the cavatelli with the creaminess of ricotta and the fresh nuttiness of peas. And she wondered what Tricia would say if she ordered thick ribbons of fresh tripe in a broth of capers and tomato to follow it.

She made a few notes to refer to later, then snapped some photographs of the menu board. The welcome dinner they had eaten in this same restaurant might have half faded from her memory by now if she hadn't been careful to record it. She was certain her brain had got foggier during the cancer treatment and never really come right again. The girls called it 'being dippy' if she repeated herself, forgot a name or where she had put her keys. Moll had learned to live with the sudden blanks and developed the habit of being careful with things she knew she wanted to remember.

Now she wondered if the treatment might have affected her judgement as well. Hadn't she been the one to encourage Valerie's little flirtation with Vincenzo? He had seemed so charming and attentive, so kind. Now, after what Tricia had said, she wondered if she'd had him wrong all along. She had to concede Tricia seemed pretty shrewd, particularly where men were concerned.

It wasn't that she was rethinking her opinion of Tricia exactly, but Moll was grateful to her. The silver bangles were in her satchel, wrapped and beribboned, and exactly the right gift. There hadn't been the smallest wobble when she handed over her credit card, and now she felt warm at the thought of the girls' faces when they opened them.

She turned to head back towards the cookery school, deciding she would hand over the gifts to them before sharing the pasta-making plan. That way there was more chance of them not dismissing the idea straight off. In the meantime, she might ask Luca for his advice on the best way to pack cavatelli to prevent it sticking or drying out. In her mind, the project was already progressing. Another reason to be grateful to Tricia.

Moll had been planning to spend the rest of her free time on the Internet, but the moment she pushed open the front door she forgot about that, for she found Poppy was back, and fizzing with excitement.

'Oh Moll,' she said. 'I'm so glad you're here. I've been waiting for you.'

'Why?' Moll was eager. 'Did you see the old lady? What did she say?'

Poppy beamed. 'We're family; there's absolutely no doubt about it now. Isn't that amazing? Thank you so much for your help. I'd never have managed to find them without you.'

'Start from the beginning,' urged Moll. 'Tell me exactly what happened.'

'I knew the moment she showed me the photograph, a copy of the same one my grandfather gave to me. Her name is Anna Planeta and she's his cousin. She had albums full of pictures, too many to look through properly. But she gave me this one to keep.' Poppy produced an old photograph printed up on yellowing card. It showed two dark-haired women sitting on a Vespa, the one in front with a baby on her knee.

'Isn't it wonderful? These are my great-aunts. Luca says I look like them.'

Moll peered at the picture. 'Maybe round the eyes and something about the smile,' she agreed. 'But you're much slimmer than either of them.'

'I suppose it was the fashion back then to be curvier, I'm not really sure. There's so much I don't know … but I want to find it all out.' Poppy's eyes were bright.

'What about your grandfather, what will you tell him?'

'I'm going to see if I can persuade him to come and meet

Anna and her brother. She says there are other cousins too. I know he'll find all sorts of excuses not to fly so far, but if he took it slowly, stopped over somewhere, then I think he could do it.'

'Yes, surely he could,' agreed Moll.

'Anna cried when she realised who I am.' The tears sprang to Poppy's eyes now too. 'They're both so old. He must come and meet her before it's too late.'

Moll reached out and squeezed her hand. 'I think so too. But it's him you have to convince.'

'I'll ring him later to break the news, offer to book and pay for the flight, find a nice hotel,' Poppy decided. 'I'm sure he'll hate the idea of leaving Australia, but perhaps if he comes back here, he'll discover he's more Italian than he thought. What you said the other day is right, Moll. It's important to know where you come from, to have a sense of the people who helped make you what you are. Right now, it feels like I've found this whole missing piece of a jigsaw and it's slotted into place at last.'

'That's really great.' Moll was thrilled for her.

'If ever I have kids, I'd want them to come to Sicily and understand what it meant to them.' Poppy glanced back at the photograph. 'I realise times were different then, but I can't imagine letting go of people I loved and knowing that most likely I'd never see them again. It must have been heart-breaking.'

'Still, you've found them now, that's the important thing.'

'But you know I can't even speak to them properly,' lamented Poppy. 'Anna hardly understood my attempts at Italian. She seems to speak only Sicilian dialect.'

'I guess you'd learn the dialect if you lived here,' Moll encouraged her.

'I guess so,' agreed Poppy. 'If I was here for long enough, I'm certain I'd pick it up eventually.'

Moll was satisfied to have done something to help. In her

job, she despaired of making a real difference to her clients' lives. Often the best she could do was to steer them towards a lesser evil. This had been so simple, yet without her guidance, Poppy might have made no progress at all. It made Moll feel almost celebratory.

Since this was the final night, and her spirits had lifted, she decided to make an effort with her appearance. There was one outfit in her suitcase she hadn't worn yet, a silky blue shift dress with a dahlia pattern she had bought cheap at the M&S online outlet store just before she was diagnosed. It hadn't been worn that summer or any summer since; had been thrown into her bag at the last minute only because it was the sort of fabric that rolled up small and didn't crease. Moll was a random packer. She hadn't expected to wear it.

But now she put it on and it looked much better than she remembered (even if it did show too much leg). She dabbed bluey-grey shadow on her eyelids and rummaged in her satchel for the bright coral lipstick she carried everywhere but hardly ever used. Resisting the urge to wipe it off again, she packed everything back in her bag and went downstairs.

She walked into the kitchen and Tricia let out a low whistle. 'Look at you, hot stuff.'

Moll blushed. 'Don't be silly.'

'No, really, you look great.'

'Well, it's a special dinner, isn't it? And all of you look fantastic too.'

Tricia was wearing a black frock that barely grazed her thighs and fierce stiletto heels, Valerie the flimsy rose gold again and Poppy a peacock-blue maxi dress, her hair falling sleek down her back.

'I think this calls for a round of my famous gin and tonics,' Moll decided.

Mixing the drinks, ice clinking into glasses, tonic fizzing over gin, she hoped she would remember this feeling. Everyone their best selves, anticipating the meal to come, somehow knowing that the flavours would sing louder because it was the final one. It wasn't a thing she could take notes about or photograph; just a fleeting moment she had to trust would stay with her in the weeks and months to come.

'Luca says he'll meet us in the restaurant at seven,' Poppy said, when they had clinked frosted glasses and were sipping their drinks out on the terrace. 'So there's only time for one gin, which is probably a good thing, given how strong you've made them, Moll.'

Moll chuckled. 'There's no point in having a drink unless you're going to have a proper one.'

Tricia raised her glass again. 'I'm with you on that.'

As they drank, they talked of Poppy's family, and Moll stared again at the photograph of two long-dead Italian women who had no idea how much they would matter one day to a stranger from the other side of the world.

They were draining their gins when they heard a whistle. Moll looked over the terrace wall to see Vincenzo Mazzara climbing the steps, his daughter bringing up the rear.

'Oh, it's them,' she said to Valerie. 'They're here.'

Tricia went to the door and Moll heard her in the kitchen apologising that she couldn't offer them a drink. 'We're meeting Luca in ten minutes, so I'm afraid there isn't time,' she said. 'But Val and the others are out on the terrace if you want to see them.'

'It is Poppy we have come to see,' Vincenzo replied. 'And we only need a moment.'

Although the sun was sinking, he still wore his sunglasses. From what Moll could tell, the bruise beneath them looked angrier and his face a little more swollen. Behind him, half shielded by his body, came Orsolina, carrying a large chocolate box from the Mazzera *dolceria*, her face twisting into a smile.

Vincenzo stopped and pulled her two steps forward. 'We are here to apologise, are we not, *cara*?'

'Yes,' Orsolina said very quietly, then fell back into silence.

'So?' her father prompted her.

'I am very sorry for the trick I played on you,' she said to no one in particular.

Vincenzo shook her arm. 'Orsolina, *cara*, that is not enough.'

Orsolina took a breath and her gaze met Poppy's. 'What else do you want me to say?' she asked.

Poppy seemed uneasy. She looked at Valerie, then back at the unhappy woman clutching her box covered in crinkled shiny paper and ribbons.

'Well?' Orsolina's tone was almost confrontational.

'It's Luca you should be apologising to, not me. It was his book you stole,' said Poppy.

'My daughter will say sorry to Luca in due course,' said Vincenzo smoothly. 'But you are leaving tomorrow morning, so there is some urgency.'

Poppy tilted her chin at him. 'No, I'm not leaving,' she said.

'I'm sorry, I understood this was the last day ...'

'It is,' Poppy told him. 'The others are going home, but I'm not.'

Orsolina's lips pressed and tightened. She threw her box down on the dining table. Her father held fast to her arm as she tried to turn away.

'There are people I want to get to know,' Poppy told her.

'What people?' Orsolina demanded.

'The family I've only just discovered ... the island they come from ...'

'And Luca?' Her voice wobbled.

'Yes, Luca,' said Poppy gently. 'I'm so sorry, Orsolina. I know how you feel about him. But the thing is, I'm beginning to feel that way too. So yes, Luca most of all.'

*

They made a gaudy group strolling down the street towards the restaurant. Heads turned, they were ogled openly, there were even a couple of whistles. For once, no one seemed to notice or care (not even Tricia). Tonight was for themselves and each other. It was for squeezing the final drops of flavour from the holiday before they went their separate ways.

There was no need for Moll to pore over the menu, as she had made all her decisions earlier. The others had a more difficult time, even though the menus they were given had been translated into English.

Luca held back, insisting they do it all themselves. 'I've taught you everything you need to know,' he told them. 'Now it's up to you.'

He was striking in a white linen shirt that showed off his tanned skin. He smelt good too, a scent that reminded Moll of wild fennel mixed with fresh air and salt spray. She was sitting on one side of him, Poppy on the other. For all that she tried not to monopolise his conversation, Moll couldn't help asking questions.

'Why is it called the Inn of Lost Flavours?' she wondered. 'Were they really lost?'

'They're old-fashioned dishes,' Luca told her, 'things we eat with nostalgia but perhaps don't often prepare at home any more. They have the potential to become lost in the future if we're not careful.'

'I think we all have that potential,' said Valerie, thoughtfully. She was drinking faster than usual, already chugging through a glass of Prosecco. 'We all get lost from time to time, but if we're lucky, we find ourselves again.'

Moll had no idea what she was talking about. 'Still, it's an excellent name, isn't it?' she said brightly. 'Luca, why don't you use it for your collection of Sicilian recipes – *The Book of Lost Flavours*? After all, your nonna's book was really lost, wasn't it?'

'Yes, but while I am very happy to have it returned to me, I don't think the flavours in it were ever truly lost,' Luca told them. 'They were there in my memory. They always would have been.'

At last they decided on their meals, Tricia predictably pulling a face at Moll's choice of tripe.

'Rubbery stomach lining ... really?' she said.

'It's traditional,' Moll argued.

'It's disgusting, but I suppose there are some things we're never going to agree on, you and I. We didn't do too badly, though, considering, did we?'

Moll looked at her. 'I'm sorry if I've been a bit prickly,' she began.

'Don't worry about it. Your prickles make you who you are.' Tricia paused for a beat or two, adding, 'I know we'll never be the best of friends, but you'll stay in touch, won't you?'

Moll was surprised. 'If you want me to.'

'I'd like to know how things turn out, you know, with the pasta idea and everything. If I can do anything to help ...'

Moll knew what she meant. She imagined that Tricia would be a good person to have on her side. 'I'll stay in touch,' she promised.

Perhaps it was greedy to eat four courses. No one else could manage so many. But Moll felt insatiable for some reason. She devoured bruschetta covered in piquant salsa, relished cavatelli creamy with ricotta, polished off most of the tomato-soused tripe, then ordered some cannoli for dessert.

The waiter came to fill the crisp shells at the table. All eyes were on him except Moll's. She found herself studying their faces instead, and she realised that not a single one of these women knew truly what their future held. Valerie would go home to her apartment in New York, Tricia back to her important lawyer's life in London; Poppy was staying here with Luca. But beyond that lay uncertainty: plans could be overturned, dreams go unfulfilled; life might tease them or let them down entirely (although she hoped it wouldn't).

Moll took a mouthful of the dessert wine Luca had poured for her, impatient for the cannoli. She was indulging herself now. There was no need for another sugar-dusted pastry stuffed with ricotta, dipped in pistachios and drowned in vanilla syrup. Yet she took the plate the waiter offered, scooped one up and dug her teeth in anyway.

Food of Love

Eight days. Luca Amore finds it difficult to believe so much has changed in that short time. While he was kneading the dough for cavatelli, while he was talking about food, while he was preserving capers and picking fennel, his life shifted and turned, it changed direction and broke through its limits. And now everything feels familiar but strange.

Today Luca is doing the usual things. Four fresh aprons hang from the hooks in his kitchen, the blackboard has been wiped clean and a new menu chalked up, plates are stacked, cutlery and saucepans are shining. The Food of Love Cookery School will soon be back open for business.

In the past, this has been his pause, a chance to make lists and take stock. But Luca has thrown away his lists, for just the thought of them was dizzying.

In his head, he churns through all that lies ahead. First they must take Poppy to meet his mother. Then they must find a place to live, for they cannot stay in his mamma's house for ever. More importantly, they must learn the rhythms of one another's moods; understand how to comfort, apologise, celebrate. Know when to draw close and when it might be better to spend time apart. Knit together in a way that will suit them both.

Eight days. Yet Luca is certain. His confidence must carry them forward, for he suspects she doesn't always feel so sure. Her list is as long as his; perhaps longer. There is a whole life in Australia she must decide what to do with: a house, a job, family and friends. Sooner or later … but not today … not this week or next.

She is making cavatelli now, still hesitantly, but not so much as the first time she tried it. Some are thick nuggets of dough, others more delicate, and she knows they will cook unevenly. He tells her not to worry; they don't have to be perfect. Nothing does.

Later they will sit on the terrace, just the two of them. They might raise their glasses to Moll, Val and Tricia, wish them good health and fine futures. Then they will eat the cavatelli she has made, sharing a bowl the way he and his nonna often used to.

Eight days, and Luca Amore fell in love with her a little more as each one went by. Now with each new day they spend together comes the hope that she loves him back.

Food of Love Recipes

CAVATELLI WITH CINNAMON AND SAUSAGE SAUCE

500g durum wheat flour (semolina flour)
tepid water
1 tsp salt
500g Italian sausage (preferably flavoured with fennel seeds and chilli flakes)
extra-virgin olive oil
½ glass full-bodied red wine
1 tsp cinnamon powder
tomato sauce (jar of passata or home-made)
grated caciocavallo Ragusano cheese (or you could use Pecorino)

Mix the flour with the warm salted water until you get a firm dough. Knead the dough and form thick spaghettoni (rolls), then cut into 1cm portions and roll them on a fork (or special wooden cavatelli board) with your thumb to make the cavatelli, which are like little seashells. When they are all ready, leave them in the air to dry. While you're making the cavatelli, keep the remaining dough covered with a towel so that it does not dry out.

Remove the sausage from its casing, break into small chunks, then sauté in extra-virgin olive oil on a medium-high heat. Pour in the wine, and when the alcohol evaporates, add the cinnamon followed by the tomato sauce. Lower the heat and let it simmer for 15 minutes.

Cook the pasta in boiling salted water; the cavatelli will float to the surface as soon as they are ready. Place them in a bowl with the sauce, mix well and sprinkle with the grated cheese.

FAVIO'S CHOCOLATE CHICKEN

6 chicken thighs
500ml Prosecco or white wine
3 tsp fennel seeds
2 cloves
30g grated dark chocolate
1–2 medium onions
4 tbsp extra-virgin olive oil
1 tbsp sugar
chilli (as much as or little as you like)
4 tbsp white wine vinegar
a pinch of salt

Marinate the chicken in Prosecco overnight. Grind the fennel seeds and the cloves together with the chocolate using a pestle and mortar and set aside. Chop the onion and soften in a large pan with olive oil, then turn the heat up and add the chicken. Keep turning as it fries until evenly golden brown.

Add the mixture of chocolate, fennel seeds and cloves, the sugar, salt and the chilli and stir in with the vinegar. Lower the heat, cover the pan and let it simmer for 30–40 minutes. If it gets too dry, add a splash more Prosecco.

CHICKEN IN AGRODOLCE

extra-virgin olive oil
2 cloves garlic
6 chicken thighs
2 medium onions
3 carrots
2 stalks celery
2 tbsp sugar
1 cup white wine vinegar
4 bay leaves
2 tablespoons capers
200g green olives
salt and pepper
1 glass white wine
fresh chilli

Heat the oil, peel and crush the garlic cloves and add them to the pan, then add the chicken and brown over a high heat. When golden brown, remove from the pan and keep warm. Chop the onion, carrots and celery and sauté in the pan. After a few minutes, when lightly golden, add the chicken thighs. Dissolve sugar in vinegar and sprinkle all over the chicken. Add the bay leaves, capers, olives, salt and pepper, stir well and pour over the white wine. Cook over a low heat and, if you like it, add some chopped chilli before serving.

(Recipes by Katia Amore: www.lovesicily.com)

Acknowledgements

When I wrote this novel, I wanted the reader to feel like the fifth person on holiday with Poppy, Tricia, Valerie and Moll. Although the story and its characters are fictional, the good news is it's possible to go to the cooking school that inspired me. At Love Sicily (www.lovesicily.com), in the beautiful town of Modica, I had the best ever research trip and my thanks are due to Katia Amore (how could I resist that surname!) and her helpers Angelo and Pinutcha. Thanks also to the new friends I made there – Hilary, Sally and Maureen – to old friends who have put up with me during the writing of this novel, and to the colleagues who have supported me, in particular those at Orion, Hachette NZ, Hachette Australia, the *New Zealand Woman's Weekly* and the *Herald on Sunday*.

Thanks again to Katia for allowing me to publish the recipes for some of the dishes we cooked together at Love Sicily. More food inspiration was found in the pages of *Made in Sicily* by Giorgio Locatelli and *My Cousin Rosa* by Rosa Mitchell, as well as countless blogs. I also turned to the blogosphere for help in understanding Moll's situation and should credit in particular an excellent one written for the *Independent* by Ismena Clout. Meeting author and journalist Rose Prince of The Pocket Bakery whilst at the Sharjah International Book Fair also helped to inspire me. And *The Diana Chronicles* by Tina Brown helped inform me.

Some places I mention are real – the Caffe Sicilia in Noto is famed for its extraordinary ice cream, the Dolceria Bonajuto in Modica (which became Vincenzo Mazzara's *dolceria*) for its chocolate.

This book is dedicated to friends old and new, and to Italy, which has given me so many stories. Here's to many more holidays there ... Oops, did I say that? I mean research trips, of course ...